T0131525

Carolina Jasmine

L. V. Vehaskari
D. A. Clark

CAROLINA JASMINE

iUniverse books may be ordered through booksellers or by contacting:

iUniverse
1663 Liberty Drive
Bloomington, IN 47403
www.iuniverse.com
1-800-Authors (1-800-288-4677)

ISBN: 978-1-5320-7734-0 (sc)
ISBN: 978-1-5320-7735-7 (e)

Library of Congress Control Number: 2019909350

Print information available on the last page.

iUniverse rev. date: 07/19/2019

Contents

The wet rancid smell from the asphalt rose in the steam from the black puddles dotted with plastic cups, gum, candy wrappers and cigarette butts washed from the sidewalks. The blue black clouds rumbled westward throwing shards of lightning and spitting flares from the electric pole. Pitch black everywhere, none of the stores along the road had life, no street lights and the traffic signal was out.

Cars inched along able to pick their way only by other headlights showing where there was life. Traffic hesitated as the drivers became aware of an SUV fish-tailing, the headlights waving from side to side scraping several cars as it spun in the middle of the street. The driver accelerated trying to pull out of the spin, the tires slipped in an oil-filled puddle and shot into the air under the dead traffic light and crashed into a light blue Prius. God only knows what the hurry was.

The screech of metal tearing into metal and powering through glass sent an acrid smell into the air. There was no time to scream. For a few seconds that seemed like hours, there was no sound, no wind, no life, only the slight rain pattering on the mangled cars.

Within minutes people were screaming, calling police and EMS and trying to see if there were any survivors. Men ran from their cars without raincoats and stopped in front of the two cars trying to figure out where one car ended and the other began. The choking smell of blood mixed with body fluids, ripped metal and asphalt caused several to vomit. The driver of the SUV had been thrown through the window, mangled and lay between the two bodies in the Prius. The bumper of the SUV had cut through the windshield and sliced the driver's jugular. Shrapnel of glass covered the woman passenger and several large pieces pierced her body, her pregnant body.

The Jaws-of-life grunted as it pulled the cars screeching and screaming apart and first responders flipped them to righted position. The bodies were laid out as the EMS team stated the time of death. One EMS began pulling the glass out of the woman's belly but snapped around when she heard a groan and saw tears streaming across the woman's twisted face. "Hey guys. This one's still alive."

"What do you mean we only get $500,000? Where's the rest of the six million dollar award? I won't have enough to pay for Melanie's medical and long-term care. What happened to the rest of the money? Wha..what am I supposed to do? I have to take care of her and it's so expensive. She's my sister —my twin."

Melissa had been a good witness. Dressed in spinster drab clothes with a voice that matched, some of the jury strained to hear her, others fell asleep, but she got their sympathy.

"I'm sorry Ms. Warren. When you retained our services, you were told we charge nothing if we lose the case and 40% of the award if we won. In addition there were many expenses. We can appeal for more money, but I think you'd lose more than what you've already been awarded."

"Explain just exactly what fees." With one hand she gripped her handbag, while the other held the chair as if it would run out from under her.

"It's a long list." Michaels leaned back in his plush leather chair and stared at the ceiling. "Attorney's fees are computed on the total amount of the settlement or judgment, including any amounts recovered on behalf of any lien holder or other third party (such as worker's compensation, Medicare, Medicaid, medical providers, health insurers and the V. A., etc…)." It sounded as if he had turned on a recorded lecture without sympathy or care. He'd obviously used it often. He continued, "…who has reimbursement rights to any portion of the recovery and any amounts recovered as compensation for the payment of any reimbursement to any such lien holder or third party."

Melissa's head throbbed and hot tears clouded her vision. She didn't understand any of those words. She choked down a sob as Michaels continued.

"Attorney's fees are computed on the total amount of the settlement, award, verdict or judgment before deducting costs, expenses, liens, or any other disbursements." His chair straightened with a bang and he stared at Melissa. "I'd be glad to get my assistant to print it for you. In the meantime I suggest you take the award and put it to good use for your sister's care."

"Mr. Michaels, you and I know the car accident killed my brother in law and the baby my sister was carrying, but something else happened to Melanie. She doesn't talk but mumbles and screams and she has no control of her motor skills."

He rocked back and looked at his fingernails as if they angered him. "It's unfortunate but these things happen."

"But, but, where is the rest of the six million? You said you'd take care of us. You promised we'd be compensated. We were told that you're one of the best lawyers around."

He stretched his arms across his desk and assumed the praying pose. "You are not the first to be dissatisfied with the court's decision. As I said, you could appeal but again I would advise against it." With a slight eye movement he signaled the two door men. "Now if you'd kindly let my assistants show you to the door."

"But $500,000 isn't enough for long term care. What am I going to do?"

Oliver Michaels didn't move. "Ms. Warren we're through here. My condolences."

The two men eased her from the chair and escorted her to the door. "What am I going to do? It…it wasn't supposed to happen like this. Mr. Michaels, please."

Chapter 1

Oliver Michaels bumped and shoved his way through the New Orleans French Quarter crowds of rowdy vampires, witches with green fluorescent foot-long drinks, werewolves, drunken ghosts, someone dressed as a tree- house, a tower of pizza, priests, Big Bird, a naked man in a barrel, two headed monsters…name it. The outlandish costumes were a devilishly clever tribute to the artistry and creativity of the New Orleanians and visitors who came to the adult Halloween party.

Michaels eyed the swarm through his eighteenth century long black nun's habit which molded around his paunch and made him look like a pregnant nun. His pungent stench and the smoke of the Cuban cigar cleared away some of the crowd. He grinned as the decadent luscious mass milled past and he wondered who was male or female and smiled because it didn't matter because you could see a Viking wearing a gold shiny skirt, a bearded male and female Cleopatra, a girl with the plague, a ballerina with a dragon head dancing with a ghost-faced cowboy.

He flicked ashes on Jesus carrying a cross and cursed himself for not asking for a bigger settlement in the Melissa Warren case. He knew she'd be a mousey sympathetic witness who'd wring tears out of a stone and he had his daughter's wedding to pay for, which his wife had planned to be the biggest shindig this social season.

As he leaned against a greasy lamp post, a pirate put a string of beads around his hood and gave him a big sloppy alcoholic kiss and moved to his next victim. Michaels wiped his mouth and spit. He pushed his way into the Cat's Whiskers and grabbed the first drink he saw on the bar. He didn't care whose it was. "Hey Buddy," said the wrestle-mania bartender as he flicked a cloth at Michaels, "That's not yours. You gotta pay."

"Fuck off. Here's the nun's third finger."

He merged with the roaming masses of costumes, rinsed out his mouth, spat, drank the rest of whatever it was and threw the go-cup in the street. The power of being incognito inspired him to feel-up those who came in reach. He enjoyed the thrill of the surprised and pleased looks. But he got the most pleasure out of the ones who tried to fight him off and who struggled. Satisfied, he threw his cigar stub in a hot dog vendor's cart full of roasting greasy hot dogs, oblivious to the stream of curses, and shoved his way through the stockyard of Bourbon Street party goers, back toward the apartment loaned to him by a satisfied client.

His head ached, sweat dripped down the nun's cap around his eyes and he struggled to breathe. He grabbed his bottle of blood pressure pills and threw some in his mouth as the elevator reached the top floor.

The key card slid into the lock and the door popped open with a whirl and click and a low luxurious voice greeted him. "Come in, come in, so there you are, Oliver Michaels all decked out for Halloween. Lovely nun's habit. Come in Big Guy, or should I say Sister? Make yourself comfortable and take that thing off."

She was everything that had been promised and he grunted his approval. Her red hair flowed around her shoulders caressing the green dress that wrapped round her like a gentle silk glove bringing out her peaks, curves and valleys. Her emerald eyes had a depth forged from the mines of Brazil. Impossible to believe they were real. She poured him a drink as he watched her every desirable move.

"Here's a soothing drink, Big Guy. It's made of natural herbs; I think you might like it. Enjoy while I just finish up here in the kitchen and then we can play."

Michaels downed it in a couple of swallows and yelled into the kitchen, "Hey, Red. This drink has a kick to it. Got any more?" He let loose a loud bullfrog burp.

"Yeah. Sure. There's plenty."

"Did you bring the goods?"

"The goods, or the natural product for male enhancement to be precise, are packaged and ready to go. But we'll give it a test run later."

"You sure are a pleasant surprise. You look familiar. Have we met?"

"Oh I doubt it." She blew him a kiss. "I did wander around National Lawyer's Association meeting in the Convention Center today. You were talking about tort reform, right? You don't want lawmakers to put a ceiling on awards paid out to suits against the medical profession, is that correct?"

He raised his eyebrows. "I thought I might have seen you there. It's hard to miss a redhead in that suited crowd but I didn't expect you to have brains as well as a hot body. That's a surprise."

"Well Big Guy, I've got both so drink up. You'll never forget this evening, ever." She poured him another glass and returned with a bouquet of flowers. "Here's some colorful oleander for you to look at while I finish cooking."

"Well Red, tort reform is actually a bunch of crap. If you aren't out to make a lot of money, there is no use in doing anything. Take it from me, and I've made a lot of money." Oliver gulped the martini, wiped his mouth with the back of his hand, and belched. "Man that stuff's good."

"Have several, but come and eat I've made you this special Mushroom Alfredo Pasta and fresh oleander salad. I know you must be hungry."

"Smells good. I hope it tastes as good as it smells. That's one kick-ass martini! I've never tasted anything quite like it. Pour me another."

"Here you go. It's made from a rare Valerian root and quite potent so I suggest you not drink too much, unless you can hold your liquor."

"Hell yeah, I can drink anyone under the table. Let me have it! What did you say it is?"

She held her glass up to the light, swirling it slightly. "This yellowish-green liquid comes from the Valerian plant, which has been used as a medicinal herb since at least the time of ancient Greece and Rome. It's so mild it can be consumed as a tea and it mixes well in a martini."

"Great stuff." Oliver wiped his forehead with a napkin and swallowed two more blood pressure pills.

"Tonight will be the first and last of many things for you, Big Guy. Here, enjoy the salad and pasta, made with special ingredients just for you. Bon appétit."

"You ate and drank well, Oliver. Now, while you're sitting there quiet. Let me tell you something. To begin with, you lied."

She twirled her wine glass as she talked. "You told me you would financially provide for me and my family." She threw her napkin on her plate and pushed back to get a better look at him. "You're a crooked, selfish arse-hole."

Half the food from his plate was eaten, his cheeks were puffed up like a chipmunk full of food, and a partially chewed oleander leaf hung from the corner of his mouth. Only his eyes moved slightly as she slowly stood up. Her stiletto heels clicked on the tile floor like gunshots.

"Please don't mind if I clean up while I talk to you. You might find my point of view rather boring and pedantic, but it is kind of you to sit still and listen, for a change." She snapped on thick rubber gloves, took the leftover food, dumped it in the sink and ground it up in the disposal, scraped the plates, poured bleach over them, and put them in the dishwasher.

He didn't move. His breathing was shallow but he listened.

"Olli, you don't mind if I call you Olli, now do you-? Humm, since you don't answer, I guess I must assume you don't object. I've learned so much about you. Your lawsuits seldom make lives better; for the majority of your clients and physicians, their lives are much worse." She sat down again facing her guest. "Do you know that because of so many lawsuits, medical companies have stopped some of their valuable research for cures or preventive innovations for diseases and infections because work in those fields risked stirring up the bloodsuckers like you, eager for suitable lawsuits? The liability was too great. But you don't care, do you."

Michaels coughed then choked. She stopped, took a deep breath, and looked at him. His head hit the wood table with a thunk.

"Oh dear, your wine glass fell." She picked up the glass and wiped up the spilled wine. "Never mind. Don't bother to get up."

She wiped his face and hands. "Oh, please don't look so distressed, Olli, are you in an uncomfortable sitting position? Here let me help you." She pushed him upright and listened to his wheezing breath. "There, is sitting straight easier?"

"Well, I am very glad you enjoyed the salad and mushroom pasta. I am quite proud of my culinary skills. In fact, I am thinking of attending the Cordon Bleu school of cooking in Paris next year, the Cordon Bleu School of Poisonous Plants. It should be quite interesting, don't you think?"

Michaels slumped over again.

"Did you notice the flowers?" She moved around the apartment straightening and placing everything in order. "This wonderful ornamental shrub comes in lots of colors. It's hardy and used as median-barriers along the highways and it's considered one of the most poisonous plants in the world."

She turned and spoke to Olli as she put on her light sweater. "Even the smoke from a fire of these sticks and twigs can give off fumes that can poison food because the two poisons, oleandrin and nerine have a powerful effect on the heart. You do know, don't you, that the salad was oleander?"

She checked and rechecked the room, kitchen and bathroom, wiping everything for fingerprints and residue from the flower pollen.

She wiped out his mouth. "Oh, I forgot to tell you, I also served you some rare exotic Australian mushrooms, the 'Angel of Death', the world's most poisonous mushroom. It's quite rare and is found around Canberra and Melbourne. Have you ever been there? You should have visited there when you had the chance." She patted his cheek. "It'll look like you've had a massive heart attack, but unfortunately you won't feel much pain because of the Valerian sleeping medicine in the martini."

She sprayed the room with air-freshener to get rid of the odor of cooked mushrooms. "Sorry Olli old man but with oleander, death is quick. So I must be on my way."

There was no pulse on his clammy wrist and no dilation of his eyes, which was an effect of the poison. She reached in her bag, pulled out a strand of black hair and put it in his fist. "There you go Olli, that's so the police will be looking for a dark-haired person."

She stood straight, drove her clenched fist between his eyes and pushed him off the chair. "You won't ever hurt anyone again."

She checked the room once more. "Hope you don't mind if I go out and enjoy the Halloween festivities. I am afraid you can't go, Big Guy. So sorry."

She turned. "Good night Olli. I have a date in Chicago. See you in hell."

No one in the crowd noticed a red-headed woman in a green dress merge into the revelry.

Chapter 2

"Elliott! Oh Elliott! Over here." Congresswoman Mildred Pelto waved to him from a few round luncheon tables away. "Elliott, our table is over here and there are some people I want you to meet."

Hard to imagine that the voice of a petite, delicately framed woman could cut like a scalpel through the conversation of over five hundred people in the immense Chicago hotel dining room. Elliott waved, smiled, and gritted his teeth. "I'll be right there," he mouthed to her.

He shook hands with everyone in reach, patted a few on the back, and greeted people he didn't know. "Hi. I'm Elliott Edgars, good to see you here." His face ached with a Hollywood smile that had put permanent creases on his tan skin.

He acted as if he were already rich and famous by carrying his six-foot two-inch frame with full extension, no slumping to accommodate shorter people, so many had to look up to him. That put him at a desirable advantage, for then he could return their attention with a courteous bow making them feel acknowledged.

As he scrutinized the room filled with members of the American Bar Association, his brown eyes hardened to a squint when he observed the others around Pelto's table; all of them became monetarily successful by winning lucrative cases. His heart fluttered from excitement and fear. He dried his moist hands on the inside of his pants pockets and his gut seized as if the last tacos he'd eaten were filled with botulism. His smile was cemented in place. He knew that they could either eat him alive or ask him to join in the feast.

He took a deep breath. Never taking his eyes off the notorious figures around the luncheon table, he walked toward them, every step firm and solid, with no hesitation in his direction or purpose. His steps were softened by the plush carpet as the clanking of the servers echoed around the room and the heavy odor of fresh-cooked food wafted from the hidden kitchen. Sweat seeped into his undershirt. He knew about all of them. The four men and one woman who could ruin anyone's career with a look, a snub, or a word shared in a quiet conversation.

Manipulative Congresswoman Pelto wore a snake's smile, her tongue flicking to feel the fear around her. She had married into lots of money and schemed to make sure there was always more coming under her control.

"Well, Congresswoman Pelto, you are looking as beautiful as ever." Elliott smiled, took her extended hand in both his hands, and bent toward her.

"Oh for goodness sakes, Elliott, I told you to call me Mildred," she said, pleased with his attention and assumed respect.

"Well, Mildred, I've heard you've continued the fight and you keep some staid old fogies jumping. Glad to know someone up there is working."

"Well Elliott," Mildred said with a laugh that was more of a deep chest snort. "You've learned to flatter early in your young career. Keep it up, it works." She patted his coat lapel.

She turned as if bestowing her regal graces on the other members of the table. "Gentlemen," she said. Without hesitation the four men turned. "This is Elliott Edgars, a very promising young candidate, uh …representative from Florida." Mildred's intentional slip of the tongue alerted them to Elliott's political potential and that he had Mildred's support. Four pairs of eyes snapped to attention and bored into Elliott.

"To my right is Senator Merriweather from Utah." With a delicate feminine handshake, he undressed Elliott with his eyes. Elliott shivered. He'd heard the rumors of Merriweather's secret life and wondered when it would be leaked to the press.

"Pleased to meet you sir, I've heard you have a strong constituency. Congratulations. I'd like to talk to you about how to build up a strong electorate, when you have time."

"This," Pelto said indicating a ruddy round faced man with a line-backer form, "is Tom O'Hara. As President of the San Francisco Lawyers Association, he controls most of the West Coast Bar Associations."

The table dipped as he pushed himself up to shake Elliott's hand. O'Hara breathed heavily and spewed a cough into a napkin. He stared at Elliott and seemed to say, "If you move, I'll have one of my men shoot you." He cleared his throat but still gurgled, "Yeah, I've heard about you." He cleared his throat again. "We need to sit down and have a talk; a serious talk, not just a 'let's do lunch' talk." His smile faded into a slight sneer and the chair sagged as he plopped down.

Elliott's stone gaze never left O'Hara and he threw the challenge back. "Let's set a date. I'm ready." He watched as the men's eyebrows rose, surprised at his bold response.

He moved around the table to shake hands with Johnny Collier and Austin Kaufman as Pelto smiled and introduced them, he knew both were known for their unscrupulous brutality and their success. There was no smile or politeness here, just direct and straight. "Mr. Kaufman, I've heard a lot about you. You've studied medicine and law and that makes you quite a knowledgeable asset. It seems it's hard to win a case against you." Kaufman glared, turned and sat down. Elliott stared at the man's back. More than humiliation, he felt evil coming from Kaufman and a clear warning.

He watched as Mildred twitched and straightened her shoulders and said, "We've kept the empty chair for Oliver Michaels who was recently found dead of a heart attack in New Orleans." The other men grunted, looked from side to side and showed no emotion. Then Collier leaned back and lifted his wine glass, "I guess we ought to give a toast to his departure. Nothing too nice, just RIP you old bastard."

Elliott believed that even if he were deaf, he could read the intentions and motives of people by watching their mannerisms, glances, dilated eyes and all manner of body language. He glanced at Pelto who patted her hair. "Well, there were flowers at the funeral. Someone put on the casket, black carnations and someone put those cheap oleander things that grow on the side of the highway."

The tension around the table alerted Elliott to the underlying disrespect these power-shakers had for each other. Collier stretched his arms and rested them on the chairs next to him and whispered, "They must've been sent by people who were glad to see him go, especially people who owed him money. You all know he was getting slow and losing his edge. He didn't notice until it was too late that I took the majority of the settlement on the last case we worked." He snorted into his napkin. "Funny he never worked with me again."

Elliott flinched; he knew there was no love lost between these fierce competitors.

He was very well aware of Mildred's snake eyes that flicked from each man as she noted and evaluated their movements and reactions. She saw mutual recognition, awareness, and caution. He watched as her thin smile tried hard to crack her Botox skin, as she gloated at how successful her manipulation was going. But under the stiff façade, he knew that any of these men could destroy her and he watched the play unfold. Shaky under her concrete demeanor, Mildred called out, "Waiter, bring me a gin and tonic, skip the ice." Three waiters jostled, bumped into each other scurrying around the tables to get to the bar. "Elliott, come sit next to me," she ordered. She slammed her bag on the table, dragged out her chair before Elliott could reach it, sat down, ignored him, and leaned across the table. "Tom, that panel discussion this morning about lawsuits affecting patient care was a total farce," she spat out, "Such a ridiculous waste of time." She turned and glared at the waiter weaving his way through the crowd with a large gin and tonic. "Collier, O'Hara, and I tried to insert a modicum of logic into the conversation but the physicians were so single-minded and set in their opinions that there was no real discussion at all. In fact," she said as she sat back in her chair and pushed back her already stiff hair from her forehead, "the pharmacist we've hired, Dr. Mark Something-or-other, walked out before the session was over." She yanked her drink from the waiter's tray, turned her back without acknowledging him, and continued. "We have to have more profitable experiences in these meetings or just cancel them all together."

Collier leaned over the table and growled through his bushy manicured mustache, "Come on Mildred, you know we gave them hell."

"You sure made 'em squirm, Collier." O'Hara wiped his forehead with the white table napkin, took several pills from a bottle in his inside pocket, and swallowed them with the red wine. Merriweather eyed the group with amusement while Kaufman methodically, determinedly, and unconsciously tore the stack of conference brochures and handouts into little pieces.

Elliott watched the power play, each person shooting intimidating comments masked in humor, toward the others. The egotistical verbal ribbing hit their marks but bounced off the hardboiled veterans for they were competent, aggressive, and confident colleagues ready to turn on each other. Sweat was beading around his white shirt collar that felt tighter now than two hours ago. He fought down the nervous tension building up by adjusting and readjusting his collar and tie yet he was still fully aware of the relaxing effect the drink was making on Mildred Pelto as she talked to the other men at the table. For now he was going to sit back and watch the intrigue.

Pelto took a deep breath and felt in control of the persons at the table and the progress of their meeting. The queen bee gloated. "Tommy, be civil now when you introduce our speaker, ok?"

"Mildred," O Hara glared at her, and said, "No one is allowed to call me Tommy but you, and never in public."

Senator Merriweather giggled as he dotted his mouth with the napkin. "Tommy, I didn't know you had a sensitive spot. My, my, you'd better not let the press know or they'll hound you forever."

"Go on, Tom," Collier yelled out. "Introduce the victim and let's get this over with. We'll heckle you both and get this session roaring. This meeting has been booooring." He leaned back in his chair, stared at the ceiling, his left eyebrow and upper lip rose in a snarl. "I hate to waste time on these losers."

Kaufman crushed the bits of torn paper into a ball and threw it at a passing waiter, "Take this crap off the table," he snapped. Small pieces of paper drifted to the floor as the waiter fought to catch the disintegrating paper ball.

The focus in the room turned to the introduction and message given by the invited guest, Surgeon General Dr. Chapel. Elliott had heard positive comments about him and was eager to hear his message about Tort Reform and to feel what the mood and opinions were from around the table, but he suspected he already knew.

Like a lone gazelle surrounded by a pride of hungry lions, the Surgeon General took the podium. His sole support came from the physicians from the earlier panel discussion, except the pharmacist, Mark Warren from Los Angeles, who'd left the meeting. Dr. Chapel looked around and with a steady, confident voice began. "Good afternoon everyone. I am pleased to be here with this distinguished assembly and even though I know that I am not in a receptive group, I would like to give the medical profession's side to Tort Reform."

"Oh great, here we go again. That same goody-two shoes is here always trying to ram a conscience down our throats," Collier moaned, pushed his dinner plate away and put his head down on his folded arms.

"Well for you Johnny," O'Hara laughed, slapped his hand on the table making the plates jump and the water glasses shake, "...that would be impossible because you don't have a conscience!" Mildred smiled at Johnny's discomfort.

Kaufman was now trying to tear up the white linen napkin. "To support Tort Reform would be shooting ourselves in the foot and taking money out of our pockets."

"That's just what they're trying to do," O'Hara warned. Kaufman frowned at O'Hara as the napkin ripped in two.

"Let's sue the docs for not practicing medicine." Merriweather let out another feminine nervous titter, which he tried to cover up by slamming on the table and laughing at his weak attempt at humor.

Elliott listened to the heckling from around the table and watched impassively as his stomach knotted up. His eyes moved from face to face recording each gesture and remark while he analyzed what viciousness and power each had and what dangers there would be working with anyone of them. He pretended to sip his wine while he wondered if he could be so cruel, if he could be like them

Dr. Chapel was beginning to wind down his presentation. Still calm and in control in spite of the jeering interruptions, he appealed to the audience, "We need both the medical and legal professions to be accountable, responsible, and qualified."

"Don't worry, Doc. We'll keep you in line!" Johnny yelled out. There was a smattering of laughter from the dining room attendees.

Dr. Chapel turned to Collier and said, "Let me ask you this. Who will you go to when you have a heart attack, a stroke, a brain tumor, or cancer? Will the doctor of your choice refuse to see you for fear of a lawsuit? Who will help you die a comfortable and respectable death?" Dr. Chapel stretched out his arms to the audience. "Can't we lead the search for a better solution?" He wiped his forehead. "Thank you for listening." He gripped the podium, turned, and with defeated heavy steps, walked to his seat.

From the back of the room, cutting through the polite applause, a voice boomed out. "Give 'em hell, Doc!"

A killing chill drove spikes down Elliott's back, the wine glass snapped in his hand as he turned to see his brother Robert push through the back door wearing a mismatched suit and not his usual jeans shorts and Hawaiian shirt. Elliott shivered, wondering what nastiness Robert was up to.

If hatred had a boiling point, it reached Robert ten seconds before he slipped out of the room. He growled half aloud, "God-damned lawyers, including my sweet talking baby brother."

Unable to control the burning rage that blinded his path, he slammed into a cart of luncheon trays, and like a bull in a rodeo, swept his arms up, smashing the china and aluminum covers, along with the unsuspecting waiter, into the gilded wallpaper.

Without stopping, he thundered out of the hotel, shoving a path through unsuspecting pedestrians and headed toward a crowded mall to disappear before the security guards pushed through the back door.

Chapter 3

Mark's head pounded from rising blood pressure which made high screaming pitches in his ears. Sweat trickled down his reddened face and he clenched his fists. The migraines, from that fall during a marathon several years ago, continued to make their unannounced angry reappearance, especially during times of stress. Thankfully, neither his hearing nor his sight was affected but for a scientist, the infrequent memory loss sent him into momentary panic until he gained recall, for he covertly prided himself on his mental abilities while always appearing humble at every turn. Men were jealous of his long, lithe body that loved running. He loved running, especially to escape from events that he had no control over and he thrived in winning.

He was a pharmacist, an invited guest to the conference on medical malpractice, and it turned out to be a humiliating free-for-all against the physicians. The jack-hammer screamed in his ears. He had to get out. He had to get away from the pompous egotistical lawyers sitting on the panel discussion. He abruptly stood up, his chair slammed against the wood floor as he grabbed his briefcase and stomped off the stage to barking laughter from Johnny Collier.

He slammed the door into the wall as he headed into the hallway leading to the exit, pushed his glasses up his sweaty nose, turned the corner and ran smack into a large, scowling, bushy grey-haired man blocking the exit. Actually, blocking most of the hallway. Mark stared. The man was twice his size so the instinct to fight quickly disappeared.

"That Johnny Collier is an ass-hole. Sorry you had to stay up there and be humiliated with all his odious, pontificating bullshit."

Mark didn't move, didn't say a word and didn't think he was breathing.

This bear of a man said, "I'm Robert Edgars. I'm not a lawyer. I'm helping out some friends by nosing around to see what new schemes the shysters are dredging up to inflict on the rest of us poor bastards. It's a private investigation into some of their- shall we say- subversive financial behavior?"

"So you're a policeman?"

"Hell, No. I'll be honest with you." He smoothed down his bushy beard, folded his hands over his stomach, and said, "Your Dad's a friend of mine. We trade exotic plants and he has told me all about his past dealings with crooked lawyers. I've also had my problems with lawyers."

He whispered, even though there was no one else in the hall. "The people who hired me know my revulsion; I have a special murderous affinity for those who run away with money from their clients and build up their own off-shore accounts like the one, who out of the kindness of his heart, took all my retirement investments. Don't worry, I get angry." He paused. "And …I get even."

Mark stiffened. "What do you want?"

Robert put his hand on Mark's shoulder and said, "Hey, listen, they treated you real shitty up there. You guys were set up to fall flat-faced in front of this biased crowd. My brother, Elliott, was in the audience and I didn't see him coming to Dr. Chapel's defense. He's as much a bastard as the rest of them."

The six seconds the men stared at each other stopped time, while each sized up the other. Robert's piercing blue eyes dared Mark to disbelieve while Mark relaxed his clenched fists.

"Dad's never mentioned you."

"Don't worry. He will. I just took him and Melissa to the airport."

"They didn't say anything about going with you."

"I surprised them. I asked Melissa to come work for me. It'll help pay for Melody's care."

"Ok." Mark stuck out his hand. "I'll talk to Dad. So you know my sisters?"

"Sure do. Sad about Melody's car accident. Real sorry there."

Robert squeezed Mark's hand. "Come on, you up-tight half-Aussi." He grabbed Mark's arm, pulled him out into the street, and said, "Let's grab a bite to eat before you have to get to the airport. There is a real hole-in-the-wall diner down the side street from the hotel where our talk can inflame the disgust we both have for unethical, self-serving, money-grabbing crooks."

Mark's head spun with mixing words from the conference panel and Robert's unusual vocabulary, making him feel like he might be hallucinating. But he let himself be pushed into a diner with French fry smells laminated into the walls along with decades of dust and dirt.

Robert ordered but Mark didn't eat. He wasn't sure what kind of meat would ooze green oil, besides Robert had disgusting eating habits which made Mark's stomach tie in knots. Robert was fascinating, knowledgeable and told stories of escapades into East

Germany with German friends, Viet Nam, the South Sea Islands, and almost any country Mark could name. At least they were entertaining stories even if they might be exaggerated. Gradually, the tension in his shoulders and neck relaxed as he listened.

Robert wrapped up the lunch leftovers and threw a hundred-dollar bill on the table. "Come on. I'll drive you to the airport. Your luggage is already in my car and you'll just make the 4:45 boarding."

"How the hell… How did you know?"

Robert leaned in close, his breath smelled of salami and garlic, and said soft and low, "Mark, you don't want to know. Remember, I am a friend of your father."

Mark hid a gag behind a paper napkin and squirmed to get out of the wooden bench. Before he could get up from the table, Robert was already moving out of the diner into the street, forcing Mark to jog to catch up. For a big man, Robert must be more muscle than fat.

Robert stopped in front of a car that was beat up and tied together with wires and cords, looking like a piece of trash. He laughed when he saw Mark's jaw drop

"Oh my god, Robert. The last time I saw a 1943 powder blue Studebaker was in a movie somewhere."

"This old babe used to belong to my grandfather and has since been—modified—shall we say. No one will steal this one. And they would be surprised if they tried."

"Why? I can't believe that pile of junk can move, much less stay together in one piece."

"Well," Robert laughed and said, "If anyone was stupid enough to try and steal it, the minute they touched the steering wheel the electric current would knock their balls off. Get in. You're ok. You just gotta know how to handle her."

The dry asphalt from the street hit underneath the car like a machine gun. The car was a real surprise. She rocketed off like a Porsche and delivered an unbelievably smooth ride.

"Robert if you don't slow down, we'll miss the airport."

The Blue Babe rolled around the corner into the departing flight lane, scattered pedestrians, screeched to a stop and gunned the motor. With a loud pop, blue-black smoke mushroomed from the tailpipe, alerting the traffic security. Robert hid his wild bushy hair under a cap and pulled it down close to his eyes. He scanned pedestrians, cops, suitcases, cars. "Nice to meet you Mark. I'll be in touch real soon. I gotta' run before the Keystone cops wanna' inspect my car."

Mark jumped and snatched his suitcase from the back seat then stood back and watched the car speed off. A shiver racked his spine as if the Blue Babe had left him with a shock. Mark stepped back and listened to the Babe speed around the opposite side of the departure lanes. He watched the blue-black smoke trail around the lines of cars, into the exit row and onto the freeway. Robert was like an addiction, a fascinating, unbelievable character you are afraid of and yet want to see more of. He was like a drug you can't stop taking. He had to ask his Dad about this Robert.

Mark stepped into the street and hailed a taxi. "I've got a job to finish."

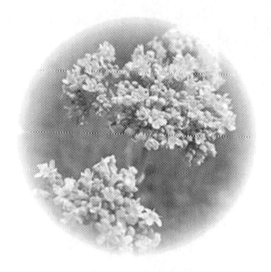

Chapter 4

Look for Room 9681, Executive Suite, and Tom O'Hara. She walked as if in deep water with her stiletto heels gliding across the hall carpet, the green silk dress barely swaying with her steps.

In her shoulder bag were red flowers. She carried the brown straw basket in front of her with both hands as if it had too many raw eggs piled into a precarious pyramid. "Easy now my dear colorful friends. The cool weather here in Chicago has made you dormant and lethargic." She whispered to the basket, "Poor little dears to be aroused soon. Oh well, we all have to do our work to get paid. Mr. O'Hara loves fruit, and he'll have a nice basket filled - with a bite!" She paused, smoothed her red hair, and took a deep breath. She stopped. Knocked on the door and smiled.

A toilet flushed and the sound of the TV stopped. The door to Suite 9681 flew open.

"Hello there, Tom," she said. "Great talk today! It was thrilling to see you excite the troops! Well done." She stepped in past the surprised O'Hara.

He slammed the door shut. With labored steps, heavy breathing, sweat beading around his face and neck, he followed her into the large sitting room. "I'm not often surprised," he wheezed. "It's not good for my health. I didn't know it was you who would be coming. You don't look half bad in that get-up. When did you start getting dressed up?"

She turned and watched the red puffy face in front of her. "You look like you've been in a hot-tub. You all right?" She stretched out her hands. "I've brought you a basket of fruit. It's healthy, you know, and good for you."

"Thank you, thank you. So you've brought a basket of fruit!" He jerked the basket from her hands and slammed it down on a near coffee table. "What about the medicine?"

She watched in horror as the fruit began to move. Her heart was beating fast and she moved so O'Hara's eyes would follow her away from the basket. Her hands shook as she pulled the medicine bottles and the flowers from her bag.

"Here are some Valeria flowers that grow on the plant where the berries come from for your sleeping medicine; its other name is the garden heliotrope. It looks a bit like Queen Anne's Lace, if you are familiar with that plant."

"No. Can't say that I am. I don't care for flowers. That's woman's stuff." O'Hara's lip curled as if he'd eaten rotten liver.

"And yes, I've brought you the all-natural sleeping medicine you requested. You can take two at a time with no problem." He snatched them from her, turned to the water decanter, poured six tablets into his hand, and swallowed them all with thick and heavy gulps.

She relaxed as the tension flowed out of her and she smiled. "The new medicine is made from the Valerian root. Two pills would have been enough," she whispered.

"This better work," O'Hara snapped. "My blood pressure's over two hundred and I've had a terrible headache all day."

"Don't worry, Tom," she soothed. "You'll be fine. It won't take long now." Her voice was hypnotic, soft, and calming. "I have a surprise for you Tom."

He blinked. No one called him Tom except his family. No one. But right now he felt hassle-free. The stress was draining from his arms and legs and left him feeling marshmallow-soft and pliable. A laugh was coming up from somewhere deep inside him. "A laugh? A bubbling sensation? Me? Am I getting dizzy? This is too weird." He sank into the thick, velvet sofa cushions.

She didn't move but watched his eyes droop and his arms fall to his sides. "There you go. Feeling better already? I thought we could celebrate a successful seminar day with a special drink-concoction I've made up from the Valerian berries." She moved with soft, cat-like steps to the bar. "Here, I'll just make it up here. The hotel doesn't charge you for using the bar in the Executive Suite, does it?"

O'Hara's head wobbled as he tried to clear his mind. "Oh shit, yeah. They charge! They smell a rich man coming down the street ten blocks away!" He struggled for words, and when he found them, spit them out as if they were poison. "I'm surprised they aren't charging for the toilet paper! I'll hand over the bill to the American Trial Lawyers Association and they'll cover it. No problem."

"Well Tom, I'm just glad to get paid! My fee is going to go up a great deal after hearing the salaries that these folks are receiving!"

He held his head in his two hands. His voice became quieter. "Take whatever you need. I'm paying you for my sleep-aids, out of my own pocket. Nobody needs to know." He leaned back on the soft cushions, closed his eyes and felt himself float. "Man! What was that stuff I took?"

The ice tinkled in the glass as she made the yellow-green drink. "I just mentioned the name. The medicine and the drink are made from the Valerian plant, which has been used as a medicinal herb since at least the time of ancient Greece and Rome. Hippocrates described its properties and prescribed it as a remedy for insomnia." She smiled with satisfaction. "I was sure it would work on you. It is a rare treat; expensive, but I'm sure you can pay for it with no pain to yourself."

"Yeah, money will get you anything. Ask me, I know!" O'Hara threw back the cocktail and wiped his mouth with the back of his hand. "Hope this works. I've got to get my sleep tonight."

Confidence and excitement tingled in her as she sat next to Tom and watched for physical signs. His eyes were drooping and he was having trouble focusing. Her voice lowered when she said, "You know, I would not have your life style for all your money. You have high-tension situations, high-risk bargains, constant headaches, and a high-speed lifestyle that can drive you crazy. First, you lose your calm, then your composure, then your sleep and, then, your mind. Is it all worth that much?"

"Yes," he mumbled, "The more money the better. I have people like you who know how to make and bring me any kind of drugs that I need to calm me and help me sleep." He rubbed his hands over his forehead and eyes. "I have to be fresh tomorrow morning!" Tom laughed in slow motion with a deep gurgle.

"Boy, this stuff works. But I'll need to be alert to catch an early plane tomorrow. I won't have any problems in the morning, will I?" His breathing was slowing and his words were slurred.

"No, Tom, no." She said through tight lips, "You won't have any problem in the morning." She clenched her teeth together, took his sweaty arm, and found a weak pulse. Nausea oozed into her throat. She swallowed and took several slow deep breaths. "Well, O'Hara,

I think you're going to OD on sleeping medicine." She dropped his arm.

With anger and force, she pushed him over. "Cheers, Tom. And Sweet Dreams. You won't sue anyone, ever again."

"How easy that was. Ten minutes. Dead asleep. Now let's get you undressed from all these fabulously expensive clothes. What good are they to you now?" She ripped his clothes as she yanked them off and threw them around the room. No tears. She yelled, "You bastard, you dirty rotten bastard." She struggled, pushed, and shoved O'Hara's body in place on the sofa. She yanked his arm up and felt a slight pulse. "I should have known that a greedy bastard like you would have taken too many pills."

"Naked as a jaybird you are so pathetic. What good is your wealth now?" She straightened up, hands on her hips, and stared at O'Hara. "Well Mr. O'Hara, you are not the first of the vultures to taste death. Oliver Michaels was first and he was well wined and dined and yet had such pains in his stomach. Poor fellow. There will be others to follow and no one is less vile than the next. You have the distinction of being the second one that I will have cleared away from this earth. There are so many...." She nudged his jelly-like pale skin with her stiletto heel as he exhaled a slight groan.

She put on heavy, thick work gloves and picked up the basket from the table. The basket handle snapped into a long fork-like tool. With slow motion movements, she removed the fruit that covered the colorful deadly surprise beneath.

She paused, took several deep breaths to calm her shaking hands and repeated to herself to go easy, very careful, and slow. Go slow. She slowed her breathing, took the forked tool, and picked up the first one.

"Oh, you are a beauty," she whispered as she lifted the sluggish coral snake out of the basket. "You beautiful darling corals are some of the flashiest, gaudiest, and most colorful of snakes, with banding of red, yellow/white and black. But oh you are so elusive and shy."

As she carried it over to the drugged lump of O'Hara, the snake wove in the air, like a breeze blowing willow tree branches. Speaking in a soft hypnotic voice she asked, "Tom, do you remember the Boy Scout rhyme about coral snakes?" She glared at the human blob. "Of course not. You thought you were too good for them, so let me tell you. Let's see, how did it go? Humm…" She placed the snake on O'Hara's neck. "Red next to Yellow will kill a Fellow." She prodded the snake. It twisted, coiled, straightened, and lunged for skin. She trembled. Her voice quivered. "Another one says, 'If Red touches Yellow, you're a dead Fellow." The coral snake hung on. Coral snakes don't strike, they bite and latch on, and pump venom into their victim.

She backed away from the snake. Shaking. Stepping with effort and staying in control. "I wasn't sure the Valerian would be enough to kill such a big lump, so I brought my colorful venomous friends along. One more coral should do the trick." She trembled as she lifted the basket and with the hook, placed the second coral near the artery to his heart. "Here is another beauty to feast on a bloated money-grubber. These two beauties have a powerful neurotoxin that paralyzes breathing muscles. It'll look like you had a cardiac arrest after you overdosed." She squinted as she watched the snakes. "I guess this was over-kill. But I had to be sure."

Without taking her eyes off the coral snakes, she used the snake-handler and pulled out a pygmy rattler. "There you go my little friend. You won't hurt anyone but you sure will give someone a scare. Go. Hide under the bed or some other place. You will be a smokescreen, something to mislead the police."

"Almost done." With caution she detached the two coral snakes from O'Hara's clammy skin and placed them back in the basket and closed the lid. "How convenient that the only hospitals that carry the anti-venom for a coral snake bite are in the South- the Deep South. Not here in Chicago!" She took a long, deep breath.

Her eyes narrowed as she watched the pygmy wind its way into a corner and curl up, its head resting on its top coil, ready to strike.

Another tremor shook her. It was done. There was no turning back.

She turned and looked at O'Hara and felt for a pulse. She relaxed, tension gone except in the hand carrying the basket.

"G'night, Tom. You are dead asleep by now. I have to go. I have a date in San Francisco. See you in hell."

Chapter 5

"My God, why did I ever agree to go to Chicago and be a part of that god-damn panel? Stupid, stupid, stupid." Mark yelled at the open sky, trying to match the roar of his Porsche running full throttle. He headed north from his apartment in Los Angeles to pick up his father at the Farmer's Market in Santa Barbara, then on to his farm in Cuyama. He banged his fist on the convertible's steering wheel, turned and talked to the empty seat next to him, "Bloody bullocks. I wanted a good vacation for Dad and Melissa." He felt a knife beginning to pierce through his right ear and he patted the empty passenger seat, "Don't worry, Luv. I'll be alright soon."

He gripped the gear shift and felt the car's power throb into his body. The smell of the sea salt, the smash of the waves on the brown sand and the calls of the surfers reminded him of why he loved driving with the top down. His skin tightened and prickled from the sun's blasting heat. He touched his face and pulled his fingers through his thinning, red hair; the memory of his wife told him that he should've put on a cap or used sun block. He shifted into a lower gear as he rounded a hill, then plunged into a view of the blue Pacific Ocean.

He readjusted his sunglasses and gunned the car up the next hill and squirmed in his seat as he remembered the humiliating and insulting meeting. He naively thought he could help mediate the Tort Reform issue. His stomach churned as he reached for the bottle of antacids, opened the bottle and tossed the pills in his mouth and with a mouth full of partially eaten antacids, yelled, "Stupid, stupid, stupid." He coughed, choked, and then wheezed. "Well, that wasn't smart."

The car, not wanting to slow down, roared a complaint when Mark turned off the highway onto State Street and headed into Santa Barbara. Replaying the events in Chicago drove tension lines up the back of his neck and into his clenched jaws. It was a conference held each year by the American Bar Association for the top ten percent of law school graduates. Mark snorted in disgust as he recalled the meeting.

Mark drove down State Street and headed for the open market where his father was waiting. "Hi. Did ya sell everything? Any leftovers to take home?" Mark called out as he reached over and opened the door.

"Nope. Gave 'em away." Dad stepped in and sat down. "Uumph, the seats in this car are so low, I feel like I'm in a bath tub. I hope my butt isn't dragging on the ground."

Mark grinned, "You're getting old. You probably give away more than you sell. "

A concerned look settled on Dad's face. "There've been a lot of changes in the twenty-five years you've been away, son. We don't have the same social services that they have in Australia and there're just so many people in need of food these days." He threw the empty baskets in the small back seat, fastened his seat belt, and adjusted his brimmed hat. "It's sad. Anything I have left over I just give away. I sure don't need much these days." He stared up at the blue foothills that surround Santa Barbara and pictured his small farm far on the other side of the rolling hills, nestled safe and waiting for his farmer's touch.

Mark drove down State Street, flew over the speed bumps, and headed out to Cuyama. Dad grabbed his seat belt and his hat. "Son," he yelled. "You're gonna ruin this car before too long. Can't you drive a little slower?"

"Hang on, Let's see how she takes the curves."

"Well, dag-nab it, drive slow enough so we can talk. I can't hear myself much less you." He grimaced, hung on to the door handle and his hat as they flew around the curves and over the hills. "Haven't had a chance to talk to you since the meeting. How'd it go?"

Mark frowned and gripped the steering wheel, wringing the leather covering. Dad watched and his eyebrows rose with surprise.

"The meeting started out well but then it got ugly. There were three attorneys and two physicians and me on the panel. Our discussion topic was, "Do Lawsuits Affect the Way Doctors Provide Patient Care?"

His father shook his head, "Man that should have been a sign for you to turn and run. Boy, am I glad I missed that one. Melissa and I took a bus tour of the city." He looked away from Mark, "I..I...I I had to leave and come home, after the tour, you know, I had to get back to my farm and Melissa was anxious about Melody."

"I'm glad you weren't there. I did turn and run but not until it was almost over." Mark swerved to miss a couple of jack-rabbits. "Must be mating season. Hey, we ate those in Australia. Want some for tonight's dinner?"

"No," he yelled over the car's loud growl. "They might be rabid."

He smashed his hat tight on his head and his knuckles turned white gripping the door handle. The wind tore at his words and made his eyes water.

Mark leaned toward his father and shouted in his ear, "Collier asked us how many mistakes had we made in the operating room or in dispensing medicine and how much pain and suffering have we caused?"

Dad flinched as the words hit him. "Sometimes, things just can't be helped." He let go of his hat and pointed his finger at Mark. "And you can never go back and change what happened."

Regurgitating the memories of the meeting, Mark drove slower and slower. "Dr. Jackson Chapel, who is the kindest man I know, said he couldn't see himself doing anything else because he loves medicine. He told us that one of his medical school mentors was quite wealthy and worked for the university, at his own insistence, for a dollar a year. He'd say to his students, that they should love medicine so much that if they were independently wealthy, they would be willing to pay for the privilege of being a doctor."

"That's how I felt. We all swore the Hippocratic Oath to treat patients to the best of our abilities." Dad loosened his grip on the door handle and patted his son on the arm. The more Mark's words tumbled out, the more he relaxed. "So it was with me," he said and looked toward the blue hills. "But that was a long time ago."

"You should've heard Pelto whine through her petite plastic-surgery nose." Mark pinched his nose and mimicked Pelto's high-pitched voice: "It is the duty of all lawyers to defend the defenseless and to protect them from any cause that besets them."

"You always were a good mimic. How do you get your voice to change like that?"

Mark slowed the car so he wasn't screaming. He shook his head. "You know lawsuits are driving up health care costs."

"Yep. That's what the folks around my farm are dealing with

every day. They can't afford to pay and the docs have to charge high prices just to make ends meet, so the docs move to cities and set up or join a big practice with other doctors to help offset the costs."

"Well, I remember you had bad experiences with lawyers. But I don't know what happened; just that I was sent to Aunt Birdie in Adelaide and stayed there over twenty five years." He watched as his father seemed to shrink several sizes and fade into the seat. The weight of the past aged him into a withered old man.

"It was twenty five years and seven months ago. I'd rather not talk about it right now son. It's more important that we deal with the small award given for Melody's care. Melissa is trying to take care of all the details but it's tough for her. It does keep her occupied though. Maybe some other time. Anything else interesting happen at the meeting?"

It was an obvious change of subject but Mark asked, "Do you remember Thomas O'Hara?"

Dad's thoughts turned his face to stone. "Thomas O'Hara. A name I've loathed for years. He's the one who led the suit against Dr. Harmon in San Francisco and Harmon was one of my medical school friends."

"Yep. The same one." Mark slowed at the crossroads and signaled right.

Dad wrung his hat into a nervous ball. "O'Hara and his team of well-paid lawyers went through forty-five years of documents of my old friend. They noted and entered as evidence every busted nose, every tonsillectomy, every broken arm, all repeat visits, and down to Harmon's own late developed incontinence. Although they didn't prove anything, it was shameful and humiliating. He wound up declaring bankruptcy and retired to Oregon to fish the rest of his life away. I felt wretched for him and his family; they were all devastated."

Mark changed the subject. "I tried to explain that most people are interested in medicine because they want to help others and aren't after wealth. Many doctors say that their profession is a calling and that it was worth the personal sacrifices they had to make."

"Hey, hey." Dad held up his hands in protest. "You don't have to preach to the choir. Even though young folks might love the career, fewer and fewer are becoming doctors because they fear lawsuits, the insurance costs, the long work hours, and the small pay."

Mark felt helpless as he looked over at his father, and turned into the mile long gravel driveway to the farm. "You know what, I ran into a friend of yours." Mark grinned and threw a curious look at his Dad. "Do you remember a man called Robert Edgars?"

He shot straight up, shocked, and then laughed. "Oh, my god. Did you run into that old bastard? He showed up unexpected, which is usual for him, and took Melissa and me to the airport."

"Yeah, I did literally run into him after the meeting. I guess you know him, then?"

"Oh, my god yes, fortunate or unfortunate, but, yep, I know him. He's a weird character. He uses highfaluting language and curses like a pirate. He's one complex, complicated, and dangerous person. One minute he can sweet-talk you and the next he's blasting like a bellows."

"I guess he drove the Blue Babe?"

"Yep." Dad slapped his knee. "Scared Melissa to death to ride in …well I was gonna say a piece of shit, but it is a true hidden jewel." Dad had a twinkle in his eye.

Mark grinned and nodded.

Dad held onto his hat, bent over with laughter. "Oh, hell yes, the first time I rode in the Blue Babe was years ago. Man what a trip we had."

Mark down-shifted into second gear and turned left into the parched dirt that once was grass. "I kinda liked that weird and frightening guy but you can bet I kept my hands tucked tight under my armpits all the way to the airport; I was afraid to touch anything." The dust billowed and curled into the air behind Mark's car. He liked talking about Robert because he realized his dad had been in Robert's company and had survived.

"Home again, home again." Dad directed with his hat. "Pull in over there next to the green house and leave some parking space 'cause every now and then, some folks come to buy plants."

They got out of the car and picked up Mark's things. "Dad you should have seen the Blue Babe speed off. I had to jump fast to snatch my suitcase from the back seat."

He looked at Mark, questioning. "But you didn't come home then, did you."

Mark shrugged. "No, I decided that I wasn't in a hurry to get back to my lab in LA. Besides, I wanted to take a boat ride around the Chicago Harbor. I thought it would be like Sydney Harbor and I was feeling a bit homesick. Besides, there were a few things that I needed to do and I thought I might be interested in the evening discussions."

"Good grief, Son, you didn't go back, did you? You must be something of a masochist." He shuddered. "Another thing, be careful of Robert. One minute, he'll cut you in two and walk off laughing but the next minute he'll charm the habit off a nun and be rolling in the hay with her. Beats me as to how women fall for him. He's always after something. Be careful. You aren't going to see him again, are you?"

Chapter 6

"Don't touch that!"

"What?" Mark pulled back. "Oh Christ. The castor bean plant. Why have you got that poisonous thing in here?"

"Sorry, son. You ought to wear gloves out here in the greenhouse." In his long pants, long sleeve shirt, thick rubber gloves and straw hat, Dad pushed Mark aside with an elbow. "Move back away, son."

"Sorry, I wasn't paying attention." Mark dusted off his hands and wiped them on the seat of his pants. He looked around in the twenty-five-yard long greenhouse, which resembled a milky plastic tent. Even though it was dry outside, inside it smelled fresh and moist. He reached out and picked a Thai mint leaf and tasted the sharp lemony flavor. "Mmm, this brings back memories of Mom's mint lamb. She sure could cook."

Dad's sombrero nodded as he gave a gentle dousing to the herbs.

"You know, before I was sent to Australia, this greenhouse was the largest outdoor plastic house in the county. Back then, folks laughed at you because we were so far from everything."

Dad winced. "Well, there were other reasons to laugh at us back then but that's all over now. Yeah, I know. I guess I was either just a fool or a pioneer. Most of the little towns around here have spread in all directions, but Cuyama is still a lonesome spot between these mountains."

Mark smiled. "The greenhouse looks good and the house looks the same."

"After your mother died, I kept her Carolina Jasmine, which she loved so much. It's grown and spread all over the other side of the house." Mark continued to duck away from the watering hose that his father used as a pointer when he talked.

"Do you ever find yourself talking to mom?"

"Yeah, sure do, even after all these years that she's been gone. Sometimes I hear her scolding me about not wearing a hat or putting on boots."

"Fucking cancer got both Mom and Yhi."

Dad watered his and Mark's shoes as he stared at the ground in memories. "Seems like there's so much more cancer these days but maybe we just know more. It killed both our wives and left us with memories to talk to."

Mark stepped away from the puddles. "Too bad you never got to meet Yhi. She had Darla Aborigine friends where we lived and they believed only the body fades away and the spirit stays forever so you can talk to them as if they were still alive."

"We wanted to come over for your wedding and when Adelaide was born but mom was too weak." The sombrero bobbed as Dad tried to wipe the tears. "I'm just glad you're home now."

Mark wiped his hands on an old grey rag lying on the two-by-four worktable. "So what are you doing with a castor bean plant?"

"It's decorative and sells well." Dad, in his gloved hands, pointed with a trowel to the large, robust tree-like plant. "It also has some health aspects to it. Tell me, when you were living with your Aunt Birdie, did she ever give you castor oil to clean out your system?"

"Oh, God, yes. Man, that stuff was the slimy gunk that gave me the shits. I've hated this plant ever since."

"Yep, the oil and the beans are poisonous, but like many lethal plants it has beneficial properties." With cautious and firm movements he picked one of the beans from under the broad leaves. "I'm sure you know that in low doses, the castor bean oil can kill malignant cells or bacteria and in some cases can increase heart function. And still, the oil from this one bean is enough to kill a person within a few minutes."

"At the time, I thought Aunt Birdie really was trying to kill me." Mark laughed.

"It might have seemed like it, but you know she was just purging your system to get rid of worms and god only knows what other kinds of evil stuff." He took the bean with a light touch and planted it into moist new soil mixed with chicken manure. "There you go. Now just be patient and you will grow into a big decorative tree."

He turned to Mark. "Don't you think it's an exquisite looking plant? Put on those gloves and feel the smooth thick silky texture, but don't break the skin of the leaf. People have started using these trees for decorative purposes all over California."

"Have they been warned that it is poisonous?"

"They've been told." He shrugged his shoulders. "They just ignore the advice and plant them anyway and enjoy the beautiful green foliage. If any animal ate the beans they would die of course, but most animals have an instinct as to what's dangerous and they stay away from the poisonous ones- except if they have extreme hunger or thirst. When you studied pharmacy, how much did you learn about the beneficial and poisonous properties of plants?" Dad's eyebrows rose in anticipation.

"We studied about most Australian plants and in most cases we looked for an antidote." Talking about Australia put a faraway look in Mark's eyes. "That continent has the most poisonous and dangerous plants, snakes, and spiders in the world. All grade school Aussie kids are taught to recognize them. You never know who is going to go trekking in the outback, and most of the time city folk don't have the sense of a platypus."

In his excitement, Dad pointed with his muddy trowel, allowing the dirt and water to drip down onto his long-sleeved plaid shirt while the sombrero bounced up and down with agreement and enthusiasm. "Yep, there is still a lot we can learn from plants. I'm glad to see that you're still interested, especially from an herbalist's viewpoint."

Mark hung his head and shook it slowly. "There have been so many unnecessary deaths due to just plain stupidity about plants. More research is needed and I've got a good group working in my lab in New Orleans. They have no hesitation in trying new things and are aggressive. Adelaide is fitting in real well there and she seems to like New Orleans."

"She's a beautiful and clever granddaughter- she's like her grandmother. All of you turned out to be redheaded like her." He glanced over at Mark. "You look so much like the twins. It's too bad about Melody." To hide his heartbreaking thoughts, Dad began to wind up the long watering hose. "Hey, give me a hand here, would you?" He struggled with the kinked-up hose. "Did you ever hear the story of a Russian spy who was murdered in London with castor bean poison?"

"You mean James Bond style with the poison in a martini— shaken not stirred?" Mark had given up caring about getting wet and muddy, and bent to help wrap up the long muddy hose.

"Hey, don't joke. I'm serious. It was in 1969 or 1970 when an anti-Communist Russian or Bulgarian spy, Georgi Markov, defected to London. It so angered the folks in Red Soviet-land that they killed him."

"Yeah, they say Markov was standing at a bus stop when a man came along and poked him in the leg with an umbrella."

"Yup. The man with the umbrella apologized to Markov, but nevertheless Markov died three days later. During an autopsy, they found and removed a hollow pellet which contained traces of ricin."

"That'll do it. We ground up some castor beans into ricin in pharmacy school, and it easily mixed with oil, powder, mist, or a pill. It's very versatile."

With his garden-gloved hands on his hips, he scrutinized Mark, pushed back the sombrero and asked, "Do you remember how much ricin is needed to kill someone?"

"One milligram is all it would take if inhaled or ingested. You would need close to 500 micrograms if you were going to inject it into a body, which is close to the amount they would have had to use to kill Markov."

"Good, you've learned your material well."

"You're working with some dangerous plants. I can recognize Foxglove, Bloodroot, Baneberry, Clematis and Water Hemlock right off the bat, but there are some I don't recognize. What do you do with them?"

"Just interested, son. It keeps me occupied, having something special to work with, and learning new stuff keeps my brain working. I keep the dangerous plants separate from all the other plants I grow and sell."

"This whole country seems more dangerous than Australia. But wherever you live, there always seems to be a few loonies out there wandering around angry and vengeful."

Mark looked out of place wearing neat khaki pants and a plaid short-sleeved shirt, now muddy and dirt-splotched. He hadn't worn farm clothes in a long time.

"Bring over those bags of fertilizer, would you? These fox-tails need a bit of a boost." As he lugged the heavy bags, his brown loafers sunk into the mushy wet ground.

"Ahh, a gentle shower is just what they needed."

"What about moving to New Orleans and staying with me? You're getting a bit old to keep up with this work."

Dad breathed in long enough to take the oxygen out of the greenhouse and slowly released it. "I don't need or desire city things anymore, Mark. Those were all in a past life when your mother was still alive. I'm just not interested. Here I have my mountains and the Pacific is not far away, and I am working with the soil. My father used to say that, …" Mark repeated the words in tandem because he'd heard them all his life. "…It was a good man who worked with the soil and got dirt under his fingers."

He snapped a dirty cloth at Mark and grinned. "Don't mock me. I'm your Dad. But it's sure good to have you on the same continent."

Mark shrugged his shoulders.

Dad finished sprinkling green fertilizer granules around the bottom of the clay pot, set the strange new plant upright and filled in around the sides with soft new soil mixed with more chicken manure. "There you go." He talked to all of his plants and swore they talked to him too, "Now, you tell me if you like that new fertilizer and I'll give you some more later. How about that?" He grinned at the plant.

"Talking to plants and animals is something the Aboriginal people do all the time. They believe all plants and animals have a spirit."

"Well, who knows? Maybe they do." He looked down and sighed deep, not noticing the water soaking Mark's leather shoes.

Mark backed away from the flinging mud drops. "You should at least get someone to help, a kid in high school, or a migrant worker. You are getting a bit old for this and don't frown at me." Mark was beginning to raise his voice.

"You sound like an old woman. I could help more people if I could practice medicine, but that isn't to be anymore. Stop telling me I'm old." He snorted then looked away and changed the subject. "Now that you have work and an apartment in LA and a lab in New Orleans, maybe you can begin to call the U.S. your home. Let's stop. I'm getting tired and hungry. Hey, grab those weeds out of the foxglove there, would you?"

Dad stood with one hand on an old hoe and the other on his hip. "Enough shop-talk. You have to have some playtime too, you know. You ought to drive up the coast to San Francisco. It sure is one heck of a drive and it's one of the prettiest in the States."

He closed the tarpaulin door then placed all the tools in the little pop-up shed and locked the door. "Tools sometimes disappear. If folks just ask, I'd loan the tools for free. I put the lock there just so they'd have to come ask me. I'm glad to loan tools for a bit of friendly conversation. Not a bad deal."

"This area is beautiful," said Mark. Both men stopped and looked out at the gentle rolling foothills undulating in hues of dark blue-green as the sun set over the mountain and began to slide somewhere into the Pacific. "There is a sense of freedom when you look up at those hills and see the big blue sky. Sometimes in the outback, you could see sky like that." They watched the sun fall behind the hills. "Mum really liked it here didn't she?"

"Yep, she sure did. Somehow, this reminded her of her home over there."

"Even as a kid, I remember watching her look up at the hills. She would tell us to feel the warm wind, smell the different kinds of land and soil, touch the leaves, and recognize them by their feel and smell. We learned so much from her. She grew up loving the land back in her home, in Adelaide, I mean."

"She taught you kids to love nature, that's for sure. She talked about her home, the wild areas, almost every day, and yet she was comfortable living here."

The two men walked between the long rows of tomatoes, beans, lettuce, and other vegetables that led back to Dad's white clapboard home. He carried a thick walking stick, "This here is my Moses-staff," he said raising it high and shaking it at the sky. "Got to keep it around just in case any of the diamondback or pygmy rattlers decide to come after me instead of the rats and mice." He poked around the plants as they walked. "It's come in handy a few times too."

Mark hesitated, searching for the right words. "...you know that I was angry at you for years for sending me away. It's been a long time now and I want to know the real reason."

A far away sadness weighed down on the old man. He stopped, took off his straw hat, wiped his forehead with his sleeve. "The brain... amazing what it does, what it controls, and what it remembers. You do have a right to know what happened back then when we sent you to live with Aunt Birdie. Your sisters already know most of what happened. I thought you would've remembered enough of what happened and wouldn't want to know the rest. I've never looked forward to discussing this with you. Let's go in for a cup of tea." He paused. "Your mom would have smiled at us having a cup of tea."

"Tea? Come on Dad. I was hoping to taste some of that Scotch I brought. You wouldn't mind parting with a bit of it would you?"

The straw hat nodded. "Yeah, you're right. I guess I'm going to need it to be able to tell you the whole story. I hope one bottle will be enough. This isn't going to be easy."

Dad folded his hands and reached across the kitchen table. The kitchen had always been the comfortable gathering place where the family problems were discussed openly. The bottle of Scotch was now half empty. "Do you remember old man Peacock?"

"Yeah. Your best friend – the pharmacist." The headache began to tingle, giving Mark a warning but like an addiction, he knew he should stop but couldn't because the desire to know the truth surpassed the fear of knowing.

"We tried to keep you kids out of knowing all this but I guess you knew part of it. I'll try to tell it in a nutshell but just bear with me if I tell you some things you might know or hopefully have forgotten." Dad sighed deeply and wiped his hands around and around. "Peacock accidently switched the prescription directions on two bottles of medicine and it killed a woman. I took the blame because I respected him and he had a huge family to feed. I was sued by a lawyer in town I thought was my friend, I lost my license and was labeled a murderer." He flicked the tears from the corners of his eyes, and with a shaking hand picked up the smooth Scotch bottle and splashed more into the two glasses. The quiet ticking of the clock now sounded like gunshots beating a rhythm with the dripping faucet.

Mark sat like a man crushed by a Mack truck, while a screaming pitch ran lightning strikes through his brain. When he tried to breathe, the smell of fear and hatred burned his nose and bile churned through his stomach and scorched his throat.

Dad waited until the drink warmed his stomach and calmed his nerves. "They turned against us. There was only one woman in the whole town who'd speak to your mom." He swallowed hard, sweat mixed with the tears quietly slipping down his cheeks. "The twins were hounded out of all activities at school and you were beat up. The last time they beat you up, you landed in intensive care and that's when we sent you to Australia to mom's sister, Aunt Birdie."

Mark, characteristically quiet, trembled, and barely able to stand, stumbled to the counter where he took a double dose of medicine, grabbed the Scotch and drank from the bottle.

"Whoa there, Son." Dad grabbed the bottle from Mark, spilling it, leaving them both smelling of Scotch. "Don't waste that good stuff. Slow down." He held the bottle up to the light. "Crap, it's almost gone." He poured the last into his glass. "Listen son. It's all in the past and we've all got new and good lives, except your mom. I think it might've hastened her death, but life goes on."

Mark swayed slightly. "I've got a migraine coming on Dad. I think I'll go to bed now. Sorry to bring up such bad memories. Thanks for telling me." He softly walked, not feeling the stairs nor the wooden floor, quietly opened the door and sat gently on his bed.

Hours later, Mark had not moved but continued to look out of the large window that faced the rolling blue hills almost hidden in the blue-black night sky. A small line of light from the setting sun traced the tops of the hills as the night birds darted after mosquitoes. He played over in his mind the evening's conversation in the kitchen. The missing pieces now all fit together and it all made sense, heart wrenching, sickening, insane sense. Dad had taken the blame; he didn't realize that the lawyers would wind up taking away his medical license. The thoughts continued beating the pain in his head until it felt like it was exploding into millions of fractures, like shattered glass. Now he knew. He was beaten up because they thought he was the murderer's son. He shouldn't have asked.

But that was all in the past and life, in some ways, had gone on. Where were all those kids that beat him up? Where are the shitty lawyers that ruined his father's life? Did they ever suffer like his Dad and sisters? Was there ever any retribution?

Chapter 7

He was waiting. John Smith Collier, trial lawyer extraordinaire: cruel, self-serving, unethical, immoral, and very rich. The ghetto taught him the thrill of malicious power and control and he threw his arrogant muscle around, knowing no one would dare oppose him.

She glided into his office, self-assured, alluring, wanting. His mouth dried up and for once in his life he didn't speak. Her long red hair swayed with the rhythm of her hips while the green silk dress formed a caressing hand around her body.

The bouquet of long-stemmed yellow flowers she carried, shouted, "Notice me."

"Don't get up from your work, Luv. I'll just put these in a vase."

His tongue felt like a prickly pear on a cactus.

"Hey Big Guy, you look thirsty. Want something to drink?"

"Sure. Just watching you, I know I'm gonna' need a lot to drink tonight."

She drifted over to the big refrigerator. "Here is one of your favorites, cherry, right?" She opened the bottle in slow motion and took a sip then poured it into a glass and stirred it with her long white finger. "Here you go. Just for you. What are you working on, Luv?"

He gloated as he flourished his signature on the documents. "Some dumb-ass obstetrician's getting sued for not telling parents their kid was malformed. Nothing's really wrong with the little shit but I'm making six figures for their pain and suffering. Got to finish it tonight as these papers need to go in by eight sharp tomorrow morning."

He tilted and emptied his drink in gulps as he watched her. Her voice was natural and flowing, low, breathy, and hypnotic, a definite turn-on. She was his vision and diversion. This one approached him on her own; there were no go-betweens. And here she was waiting in his office. Money and class oozed from every delicate inch of her creamy soft skin to her emerald earrings.

"Bring me some more of that from the fridge, will you, while I finish up here. That last one had a slight bitter taste."

"Sure Johnny, and don't worry about the taste, I added some stimulant that should arouse your interest a bit later."

"Mmm... I won't need any additives. You have no idea what you're in for." His jaws tightened and his fists clenched. "You know, Red, you look a bit familiar."

She smiled, turned toward the fridge. He patted her butt. "We bumped into each other last week in Chicago. Hold on, Luv, I need to use the ladies room. I'll be right back." She glanced at him over her shoulder. "Don't go away," she said and winked.

"Honey, I ain't going nowhere until you and I get up real close and personal." Johnny smacked his lips, and ran his fingers over his mouth. His tongue felt thick. "I wonder if the air-conditioner is working alright; damn woman's making me hot. I'm beginning to sweat like a red-neck's mule on a summer's day." He wondered where he bumped into her, as she was definitely a body not to forget. He pulled at the stiff white collar of his Italian silk shirt and shifted through the papers trying to remember where he'd stopped.

She returned, picked up a stem of yellow flowers; her steps barely making a sound on the plush carpet, her every step was a cannon's roar in his temples as she trailed the flowers along the furniture. The double doors swung open to the decorative-iron balcony surrounding the cream-colored marble floor. Her long slender fingers squeezed and twisted deep wrinkles in the heavy dark red velvet curtain as she steadied herself. She took a deep breath at the panoramic San Francisco bay, spread her arms out wide, and called out, "You know, you've got it real good here, Johnny, on the top floor of the Fairmont. The whole world's at your feet, literally. It looks like you can see around the world."

The tender sea breeze caressed her hair and tightened the dress around her body. Johnny's heart beat like a bass drum rumbling through his chest down his arms and into his legs.

"There is nothing like the night view; it's so much more beautiful than New York, Melbourne, or Chicago. It is breathtaking." Her deep melodic voice sighed softly. Her voice was hypnotic and spellbinding.

She traced the lines of the silhouetted buildings and mountains with her dancing fingertips. "Look how the wispy white clouds wrap around and caress the soft grey-blue rolling mountains that deepen into a midnight blue as they inch down into the ever changing sapphire water. That huge bay seems like purgatory, a comatose black revealing a gulf of endless death."

Johnny sat spellbound watching and listening. "Red, I hate poetry but the way you talk it up, I could almost begin to like it." He took a few quick breaths and pulled his tie loose. He shook his head to get rid of the buzzing. For one of the few times in his life, he was beginning to lose control and it frightened him- but just a little.

Her voice was like a lullaby as she turned and leaned against the balcony. "Have you ever noticed that surrounding the bay? You can see the twinkling lights of the homes and businesses from Sausalito to Oakland and Berkley. They wink to each other while they wait for the blanketing clouds to move in from the Pacific to cover them with chilling moisture." Her smooth voice, like a cradle song, rocked him into soft numbness. "Far to the left, I can see a slight view of the Golden Gate Bridge which is disappearing into the unconscious-inducing fog. It's so relaxing, so relaxing, so relaxing."

The sweat trickled down his face into his silk collar and fogged his glasses.

She breathed a deep sad relief, for the view gave her a promise, a death promise long overdue, and for some of the injured, the pain would subside and close an unpleasant period in their lives.

He looked down at his desk not focusing on the work in front of him. Concentration was out of the question. "God I'm thirsty. Get me some more drink, will you Red? I feel like I've been on a desert all day."

He looked up from his desk and watched her slow sway to the refrigerator. She poured the cold liquid in his glass and held it between her breasts leaving a wet imprint. His pen slid from his moist fingers as he watched her. "Good God, woman!" The cool perspiration from the glass snaked down the glass of red sparkling juice cooling his hot sweaty hand.

She placed the vase of flowers on his desk. "How do you like the flowers I brought you? They're Carolina Jasmine." She stroked one of the long branches and continued her hypnotic sing-whispering. "They're like the ones growing around your childhood home in Alabama." He blinked as his head snapped to attention. "It's one of the most beautiful yellow-gold native flowering vines in North

America which spreads aggressively covering trellises, wooden fences, walls, and trees. You can drive through the hillside and see this welcoming sign of spring." She whispered, "They are also... very... poisonous."

"Gorgeous, I don't care about flowers but I'm racking my brain trying to remember where we met in Chicago. Can't believe I'd forget you." The dampness was trickling down the back of his neck to the swayed curve of his backbone. He wiped his forehead with a red linen handkerchief as he emptied the cool liquid down his parched throat.

"You will remember later, no hurry. I'll be here to help you, don't worry. You were too busy. You didn't have time to notice me then."

"You liked what you saw, right Doll?"

She took a deep breath and spoke slowly, "Johnny, famous Johnny, it's hard not to notice you even from a long distance. You walk with a swagger, dress in thousand dollar suits, five hundred dollar shoes and God knows the price of your cars. You are very rich as is shown by the gaudy gold rings, the fragrant Cuban cigars, and the gold chains around your neck. With all your wealth, you've become a very attractive man."

He watched and frowned, "Well, Red, all I can say is that you have good taste...or a good eye for expensive things, which, yes, I have a lot of. And if you are good, I mean real good, you might get some of the same things." He wheezed as he laughed and she turned to watch him chuckle to himself.

"Come, my love," she crooned in a low Greta Garbo voice. "Try to remember when we met."

"You've got me so damn hot and bothered, I couldn't remember anything right now," he said. Again he wiped his face and hands and tried to focus on the blurred documents on his desk.

"Remember in Chicago, Johnny? 'Do Lawsuits Affect the Way Doctors Provide Patient Care?' We were both there." She turned and smiled at him and licked her lips. "Come, my sweet, think hard, you will remember."

He frowned in concentration. "That week in Chicago... the ridiculous, ludicrous meeting with the doctors. Those sanctimonious doctors and political do-gooders who think they can control the legal system we've spent years building up." He snapped the pen in his hand as he recalled the meeting. "Now they want to control how much money we make off them and the medical companies with Tort Reform. Fat chance! Those puffed-up, pious doctors who think they are God and are above control. HA! If they are going to play God, then they'd better be ready to pay for hell! The whole meeting was a mockery."

The romantic moment was gone. Through squinted eyes he glared at his guest. His heart was beating faster and he felt a squeezing on his left side. "You were there?" He gasped and tried to catch his breath. "Let's see, I was there for two days..." he struggled for breath, "when could we have met?" He wiped his face and neck, the red handkerchief now dark with splotches. He pushed himself up in slow motion and turned with a flicker of recognition and shock, "Oh my God!... How the hell.... Yousonofabitch..." He lurched across his desk, reached for his phone and fell to the floor with a dead-man's thud.

She was in no hurry as she walked over to where he lay gasping, knelt down and lifted his head. "Here, my Luv, let me give you some more water. Now, now, don't spit it out. Here you are, the once hot-shot Johnny Smith Collier, lying in front of me sweating, panic-stricken eyes bulging, fear running through your mind and what is left of your body."

Johnny gurgled and spewed out yellow-green vomit.

She dropped his head on the floor and stood up above him with her green silky dress gathered up around her thighs, swiveling her hips above him. "Dear Johnny, oh how surprised you are to see me here!" She giggled, "Oh, you should have seen the look on your face when you realized who I am! Aren't you surprised to find me here all dressed up, sexy, silky, alluring, and my stilettos shaping my long, thin inviting legs."

His eyes bulged. His arms and legs twitched as he tried to move.

She slid onto the desk above Johnny, waved her legs and caressed them with the wet glass in her hand. "You always had a soft spot for long legs and long flowing red hair, and bright red lips. Do you like the transformation? It's been just a short time since our last meeting. How could you have forgotten me?"

Cool, calculating, she bent down, checked his pulse, felt for a temperature, and checked his pupils.

"Hum, let's see now, yes, it might take several hours for your body temperature to lower, and gradually your skin will become cold and clammy and your pulse rapid and feeble. Then you'll have dropping of the upper eyelid and lowering jaw, squint and double vision. Your respiration will become slow and feeble, shallow and irregular, and death will occur from centric respiratory failure and your heart will stop. Consciousness is most often preserved until late in the poisoning, so you will be able to hear and understand me quite clearly until the end."

"In most cases, the effects begin in half an hour, but sometimes it is almost immediate. Johnny, it looks like you might be having a heart attack again, at least, that's how it'll appear. What a shame that there is no one here to help you. Too bad you couldn't reach your medicine or your alarm. What a shame." She walked around the room wiping away fingerprints.

She watched as his heaving pushed some of the poison into his lungs choking and slowly drowning him. "Someone should come to help you. Oh well, I don't hear anyone coming, do you? How does it feel Johnny? You can't talk? Hard to breathe? Good. Good. This is going faster than expected. Almost over now."

"Don't worry Johnny," she leaned over him to check his pulse again and patted him, "you're not the first one to die and there will be others to follow. All are slithering, poisonous excuses of human beings who delight in ruining people's lives. How many more like you will I be able to reach, to put out of our misery, and to give us some kind of closure?"

"Good that you called and told your henchmen not to disturb you; they all know your reputation with the ladies. The cameras in the lobby will show only some insignificant person walking in with a bunch of yellow flowers, nothing more. Hopefully they won't check the camera in the bathroom where I'll change. Hummm, Let's leave some clues for the police, shall we?"

She pulled out two martini glasses from her bag. "It was easy enough to borrow these from the Tonga bar down stairs. She wrapped his hand around one of the glasses. "There you are," she held them up high, "one is yours and one has red lipstick." She placed them on the small end table. "I hope you had a good time together before your heart attack. What a way to die—anticipating an exciting evening with a scrumptious redhead! Way to go Johnny!" She tested his pulse, "Humm, almost gone there old man, almost gone."

She reached into her bag and carefully unwrapped a plastic card, and pressed it onto the side of the glass with lipstick. "And just to tease the cops and give them something to puzzle their little pea-brains, these are fingerprints from an old neighbor of mine. She held up it to the light and inspected it. "Oh boy, those hints ought to give the police pause. Oh, this is so much fun! Wish you could enjoy this as much as I am."

"Let's see, oh yes, there's one more bloody thing that a lady might leave behind. I left it in the bathroom; what a gory, yet ingenious touch. That should give the police something interesting to ponder. I wonder whose DNA's on it."

"Ok, room clean, no forced entry, no fingerprints, secretary gone, cameras off, medicine in the bathroom unopened, telephone dropped far from body. Everything looks alright."

"G'night, Johnny. I have a date in Florida. See you in hell."

Chapter 8

"Good god, Robert! I can smell you from ten feet away!" Elliott looked around Robert's house full of hoarded goods.

"Good!" he barked. "It keeps people away. Anyway, I don't believe in bathing 'cause too many healthy germs will wash off and I'll get pneumonia and deodorant has evil chemicals that'll eat your skin away. Besides, I don't like people anyway."

Elliott watched over the rim of his coffee cup. About one hundred pounds overweight, Robert wore the same faded extra-large blue and red checked flannel shirt, even in hot humid weather, and ratty blue jeans, tied up with a rope because belts made him sweat, when tucked under his enormous belly. God knows when the clothes were last washed. Following him around was an incessant slapping of his rubber flip-flops when he shuffle-walked. He was supposed to be some kind of Secret Service agent or CIA or something nefarious and because he was so offensive and disgusting no one would suspect him of being anything but a stinking bum. Rather good cover for an agent.

"Is my itty bitty baby brother upset by my aromatic body?" Robert sneered and whined. Although debonair and in-charge everywhere else, in Robert's presence, Elliott felt small and overwhelmed—a result of being bullied by his older brother all his life.

Elliott thought it was more like puking than just being upset but aloud he said, "It just takes time to get used to you since I haven't been to your house for a while." He watched with caution and disgust.

Robert's brutal blue eyes peered out from the wild eyebrows and uncombed salt and pepper mane of shoulder length hair that grew and tangled with the long bushy grey beard full of old splattered and dripped food. Flies looking for a meal would sometimes become entangled in the curly hair, trapped and buzzing frantic to escape. The visible part of his face was the translucent white hiding underneath the brown sun blotches that pockmarked his face.

Elliott shook his head and covered his nose with his hand. "How can you be so disgusting and yet have women fawning all over you? One even married you for a few months."

"Simple, brother!" He brightened up. "I bat my baby-blues, plead helpless and in need of comfort. Works every time." He grunted a laugh. "They can't help wanting to clean me up." He pinched the top of his nose, blew snot into his hand, and wiped it on his shirt.

Elliott gagged. But no matter how disgusting, he needed his brother's help. The words slipped out before he could stop them. "You ought to clean yourself up."

Robert lifted his head, burned holes in Elliott's chest with hatred in his eyes. "You god-damned goody-two shoes." His words slithered out, wrapped around Elliott, tightened, and poised to strike into the base of Elliott's life. He shrank into the scratchy red sofa, fearing and hating what he knew was coming next.

Robert's voice grew. "It's always been about how cute you were and how smart and how nice." Robert stood and lumbered toward him, the crescendo in his voice now reaching ear-piercing range. "I hated you so much I wanted to kill you." Robert clenched and unclenched his fists. "You got all the attention and me, big brother, I got smacked down." He stood over Elliott and pinned his arms to the sofa. "You took all the love and attention from our parents that I craved. You," he bellowed so loud the words were almost incomprehensible. "You… were… adopted."

Sweat poured down Robert's bulging red face, his eyes constricted in a narrow squint, he squeezed Elliott's arms. His voice lowered into a menacing growl. "You were the son of an alcoholic-druggy-prostitute."

Dead silence. Neither man spoke.

Elliott relaxed enough to let Robert know that he would give in, again, and do whatever was needed. Guilt was a great motivator. "I know," he said. Elliott looked down and pretended to be humbled. "I didn't choose my mother and no one knows who my father is or was." In order to survive Robert's onslaught, he knew he had to be self-effacing. "I was lucky to have the family I grew up in and get a good chance at life." He knew this line by rote.

Robert relaxed and stood over Elliott. "And…?" he demanded.

"And I was lucky to have you for a brother." Elliott hung his head and swallowed the bile in his throat.

"Good, glad to know you feel that way." Robert shuffled back to his chair and his iced coffee.

Elliott let Robert feel in control. He still needed his help so he praised him. "It's not so surprising that you're now a private detective."

Robert flashed him a threatening look. "How so?"

"Well," said Elliott as he sipped his coffee, grimaced, replaced the tumbler on the coffee table, and held his stomach, and sat back in the rough red sofa. Robert liked to "cut and chew" his coffee so you never knew if you were drinking strong coffee or cigarettes. With Robert, it could be both. "You sure have a lot of secrets in your past and quite a few unexplained events. And you've had a few run-ins with the law, but you've always managed to get off. How?"

"It's none of your damn business."

"I've often wondered." Elliott eyes roamed over the German paraphernalia on the walls: the wooden plates, the oil paintings, and the cuckoo clock. "You've hated any establishment and rules or discipline of any kind. You rebelled against everybody and everything, yet after you were thrown out of the last college, you enlisted in the army. Why?"

"Better than going to jail. Almost," he snarled.

"Yeah, but somebody with your violent history should have been sent to Viet Nam, but instead, you got a cushy Berlin posting. BERLIN for god's sake."

Robert tilted his chair and put his feet on the table next to the half-chewed cold pizza. "Made friends with a sort of secret service group. Somebody owed me a favor." He brushed pizza crumbs out of his beard.

"Did you get into trouble over there?"

"Naaaw. Innocent little ole me?"

"Asshole. Did you get caught?"

"Yeah. Lots of times. But I had Green Beret friends in a so-called organization, and we got thrown in the brig just for show. Wasn't in for long. Got caught most of the time for getting out of the East German side."

"What the hell were you doing on the East side of the wall? You know you're bat-shit crazy!"

Robert chuckled. "Yeah. Keeps most people away."

He picked his teeth with a fillet knife. "But you're here and you don't make social calls to your older brother. Whadaya want?" He took the knife and began cleaning the dirt from under his nails.

Elliott took a deep breath, locked eyes with his older brother. "It was hard to miss your dramatic exit from the meeting in Chicago. What were you doing there? We both know how you hate lawyers and politicians."

"Does it bother my itsy-bitsy baby brother?" He put on an innocent face with pointed eyebrows mimicking his prayer-like hands. "I was just looking for education and enlightenment...."

"Bull-shit."

...and maybe some shyster to kill. Maybe the one who stole all my retirement investments."

"Ah. Now that makes sense. Not that you often make sense."

The chair slammed to the floor, pizza flew across the room spreading a cold stale smell. "When I find him or her, they'll wish they were dead before I'm through with them." He stabbed the knife into the table.

Elliott flinched. Nervous sweat dripped down the sides of his face into his collar. "I'll be sure to warn them if I run across someone advertising that they have your money."

"You're just like the rest of them." The growl came from the pit of his stomach. "What- do- you-want?"

"Just something up your nasty diabolical path. I want you to investigate the people who were sitting and lunching at my table. All are lawyers and all in politics. Dig up any dirty stuff you can find on them. You should enjoy this and you'll get paid."

Robert raised one eyebrow. "Find by any means?"

"Just don't tell me how you do it." He tasted coffee or cigarettes in the back of his throat. "What I don't understand is why someone hasn't killed you yet."

"Who said they didn't try?" Robert put a straw in his ice coffee. "Besides, more than one heavy-weight politician would soon commit suicide if certain information in an off-shore account was released to the press, among other scandalous shit." The sucking rattling noise from the straw on the bottom of the long cup was the lone sound in the room. "That's my personal insurance."

Elliott was frightened at what he might have started. "I need some fresh air. I'm going outside."

"Yeah, come on, I'll show you some of my new acquisitions." Robert threw his cup in the kitchen sink and lumbered out the back door. Elliott noticed chewing tobacco next to the coffee pot and quietly put his cup in the sink.

"God almighty." Elliott followed his brother and slammed the screen door.

He stood amazed at the thick jungle of flowers. The warm moist Florida weather was conducive to growing anything but desert plants, and filthy, dirty, uncouth Robert had created a luxuriant, vibrant blaze of color. There was abundant Carolina Jasmine filling the fence with yellow flowers while bustling white and red poppies, white clematis, and nightshade clung to the oak trees. The foxgloves were various crimson and pale pink, some with numerous dark red spots, each bloom surrounded with a white border. There were flowers and strange vines with long pea and seed pods from Africa and Indonesia.

"Oh, my god, Robert. This is beautiful and it smells great." Elliott breathed deep. Each direction he turned was a different variety of brilliant flowers and smells.

"I love the Foxglove," Robert said and pointed to the blue and pink bell shaped blooms. "It's a favorite of the honey bees. It's human-vermin and industrialism that's killing the bees, and without bees, we'll all die." He shot out long brown spit while Elliott paled at the remembrance of what he must have drunk.

"Look, little Buddy, I kept the roses you love, and under them I planted different varieties of Hellebore."

Elliott stood back and admired Robert's work. "This is probably the best thing you've done in your life. Mom would have been proud."

Robert spread out his arms and turned in a circle. "Look Little Brother, look. All you see, smell, and are amazed at, all except your roses, all are deadly poisonous. Any one leaf, berry, or flower can be lethal. This is a garden for killing."

Elliott nodded stupefied. Robert was dangerous, evil and they were brothers.

Elliott prayed quietly, "God help me."

Chapter 9

Robert never condescended to answer his phone. He felt disgust for people and believed that there was control and power in ignoring a caller. He even recorded an obnoxious message to ward off unwanted calls.

His phone rang and the message clicked on. "Hello your own God-damn self. This is Robert. Leave a message. I might call you back or not, depends on how I feel or if I like you or not. Beeep...."

"Uh, hello, is this Robert? This is Mark. We met in Chicago and my Dad said that you two are friends. I'd like to talk. He said you know a lot about importing exotic plants and I have a lab in New Orleans where my lab techs and I are working with different specimens. Give me a call. I think we might be able to work together. Bye."

Robert waited a few days before he returned Mark's call. "Hello there, Mark. This is Robert. Give that old buzzard of a father of yours a big sloppy kiss. He's a good SOB. I'll be glad to meet you in New Orleans. I know people there. I'll meet you in a week."

NOLA Phytoceuticals: Plants with a Purpose

Peggy walked into the lab carrying a tray with jars, beakers, and Petri dishes filled with various colors of green and yellow plant parts mixed with a concoction of cream. "Adelaide, we've got enough samples to last a lifetime." She carefully placed the tray on the white countertop, pushed her mousey brown hair away from her triple-thick black-rimmed glasses and stood back to look over the containers.

Adelaide shifted files, correspondence, and order sheets in her arms to look at the new samples. "Well, as long as my father keeps finding financial support for our research, we shouldn't have money worries for a long time. It looks like we might have another grant and we're getting more supplies soon."

Peggy smiled as she pushed the glasses back up her sweaty nose while Adelaide poked and smelled one of the mixtures. Peggy wiped the counter with disinfectant then took off her disposable gloves and threw them away. "Addie, you look so much like your father."

Adelaide was a perfect mixture of her Dad and her Mom with surprisingly beautiful results. Her coloring and body structure came from Mark who was tall with long lithe arms and legs and a sinuous body: a swimmer's body, taut, and trim. Her rounded facial features, from her mother, Yhi, softened the sharp angles of Mark's face, while her amethyst colored eyes reflected the ocean blue. She had the same reddish hair as Mark, but hers flowed like honey and it sparkled when glints from the sun shone on it.

"I look like my father but I have the spirit of my mum." She took a deep breath. "She died a while ago."

"Sorry. I know you miss her. What was she like? Can you talk about her?"

"I love talking about her because it brings her spirit closer to me and I can see her clearly." Adelaide sat on the lab stool and began to swing back and forth as if she were rocking a baby. "My grandparents immigrated from Ireland or Scotland; we were never sure since they didn't talk about it. When Mom was born, she was given the Aboriginal name of Yhi. She spent her youth on a ranch with her parents, my grandparents, and brothers and the local natives and felt freer with her Aboriginal friends than with her Caucasian friends. With her native friends, she would wander the outback and learn about different ways of life and loving. She never understood how in some regions of Australia, there was prejudice against the Aboriginals."

Peggy placed the samples under the warming lights and turned to Adelaide and said, "You are a wonderful storyteller. Tell me more. We need to wait on these samples anyway."

"Mom loved the stories, customs and ceremonies of the Kauna people. Those are the Aboriginal natives who lived near the ranch. In university, she collected stories, customs, and ceremonies of the native people and became an English teacher. Mom and Dad met in the university." Addie grinned as she remembered that Mark had called Yhi a hippie and mom in turn had called him a Yankee invader.

"Does the name Yhi mean anything?"

"Oh, yeah. It comes from the Goddess Yhi, who was the goddess who brought the seasons, the rains, the North Star, the moon and all stars in the heavens."

"Oh, that sounds just lovely." Peggy was mesmerized.

"I didn't know it at the time, but mom was dying of cancer and she kept telling me the story of Yhi over and over. Now I understand why."

Peggy blinked and waited.

"To tell the story actually would take two or three days but a brief form goes like this. The time that the Goddess Yhi lived on the earth with the people was called the Dreamtime. When Yhi was on the earth, it was filled with flowers everywhere making the land fragrant and making soft places for the people to sleep, and, oh, how sweet and fragrant were their dreams. Yhi's husband, Baiame, the Father Spirit, lived in the sky and was lonesome for his wife. When Yhi returned to the sky to be with Baiame, all the flowers disappeared and the people were very sad and wept all the day and night." Adelaide looked around the lab but saw only the sands, long grasses and scrawny trees of the outback. Without her realizing it, her arms wove, danced, and expressed the story while her voice lullabied it.

"Baiame felt sorry for the people and called them up to the top of the highest mountain where he gave each of them, all the flowers and seeds they could hold. Happily the people returned to their tribes on the grasslands and spread the flowers and seeds wherever they walked. The flowers were not as lovely and as abundant as they were when Yhi lived on earth in the Dreamtime, but never again would the Earth be without flowers, and the Great Spirit would continue to watch over his people. Because the Goddess Yhi loved the people so much she promised to return every morning to light their day."

Adelaide shifted on the stool, paused, dropped her arms in her lap, swallowed and held back tears. "Mom would hold me next to her emaciated body, nothing but thin skin on her bones, and tell me that, like the Goddess Yhi, she would always be in the sky looking after me, and that every time I saw beautiful flowers, to remember that she was near and was trying to give me joy."

Tears were streaming down Peggy's cheeks, fogging up her thick glasses. She cleared her throat and changed the subject. The magic moment was gone. "I like working with you because it seems you breathe a life into these plants your dad sends us and you have an instinct for what experiments we should be doing. I've learned a lot from you."

"We make a good team, Peggy." Adelaide stood up, shifted the pile of files and looked at the last order form. "Have you opened up the last plant samples from my father?"

"Just getting to it now. I've gotta get fresh sterile gloves. I'll be back soon."

Peggy, pushed through the door, trudged down the long hallway and headed up the back stairs to the main department offices. She passed one of the maintenance men who said, "Hi there, Peg the Lab-Rat. How ya' doing this fine day?" She waved, head down, not looking left or right and scurried down the side of the hall hating herself for being a simple lab-rat with no respect, not even from the janitor. She'd always kept quiet, followed the rules and tried to be perfect and accurate in her work. She grabbed a box of gloves from the supply cabinet and ran.

Adelaide was waiting. "Peg, I think you'll need more than gloves to examine these new samples. You'd better get into the protective suit." She held out the hazmat suit and snapped the fasteners after Peggy stepped in. She patted the arm of the suit and asked, "Peg, is something bothering you?"

Peggy spoke in a voice muffled through the mask. "I'm upset because the maintenance men call me 'Peggy the Lab-Rat.' God how I hate that name. I hear it everywhere. I just smile, but it sends freezing cold shivers down my back every time. Every time. You'd think that folks would know when a nickname hurts."

Adelaide relaxed. "Calm down before you handle that last package or you'll melt into a puddle of water." She walked back into the office. "I'm right here if you need me," she said and closed the door.

Peggy talked to the door as it closed. "I feel just like one of the three witches in Shakespeare's Macbeth. Double, double, toil and trouble, fire burn and cauldron bubble. That's what I do. Mix, heat, measure potions, add color, mash and grind leaves and sticks."

Peggy felt the trickles of sweat running down her back and around her cheeks. She knew she was protected, especially wearing the face mask covering her own thick glasses, but she thought she looked like a cartoon character and felt like an old fashioned deep sea diver. Mark had insisted, but she thought it was over-kill, especially since she was the one baking, boiling and sweating in all the get-up. She slammed the last package on the counter top, rested her head on her thick covered-up hands and took a deep breath.

The office door creaked open and Adelaide walked over to Peggy. "I just can't look at those receipts and invoices anymore. Need help? Do you think I need to suit-up?"

"Yeah, I could use some help. I think if you just stand back a bit and look at what we've been sent, then you don't need to suit up. Maybe look up the references on the computer."

With long tongs, Peggy picked up one of the new samples. "The tag on this one says it's from South Africa and is a poisonous succulent called Euphorbiaceae. What does the computer say?"

"Hang on just a sec. Humm, it looks like the picture here. Man is it strange. One stalk looks like a long green pencil which grows into a bush shape with as many as fifty to over one hundred pencil-stalks all together. It also says that these are popular in desert regions because they don't use much water and they are slow growing."

"Is it good for anything?" Peggy squinted through the thick goggles and mask.

"It says here that, 'Even though this is best known for its poisonous content, parts of it can be used for medical and industrial applications.' Wait, wait, down at the bottom it states that, 'The latex or the creamy white substance in the stalks is very poisonous but can be used for medical skin creams such as cracked skin and other skin disorders.'

"I bet we could make it into an ointment, if we mix it into a cream or oil. It might turn out better than the rosary pea did. It feels- through the gloves- like it could be silky. Of course it would have to be diluted and tested on rabbit ears to see how it would affect their skin. It might take out wrinkles or lighten the skin."

"Well, there you go." Adelaide looked up at the pointy green stalk. "That's the sort of thing my father is trying to have us develop, and we've got to come up with something new and different that is going to be marketable. I wish it would magically take off fat or increase sexual arousal. We could make a lot of money."

Peggy snatched the tongs, and tossed them on the counter where they bounced and clanked into the metal cans. "Some of this work scares me."

Adelaide flinched. It was rare when Peggy showed any emotion. "Ok, Peggy. Take a deep breath; pick up the tongs, and concentrate. This has been a long week. Just think, if we can find some new use, we might get rich."

In her thick suit, she waddled over and picked up the tongs and went back to the Euphorbiaceae. "I sure would like to buy that shot-gun house in the Garden District I've been looking at. But also," she said as she turned and waved the tongs at Adelaide. "I'd like respect. Respect from the maintenance persons… everybody. I'm treated just like a lowly lab-rat and nothing else."

Adelaide didn't risk getting any closer. "But Peg, we *are* lab-rats right now and please don't cry in the suit. You'll get it all steamy and you won't be able to see."

Peggy sniffed. "You know who is real gentle and treats me with respect?" She resumed cutting off small green plant bits and placing them in different vials. "The man who calls and talks to Mark every now and then. He has such a soft voice and he calls me 'Babe.' He loves music and flowers and is full of questions. It's obvious that he knows a lot about botany because he travels all over the world too, collects all kinds of plants and seeds and brings them back even though he shouldn't bring them into the country. It's illegal, I know, but it's not my problem. He's nice. He never told me his name but just refers to himself as Mark's plant-friend and when I tell Mark who is on the phone, Mark rushes to the phone and runs into his office and closes the door. Men are so weird."

Peggy stopped to take a breath.

"Mark's plant-friend who travels a lot?" Adelaide's mind was swirling with thoughts. She rested her head on the computer top and groaned. "Oh no."

Peggy began swiveling in her high lab chair and talking as fast as her heart was beating. "But you know he also talks about literature sometimes."

Adelaide wasn't listening. She'd heard Mark and Grand-Dad talk about Robert. Her face pulled into a deep frown. She groaned as she wondered how she could diplomatically explain Robert to Peggy without hurting her.

Oblivious to Adelaide's inattention, Peggy sped along, "We seem to have a lot in common. Strange, we can have such nice conversations and I don't know his name. Whenever I ask, he just laughs and tells me to call him by Ernest Hemingway's nickname, Papa. His voice is soft like creamy chocolate, smooth to listen to; you could just dive into it and drink it up. I wonder what he looks like. He sounds sensuous and must be at least a bit good looking. He knows so much about everything and it is just real nice to talk to someone who knows a lot about different things. Our talking can go from music to football, to countries around the world; he's been just about everywhere, and we talk about all kinds of birds and flowers. He must have a wonderful garden full of all sorts of wonderful exotic things."

"Oh cripes, Peggy, pay attention, you almost spilled that stuff. You sound like you have diarrhea of the mouth. Watch it."

Peggy arranged the samples on the counter top and bent over them pretending to scrutinize them. She sniffed but was unable to wipe her nose through the mask. "Sorry."

Adelaide put her hands in her lab coat pockets and walked up to Peggy. "Sorry I snapped at you. You got carried away there. Maybe you're over-heated in that suit, and you look like you are getting ready to walk on the moon."

"Yeah, well, Mark insisted on me wearing this thing but it's hotter than 'you know what' in here. It's a bit overdoing it, I think."

"Finish with that Euphorbiaceae and get cleaned up." Adelaide walked away and said over her shoulder, "Dad's plant-friend, Robert, is coming by this afternoon and we need things to look real professional and productive."

"You mean Papa?"

Chapter 10

"Papa?" Adelaide asked surprised. "He's no papa that's for sure." Adelaide stiffened and her voice rose above her normal gentle manner. "Don't talk to him except when necessary and never tell him anything we are doing in the lab and don't tell him what plants we're using. It's not safe."

"What do you mean not safe? He's like a protective father."

"Oh, good god, Peggy." Adelaide stopped, took a deep breath, leaned close to Peggy and in a soft whisper explained, "He is not to be trusted. Dad and Grand-Dad said he could steal our ideas and sell them to a pharmaceutical company or cosmetic company and HE would be making all the money – not us."

Peggy stood with her hands on her hips, the piece of Euphorbiaceae waving from the end of the tongs and her breath fogging up the plastic mask of the hazmat suit. "I don't believe you.

He just talks about me and asks about how I am doing. He is just concerned about me. That's all."

"Peg, you have to get out and meet more people. He's using you. He's being nice to you so he can find out what we are doing here." In spite of her anger, Adelaide had a difficult time not laughing at Peggy in the protective gear, waving the plant pieces with the tongs.

"Uh…uh…uh..," she stuttered. It's hard to believe. Mark likes him. They talk a lot on the phone and Mark is always excited to talk to him." Peggy pushed back the hood of the hazmat suit so Adelaide could see Peggy's hair matted to her head, her thick glasses steamed up and sweat dripping down her cheeks.

Adelaide smothered a giggle. "Dad and Granddad said to just be real careful what you say around him. And don't tell him anything about the lab."

"What does he look like?"

"According to what Dad says, he won't be like anyone you've ever seen before."

"Whaaat?" Peggy turned and stared at Adelaide.

"Just wait. We'll both see. Get out of that suit and clean up." Adelaide hesitated before retreating into the office. "And, oh, yeah, you've done great work."

Peggy's mouth dropped open as she stared at the closed office door.

The cool air hit her as she began to peel the suit from her arms, but a slow-simmering anger began as she slowly began to realize that she was the one who had worked all the extra hours. She was being used while Adelaide and Mark were making the profit.

Peggy's sharp tight face grimaced as she continued to emerge from the suit like a mummy from its encasings. She fumed as taunts of Peggy the Lab-Rat ran circles in her mind. Anger steamed with the steam from the suit. She ripped the pant-legs off her feet. *Stupid. Stupid. Stupid. Why couldn't I see this before?*

She threw the suit into a corner, missed the stool and through her foggy glasses looked at her reflection on the cabinet door. Her face was red, hair matted and plastered to her head and her clothes were sticking to her body as if she'd been swimming in them. She leaned close to the mirror, wiped a clear circle and whispered. "Well, Peggy the lab rat will show them how stupid she is." She pushed all the vials and samples together in one big pile instead of sorting them out and determined to keep her work secret, change the formulas and rearrange the procedures. She snapped her fingers at her reflection. "Oh ho ho, just wait."

"Hi Peg, you shouldn't stay in that hazmat suit so long. You look almost apoplectic. Are you OK? You're red as a beet." Mark pushed through the lab door.

Peggy whirled around surprised. "Oh, hi, Mark. Yeah, I guess I was in there too long. Sorry, I'll be careful next time. I should've put on the timer."

"How's the cream for the new seeds working out?"

"Oh, yeah, uh, it's fine Mark." She stammered at first but then as she talked about the new concoction she made, her enthusiasm increased and words poured out of her like water falling over a dam. "The cream has a very smooth texture, warm to the touch, easy to mix up, and the plant components dissolve with no problem. I added some Scottish heather fragrance to the cream and it gave a pleasant scent with no trouble and it seems like the fragrance will last. But you know this batch might be deadly as I haven't diluted it yet. We need to test it out in very tiny drops on the rabbits first to see how skin will react to it. Do you want me to call the Animal Research Center on the North Shore and set up an appointment? We could go out there to experiment as soon as we have the animals."

"No, no, that'll be alright, I'll take care of it." Mark picked up one of the samples Peggy had made.

"Oh, Mark, you shouldn't be holding that jar without gloves. We don't know how potent it is yet."

"Oh, don't worry, I've got thick outback weather beaten skin, toughened by the unrelenting sun from Down Under. I'll keep this safe. Don't worry. I want to show it to a client of mine who's going to come by today, Robert Edgars."

Peggy looked up in surprise. She mused to herself, *So, that's his name. Papa is Robert Edgars.* She swallowed hard. "What time will he be here?"

"No one ever knows when he'll show up. He's a strange fellow, no he's just plain bizarre. You'll never see or know anyone else like him. Watch out because he's devious."

"Why do both you and Adelaide say the same thing about him?"

"Maybe it's because she's heard Dad and me talk about him. You'll say the same thing after you meet him."

"How long have you known him?"

"Not long enough. Clean up the lab and don't let him see what you've been working on. Don't talk about anything specific about the work you are doing. OK?"

"You two are scaring me. I don't know if I want to meet him or not."

"Too late. Here he is." Mark put the vial on the counter top and turned to greet a barrel of a man bursting through the door. "Robert, you bloody bushranger. Good you could drop by. Glad to see you didn't dress up for us. Shit you still look like you just walked off the beach. A show-pony, you'll never be."

"You're a mongrel bastard son of an Aussi convict. Hello your own god-damn self. What have you got to show me?"

"Robert, this is Peggy, you haven't met. She is most essential to our lab work. We couldn't do anything without her."

Peggy blushed either from the heat of the hazmat or from the unexpected compliment from Mark. Robert attention snapped toward Peggy and his eyes bored holes into her eyes and down into her stomach. In a flash his gaze softened into loving, romantic, and sympathetic. He stepped toward her, with tenderness took her hand, held it and planted a messy juicy kiss on it, almost like slurping. "Pleased to meet you at last, my dear."

Peggy gasped and stepped back. She couldn't breathe either from the shock of Robert's appearance, the smell, or from the stun of putting his voice to his face. Nothing fit. Here was the sweet, sensitive, crooning voice in a man of nearly three hundred pounds, stinking, and wearing ratty, torn khaki shorts held together with a rope and a dirty old Hawaiian shirt. In his hand he held an old straw hat and he was wearing rubber sandals. It couldn't be the same person. Papa's voice belonged to a man who was trim, sexy, tall, dark hair, and lots younger. Her head pounded and her thoughts screamed, "*NO, this could not be the same person.*"

"Have I overwhelmed you, my pet? You are much more beautiful than your voice told me. I should have known you would be as petite and gracious as you are. You are so delicate and, I bet, delicious." He smacked and licked his lips

Peggy took another step backward.

"Hold off, Robert. Let's go in my office and talk." Mark stood between Peggy and Robert and motioned to his office where Adelaide was standing in the door and watching all the activity. "This is my daughter, Adelaide."

Robert turned and stared at Adelaide from breasts to crotch. His chuckle was low and wicked. "Oh yeah, I bet we could have a good time- unless I was stoned, of course."

Adelaide moved to the side, as Robert stalked into the office barking at Mark. "Let's get to it. Talk business. What new concoctions have you two been cooking up?" The office door closed.

Peggy stood and blinked at the closed door. Her mind buzzed.

"What the hell was that, who .., what just happened?" She stumbled out of the lab into the cool hall and down to the bathroom. She stripped off her blouse and skirt. She didn't care who came in. She shook all over. Too much had happened in the last hour and she couldn't take it all in. She had to cool off her body and calm her thinking. She washed herself with the wet paper towels and stood drip-drying. She trembled as the warm air hit her wet body and she grabbed her arms around her in a protective hug. Was this due to fear or shock or a sexual appeal? Well, it dang sure wasn't sex appeal anymore, if ever there really was before.

She began to dress even though her clothes were soaked and sticking to her skin. She looked at her wet reflection in the mirror and breathed deep as instructed in the yoga book. She counted slowly but couldn't remember how far to count, then she tried to organize and rationalize her thoughts. One: Seeing and smelling Robert had been a shock. Two: They needed her techniques. And Three: Did she want to be involved?

She braced herself against the wall and tried to imagine what if any part of this process she could control.

"Peg? You alright?" Adelaide pushed through the swinging bathroom door. "You don't look so good."

"Yeah," Peggy said. "Well, I gotta time myself next time I crawl in that astronaut suit. I thought I was going to pass out. I just got so involved in the new cream. I'm alright. I just gotta' cool off."

"Well, soon as you're ready, Robert wants to talk to you. Seems he's interested in you quite a bit. He keeps asking questions about you. Remember, don't tell him anything about our work in the lab. Ok? Got it?"

"Yeah, yeah, ok, no problem. I don't know if I can talk to anyone right now, anyway. Give me a few minutes. I'll be there soon."

"OK. Don't be too long. He's creepy. He might just as soon

disappear as hang around." The bathroom door swung shut and hit her as she walked out.

Peggy wiped what she could with the paper towels, steadied her breathing and looked again in the mirror. "Stay calm. Stay calm. Deep breath. Ok, here goes."

Chapter 11

"Hey Little Sparrow. You doing alright?" Robert called from the tall stool in the middle of the lab.

"Yeah, I just got hot in that protective suit."

"What the hell's that for?"

"Oh, well, it's just to be careful. No real danger."

"It sure is good to see you face to face."

"Why do you call me little sparrow? Because I am so plain?"

"Oh shit honey, your gentle spirit will never be plain. Do you know who else was called Little Sparrow? Edith Piaf, the famous…"

"I know who Edith Piaf was. We've talked about her before, don't you remember?"

"Well, you seem to remember things with ease, not so easy for an old man like me. Do you want to go get a cup of coffee or something?

Let's get outta' here for a while. Tell Mark to go screw himself. He can do without you for one afternoon."

"One whole afternoon? How long does it take you to drink a cup of coffee?"

"Let's go over to Café Du Monde. It's fun to watch the tourists get all that powdered sugar all over 'em. Do you remember when Clinton came here? Somebody must have hated him tons because he was served beignets heaped high with that sweet powder and he was wearing a black suit. Oh man, that was fun to watch. The prez snorted and blew the shit all over him. It was hysterical. The Secret Service couldn't keep from wetting themselves laughing so hard."

"You were there?"

"Uh, naw. A buddy told me."

"You said, 'It was fun to watch.'"

"Crap, you don't miss a beat, do you? Come on Daalin', let's see how much we can get all over us and maybe in some new moist places."

The fifteen minute walk was easy for Peggy but Robert rolled from side to side like an old sailing ship and was sweaty and breathless.

"What did you tell Mark about us coming here and having coffee?"

"I told him that he could sit on his thumbs and not to wait for you to come back to work today. I was glad to see him worried. Serves him right. At least you'll get an afternoon off."

Peggy walked an arm's length from Robert, eyeing him occasionally and tried to size him up. He was crazy-fun in a weird sort of way, but that's ok because in the South, eccentric people have always been accepted and some folks brag about all the nutty things their strange relatives do. There was no way she trusted him now or felt any sexual attraction. He was a smooth and sleek talker but a true scam artist. She glanced sideways, "I bet you have a lot of stories you could tell."

"Hell yeah and some could land me in jail."

As usual toward evening, the soft moist breeze waved through the French Quarter making all the locals walk slowly and the tourists sweat like farmer's pigs standing in a July sun. Peggy mused as she watched them scurrying around like tomorrow was coming too soon and they would die. She wanted to tell them to move slowly and sashay like real southern women and take life easy.

Café Du Monde was full as ever but you could find a little table somewhere in the overcrowded open-air café, and if you waited long enough you could get one by the side where the breeze blew in from the river.

She adjusted her thick glasses. "I love this old place. I can get a cup of coffee anytime 'cause it only shuts down for a hurricane."

"Hell yeah, ain't no other place like the 'Big Easy'. I've always enjoyed this city. Do you know that during one of the hurricanes, one bar didn't close? The police and the National Guard were stationed here in the Quarter, and the bar made a killing. Also, the city was so locked down that a rat couldn't get through the blockades, but somehow there were a few strippers who slipped in and they made tons of money. They were the only women in town and they were at the only bar. What a wind-fall." He slapped the aluminum table and whistled, "Ooooeeee."

"Yeah, we heard something about that. But there're so many stories that you never know what to believe."

"Yep, Babe, and there is no other place like it and no one makes the dark coffee with chicory as good as these folks. You know the people here started using the root chicory during the civil war because they couldn't get the real coffee. Most the time it was so damn strong you had to add half a cup of milk to it, so there you go, cafe au lait."

"Yes, I know about chicory and you seem to know a little about a lot of things, don't you Robert?"

"Aw, shit, I know lots of useless information that clogs up my brain, just useless crap."

"Uh, right, all useless?"

"Well for instance, do you know where beignets come from?"

"Yes. From the French who got thrown out of Canada by the Brits." Of course she knew. "Here they come." Peggy picked up a beignet and licked the sugar from her fingers.

He slurped is coffee. "Hey Babe, I want to talk to you about your job at the lab."

She stiffened and chills shot through her spine. "Oooo kay. What about my job?" She took another bite.

"Don't pretend that you like doing crap work for Mark."

Peggy flinched.

"You're doing all the work and he's getting' rich off you."

The knot in her stomach felt as big as the cup of coffee in front of her. She couldn't swallow for fear she would throw up, so the coffee stayed in her mouth becoming luke-warm and discoloring her tongue and teeth. She stared at Robert. She had been warned he was up to something and now here it came. Was she ready?

"Look Babe, I can see who is working and who isn't. I know quality when I see it. I get around."

She swallowed and stared.

"I know you live alone without any cats or dogs, you work twelve to fifteen hours a day and on weekends too. You go to mass on Sunday on your way to work; you like to sit in the back so you can scoot out and get to the lab faster without being caught by anyone you have to talk to."

She burped up the swallowed coffee, some shot up into the back of her nose, and she felt sick. He knew too much.

"No one writes to you except the occasional former student you helped pass a stupid little exam. You clean your own apartment, which is two rooms, and your closet has only a few clothes. You are lonely and you've fixated on Mark."

Peggy gasped with a mouth full of beignets, then sneezed and spewed an eruption of powdered sugar and coffee all over the table, Robert's straw hat, Hawaiian shirt, and face. He looked like a harlequin. She froze.

Robert froze and then roared a bellowing laugh that turned heads from shocked tourists and waiters. The tears rolled down his cheeks cutting little rivers in the powder. He hacked, and coughed while the crowd laughed with him.

"Oh Babe. That's about the funniest thing that's happened to me in a long time. I've never been so white. Oh God. Give me some more napkins. Shit, that was funny."

"Glad you're not mad."

"No. no. I'm not mad at all. Just whiter and sweet…wanna lick me? Hee Hee, god that was fun." He paused. "No, really, look, I want to give you the opportunity to make some big money. Easy money. You'll have more money than you could ever dream of. I need to know if I can trust you because this has to be absolutely secret. No one must know or there will be major trouble."

"Robert, this sounds real bad. I'm outta here." Peggy wiped her hands and reached for her bags, also sprinkled with powdered sugar.

Robert gently touched her arm. "No Babe, wait. I know what it's like to be poor. I know what it's like to watch the big money kids get ahead, get the scholarships, get the big jobs. I know what it's like to get passed over for some dumb shit who's got a rich Pappy. I know what it's like to work so much that you think you have no brain left and they still want more out of you. You come from a poor family like I did and you are struggling, aren't you? You deserve more and I want to help you get more out of this life. I see you as a deserving person, a hard working person who is not getting ahead. You're stuck. You're stuck in a job doing all the work and getting just above minimum wage. And you'll be stuck there always if someone doesn't help you. I'm here and I will help you. It'll be so easy you'll laugh when I explain."

Peggy watched the tears and the sweat mix on Robert's half-wiped face. The sugar was caked around his scraggly beard, moustache, and the hair hanging on his shoulders. She wanted to laugh but didn't dare. He'd touched a tender spot. She knew she was going nowhere in her career. She'd worked and paid for college herself even though it took a long five years. It was hers and she did it alone. But she was still earning just above minimum wage like he said. She listened, intent on hearing him out.

"Don't be afraid. It's not drugs. There are no convicts involved, no mafia, no contraband, no illegals. Just shut up and listen. No one's gonna hurt you. It's not dangerous for you. You've been alone too long. I just want you to get married."

Chapter 12

"Married?"

Peggy watched through her thick glasses, suspicious and disbelieving. There was no way she'd trust Robert. She'd listen, but scrutinize and then dissect it all. She was a scientist after all.

"I got into some trouble at college. The sons of bitches made me join the army just to keep my ass out of jail." Robert began his long, drawn out tale while they sat at the small round table strewn with dirty coffee cups and powdered sugar.

"I had no choice. Just because the asshole small-minded college jerk-offs didn't see the humor in my planting a little bunch of cherry bombs in their office mail box. Well, they said I had to join the army or they would prosecute me. Motherfuckers. So there I was, stationed in Frankfurt, Germany, out of uniform, in a bar getting drunk and this scrawny guy, about twenty years younger, comes up to me and wants to practice his English. Just then some of the old farts in the back corner stand up and start singing the goddamn Hitler songs. And the place went crazy with the younger ones throwing food and crap at the old codgers."

Robert laughed uproariously telling his story; he waved his arms throwing sugar in the air. Locals, who relish any assortment of characters, were enjoying Robert's antics but the tourists averted their eyes, thinking he ought to be locked up. Maybe they were right. Robert leaned in close and whispered. "Well, I learned German as a kid when the family was shipped over there, so I got along real well with the natives."

Robert wiped his mustache and smoothed down his beard. "Well, this bony kid's name is Gerhardt, and we kept getting more and more drunk. Crap, I don't know how I got to his house, but I stayed with him and his mom the whole weekend and every free day I had for the rest of my time over there. I lived with them like I was a son. I never hung out with the Americans, because they're a self centered bunch of whiney-assed bastards. Gerhardt and I stayed out of trouble most of the time, then once we snuck into East Germany just to see if we could do it and we almost got our butts shot off. Man did we laugh about that later.

"Anyway, Gerhardt's mom got cancer. When she died, Gerhardt didn't have anyone in Germany who meant anything to him and he wanted to come to the US so I invited him over for a couple of months. He traveled all over the states and decided he didn't want to go back to Frankfurt. He wants to stay here but he just has a tourist visa and he has to return in a few weeks. He found a job here as an electrician and is making more money under the table than he did back in Frankfurt. He is a very hard worker and willing to do anything to stay."

Peggy didn't respond and didn't blink but just continued staring at Robert.

"He sold his mother's house and has $100,000 in the bank with all he's saved up and he wants to live here."

"So you met in a bar in Germany, you spent most of your free time in bars and sneaking into East Germany?"

"We were strong, arrogant, fighting bucks and got into all kinds of shit, but most of the time we never got caught; besides Gerhardt's too much of a wimp to really get into trouble."

"Most of the time?"

He clenched his fists and ground his teeth looking like a corked bottle of explosives ready to explode. She waited. He wasn't telling the whole story and if he were going to have a temper tirade, she wouldn't be scared. He wanted something and she'd wait to hear him out.

The table tipped as he leaned on it with his heavy arms. "Well, Babe, there are things we did that were stupid and rebellious, but that's all in the past." The blood in his jugular began burning and beating into his head.

"So what was it that made you determined to get into East Germany and almost get killed? What could have been so important? Not just the joy-ride. There had to be money involved, right?"

"You're missing the point here. Poor Gerhardt needs a chance to start over, to begin a new life, and he needs someone to help him."

"What is he running from? Why does he have to start over?"

Robert slammed his fists on the small metal table, scattering and smashing the coffee cups and beignet plates on the concrete floor. "God damn you to hell. You aren't listening." He stormed off pushing waiters, tables and tourists and headed down Decatur Street toward the open air French Market while Peggy helped the old Vietnamese waitress clean up the spilled coffee and broken cups.

She was paying for the coffee and damages when Robert came back. Now she knew he needed her. She waited and watched.

"Hey, I'm sorry. I have this hearing and a slight memory

retention problem. I have to say everything I am thinking before I forget it. You gotta let me finish my thoughts and sentences. Here, let me pay for all this."

Peggy stood motionless and wordless and waited as he pulled a wad of bills from his pocket.

"Here, Babe, let me explain a bit more in depth. Walk with me up by the ole' Mississippi." He took her elbow, gently steered her away from the crowds and up over the railroad tracks to the walkway top of the levee.

"I guess you've figured out by now that Gerhardt needs to get married to an American, as soon as possible. He is willing to pay you all he has, $100,000 and he will continue to work and give you money. You will not have to have sex with him, unless you want to. Could be fun. He's a nice guy and won't hurt you. I promise. As I told you, he's a real wimp."

"It is illegal, Robert, you know that. Why me? There are other women who would jump at such a chance. What haven't you told me?

"Oh, Babe, you won't be sorry 'cause this is a chance in a million. It's an opportunity you won't want to be left out of. This is a chance for you to become wealthy. And you have the talents to pull this off. You have the know-how to make us all very rich."

"My talent and my know-how?" Her eyes widened. "Oh..The lab... but what's that got to do with marrying a German?"

"Gerhardt is the only one who knows about a very special plant and you know how to develop and prepare solutions. You know plants are a hobby of mine and if we imported them to grow and sell here, we could become rich as snot."

"You know it's illegal to import plants. And what will make us wealthy?" She folded her arms over her small breasts and tried to look fierce. "Drugs? I am not having anything to do with drugs. Count me out. This discussion is over." She turned to walk away, and wondered how much he wanted her and what else he would offer.

"Okay, okay Babe. Wait. Don't go away just yet." He caught her gently and turned her around. "You see, because the plants were on the other side of the Berlin Wall and we had to sneak over into the East to get 'em."

"You endangered your lives for plants? What could be so valuable for you two to risk getting put in a Soviet prison? You're out of your minds."

"Babe, you've never gotten your hands on any plants like this. They were grown by Gerhardt's grandparents before the war. The grandma used to mix it up and sell it as a natural concoction as an aphrodisiac for men…, to get their dicks up. Don't you see what a fortune we could make? Every man on the planet would pay anything for this lotion or pill, or whatever. You would be wealthy beyond your wildest imagination."

"An aphrodisiac from a natural product and only you and Gerhardt know where it's grown or what it can do?" Her eyes widened as she saw the potential.

"As far as we know we are the only ones. His grandma never told anyone and both the old folks died right before the war. Gerhardt's mom kept the stories to herself but told Gerhardt when he was having trouble "getting with the girls." His mom had kept some of the dried leaves and when she made a potion for him, he went down to the red light district and was fucking like a rabbit for three days. Man he was wiped out. We guessed his mom made it a bit too strong. Anyway, after she used up all the leaves, we went back to the East to get some more."

"Did you find any?"

"Well, yes and no."

"Great. This is a huge cock and bull story. Is there anything true in it?"

"Well, now we know where it is grown and we can get back into the part that was East Germany but…"

"But what?"

"There is a factory built on the ground where they grew. We would have to go back and look around the woods and see if we could find it growing. Gerhardt's mom said that it was all over the area. We just have to go back and find it. He has relatives there we can stay with."

"So, go back and look for it. Why do you need me to marry Gerhardt?"

"If he leaves the States, he can't get back in for another three years."

"So he's here in the States now?"

"Yes. He's here visiting me. But listen, if we find the plant again, we will need to get it back into this country so you could find the correct formula or mixture so we could sell it. If you marry him, he can travel back and forth as much as needed. We could also try to grow it over here."

"So I would be doing all the work again."

"Yes, but Babe, you would be getting the money and wealth as soon as we got to selling it. And this time there will be no middle person to take it away from you- no Mark and no Adelaide. Just you and me and Gerhardt."

"Robert, there are all kinds of natural products on the market. What makes this one so different? If it doesn't work, we'll be in big trouble."

"This one works better than any other natural products on the market, trust me, I've tried them all. It should be easy to grow, I would imagine, since it has survived a couple of world wars and it grows wild in the forests. It should be cheap to make and we can sell it for any high price we want. We'll make a killing. Besides as a natural product, it avoids the FDA regulations. It's almost legal. The only thing is getting it into this country."

"That's smuggling."

"Don't worry. I'm working for the SITC."

"The what?"

"The Smuggling Interdiction and Trade Compliance. It's a division of the USDA and I kinda' work for or with them,… kinda'. I can get anything through."

"Marriage. Aphrodisiac. Smuggling."

She stood looking out at the powerful Mississippi and the dark blue sky with a few stars that dared to appear on such a hot summer night. The lights strung up on the Crescent City Connection Bridge reflected in the thousands of waves in the constant river flow. The river's powerful current pushed around the crescent city and into the Gulf of Mexico rushing past her, like most everything in her life. Until now, she felt as if life's events had pushed her without her consent. As she weighed the risks and danger, it scared her to think she might go to jail and she'd heard what happens to women in prison. She turned and looked at Robert wondering what Gerhardt was like.

"I don't know, Robert. I'll have to think about it."

"Well, Babe, we don't have much time. Gerhardt has to go back in three weeks. We're both here in town, now, staying at the old Pontchartrain Hotel on St. Charles. Can I bring him around to meet you?"

"Shit no Robert. I've never seen you until today. I don't know who you are and I don't like being used for your get-rich-quick-schemes. How did you know about my going to mass, that I don't have cats or dogs? How do you know who writes to me or how many clothes are hanging in my closet? How do you know that stuff about me? Who told you? I don't trust you." She surprised herself. She'd never said "shit" before.

"You don't wanna know. Don't ask. But I'm giving you an opportunity to be very rich. You're just going to have to decide if you want this or let it pass you by. I can find another lab-rat and you will just be in the same place you are right now, never getting anywhere, never having any money, never getting screwed for fun, never having nice clothes or jewelry and you will become old and bitter. You decide. I'm giving you a chance to get out of the rat's nest you're in. I'll come get you tomorrow and you tell me what it is you want for the rest of your life, gray boredom, or a chance to have a nicer, different life."

Peggy frowned at Robert. How could she have fallen for his crooning voice? She hated him and yet she considered opening Pandora's Box.

Abruptly, Robert touched his index finger to the brim of his straw hat and said, "G'night, Babe. See you in the morning," then he flip-flopped off toward the Quarter while she stood looking at the river. She tried to calm herself with a protective hug because up to now her life was stable and secure with no positive or negative swings, just a flat-line of a life. Yes, a flat-line of a life.

In the sticky heat of the summer night, she shivered, afraid to breathe. She murmured to the fearsome river that rushed by, taking no notice of her. "What? What?" She hung her head and whispered into her folded arms, "What am I going to do?"

Chapter 13

Robert jerked open the front door of his small clapboard house in Florida. "Hi Mark. Saw you coming. Glad you could make it. Come on in the back and see my menagerie of plants."

"Hi Robert, It's been a while since we've talked and since I have a meeting in Tampa, I wanted to check on Melissa. I also want to see this wonder plant you talk about…Granny something."

Yeah, Granny's Lily's outside, the wonder plant I told you about. The damn thing grows like a weed in this humid Florida weather where it's a damn sight warmer than East Germany and it's just taken off like a son of a bitch."

The backyard was a chaotic jungle. "Good god, Robert, how do you find anything out here?"

"I don't. I let Melissa do whatever she wants out here but I warned her to always carry a phone so if she gets lost she can phone someone."

"How's she's working out? She knows as much about plants as I do even though she's never studied them in university. She's had it pretty rough these past years."

"She's a great little worker. Sure got a way with flowers. She's got the greenest thumb I've ever seen. I pay her so she can take care of Melody." Robert sucked in his right cheek and spit out the chewed up toothpick. "She's fixing some sandwiches and'll be out in few."

"I help financially as much as I can but she's taken charge. I guess twins are always close even though she was always the quiet one and Melody was like her name, always singing and dancing." Mark looked out over the garden. "I worry about her."

"Hello, dear brother, how's Dad?" The screen door slammed behind Melissa as she carried a tray of sandwiches and ice tea out into the back yard. She kissed Mark on the top of his head. "You're getting a bit bald." Melissa set the food on the table. "Ok you two. There's no tofu this time but vegetables and fruit, so no complaints. Amazing what exotic herbs you can find in Robert's garden. They're safe. I tasted them all. So eat."

The sun played hide and seek through the oaks, bamboo, and sweet olive, giving a lulling feeling and fragrance to their secluded spot.

Mark became melancholy. "I want to tell you a story I just heard about a doctor-lawyer I met in Chicago, who is here for this meeting." They sat and watched the birds playing around the waving branches. "There couldn't be a more reprehensible person alive than Austin Kaufman. He attended medical school in Chapel Hill and was thrown out, so they say." Mark looked into the past and remembered. "Rumor has it that as a third year student Austin was rotating at the Veteran's Hospital when he was expelled."

Melissa held her sandwich in her lap as Robert broke his into pieces and threw into the bushes for the animals and birds.

"Austin was quite good looking but I wouldn't say he was hot. He's still quite tall 6'5", thin with high cheekbones, diminishing dark hair and looks a bit like a horse face but he thinks he looks like Sean Connery. He swaggers and barrels his way through meetings or groups of people standing around talking and without being invited, he voices his opinion and if he listens to another's view, he scorns it as being too pedantic or irrelevant. He has made a lot of money through just bullying his opponents; no one wants to face him in court."

"So he's a lawyer?" Melissa collected the used cups and plates. "He sounds horrible."

"Let me finish. The story goes that he was a medical student at the Veteran's Hospital, where there was a special patient who was liked and cared for by most of the students and residents. He was a kind but mentally stunted veteran of the war. He'd seen and taken part in more than his mind could hold and he regressed into a simple world where there was no fighting, no bombs, no gasses, no dying, and no killing. Depending on how you look at it, he was one of the fortunate ones who never had to experience the atrocities of the war through memories. His family abandoned him at the Hospital and never came to take him home. He was in his own gentle giant world. He was diabetic and weighed close to three hundred pounds. His arms and legs were so large that the blood vessels had receded into the fat which made drawing blood almost impossible. None of the medical students were able to draw blood, but a few of the resident doctors were capable of finding some thin veins. The gentle giant never complained, in fact he had not spoken a word in many years but you could get answers from him by watching his eyes which were expressive, tender, and kind. His mental state had also rendered him near catatonic without being able to move."

Robert leaned back and lit a cigar. "This story ain't gonna have a good ending."

"To everyone's surprise, Austin was able to obtain several vials of blood every day from the gentle giant. At first he was praised for his unbelievable ability to obtain blood from the diabetic patient. Then as his ability to get blood every day increased, the residents and the doctors became suspicious. They went several times a day to check the giant's arms and legs to see where Austin had taken the blood. Much to their surprise, there were never any bruises or needle marks on his arms or legs. Now the giant had lots of black hair all over his body; some even referred to him as the "dark cookie monster.""

Melissa sat down with the dirty dishes in her lap. Her breathing slowed as she listened to Mark.

"One of the doctors brought Austin into the hospital room where the gentle giant was lying and asked him to demonstrate how he drew the blood. The giant's eyes flew open and moved rapidly back and forth and he started grunting- a sound not heard before from him. When Austin neared the bed, the giant began to shake. A nurse standing by took his blood pressure, which read 220/135. Austin was sent from the room and little by little, the blood pressure receded. The alerted doctor began examining every square inch of the poor man's body. The doctor was horrified, outraged, and livid when he found needle punctures at the tip of the sternum, which protected the giant's heart. He was found to have internal bleeding around the heart because Austin had been getting blood from the heart."

Melissa hid the tears welling up in her eyes. Robert watched.

"The mute man couldn't resist and couldn't complain. Nothing could be proven as there were no witnesses; Austin was never prosecuted but due to the circumstances and his gross unethical behavior, he was asked to leave medical school. And guess what he did then? He went to law school and has been suing doctors ever since. Bastard!"

"My God, Mark." Melissa's stone-grey face frowned. "Is this Austin person going to be at your meeting?"

"Yeah. What a joke."

Melissa rose and took the tray from the table. "Robert, you know that Mark has become a pacifist due to both mother's influence and having lived all those years with the indigenous people near Adelaide. He learned that everyone and every living creature has a right and a responsibility not to violate others rights, life, and freedom."

"But it's acceptable to kill for food or for self-protection or protection for another human," Mark answered. "But isn't it the same for this medical-legal struggle? Isn't this all about a fight for protection of persons in the medical field, a fight for their lives, their freedoms, and their happiness?"

"Somehow I agree with the conflict of the paradox of rights." Robert blew smoke over the table. "The conflict that everyone has a right to use any means necessary to prevent deprivation of their civil liberties and that force could be used if necessary."

"Crap, Robert. Always the militant. You'll get us all killed."

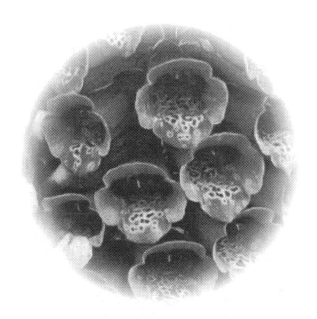

Chapter 14

Austin Kaufman walked along the shore of the Gulf of Mexico just north of Sarasota Beach; his body was reddish-brown from recent sunning. He swaggered in his Speedo and danced, or what looked like dancing, to the music in his ear phones then stomped on the sand castles built by the shore. While sipping his vodka and ice he strutted and believed that men looking at him were envious of his good shape and that women thought he was hot. He had no lack of self-confidence. He stretched his arms above his head and let out a contented sigh then saluted the wide blue sky. "It's great to be Austin Kaufman." He knew he had the perfect life. He watched the sun inching to set and sneered that sunsets were overrated and a bore.

He mused that it didn't hurt his ambitions now that Collier, Michaels, and O'Hara were out of the picture. He sucked in his already taught belly and flexed his butt muscles. With those three out of the way, he knew he'd have more visibility and more opportunity to spread out his control if he could get rid of that annoying Mildred Pelto. Kaufman downed the vodka and threw the glass into the sea. He knew it would be easy to take care of the sanctimonious Merriweather from Utah who wouldn't want his perverted private life spread out in the Salt Lake City Herald. Kaufman nodded, sure that bribery would be the way to go.

He looked from the beach toward the small bungalow that had been loaned to him by a happy client. The area was quiet with just a few local snow birds hanging on refusing to go back up north. He cleared his throat, spit on the beach and kicked sand at a seagull. He flexed his muscles again preparing for tonight's redheaded surprise.

He trudged through the sand up to the bungalow, showered and wrapped a towel around his tanned waist, slowly massaging his private parts as he dried. He had trouble lately in that area and the redhead surprise was a courier of natural products which might help in that region, as he was sure they'd soon find out. It was mentioned that if the product were successful, it could be produced locally and in turn make an insane amount of money. Because it was natural, there wouldn't be any FDA control.

Dressed in tight skimpy shorts, Kaufman pushed the window curtain aside and licked his lips. "Well, well, well, here comes my delivery babe, now." He watched from the second floor as she slowly stepped out of the convertible with long legs that seemed to take forever to reach the ground. She had long wavy red hair, big sun glasses, and a bunch of purple flowers. "Crap. Not flowers. Hope she's not the romantic type; those are hard to get rid of."

She walked slowly up the short flight of stairs, beach bag slung over her green dress, flowers in one hand, self-assured, and confident.

He opened the screen door and ogled her body from breasts to toes. "I am looking forward to getting to know you." He took a long drink of his vodka. "Any trouble finding this place?"

"No problem, Big Guy. I got good directions. How did you find this hide-away?" She took his drink from him, sipped it and sat on the sunken cushions on the wicker sofa letting the green dress fall to mid thigh.

"I won it for a client in a class action suit; the defendant lost it and everything else he owned. I can stay here for as long as I want, whenever I want. Not the classiest of places, but it'll do. I need to work on my tan. And you brought flowers, how queer of you, or should I say gay? Doesn't matter to me. I can go either way."

"I just picked up these purple foxgloves near the grocery store from a peddler on the street; he looked like he needed the money," she crooned. "Your hideout is rather quaint, but not as luxurious as your customary resorts. Did you know it was this rustic?" She crossed her long tan legs, slipping her short skirt further up her firm moist thigh. Austin wet his lips as he stared. It took a while before he could make his mouth and brain register to answer. "I'd seen the pictures."

"Well, I have a long drive back to Tampa tonight so let me show you what I have here for you. I won't be able to stay the whole night."

Austin stood, anxious for the new meds. "Ahh… a natural herb for 'male enhancement', and we're going to test it out to see if it works, I'll consider investing in it and I'd better make a killing."

"At least someone will make a real killing," she whispered.

He snatched the packet from her. "Let's see what it looks like. Have you tried this out yourself?"

"Oh, yes. Have no fear. Several of my clients who've had such difficulties, have now become fervent worshipers of this magic pill."

"Give it to me. Let's get on with it. I can't fuck any of the locals in this hick-town, it's so back-country, I'd be afraid 'cause I might get some goddamn red-neck boyfriend up here with a double-barreled shotgun up my ass."

"Hold on to your shorts, Big Guy, because I have another surprise for you. Here is something else. Some natural crack cocaine made out of flowers. Do you want to sniff? There is no harm whatsoever. You'll be so amazed at the relaxing and euphoric feelings and visions it will give you. Take a gentle snort to relax you before taking the little green pill."

"Sure, why not. It's been a long hard conference trying to bat some sense into those pansies who want tort reform. Let's have a go at it. Why not? What's the name of this stuff?"

"Well it has many names because it is such a common plant. So we've kept it a secret so others can't steal it."

He rubbed the powder between his fingers, "This powder isn't white but a bit brown in color. Is that alright?"

"Oh yes, that's the way it grows. No problem. Here just use the razor and chop it up a bit finer if you wish and then sniff away. You'll be surprised at how fast it works. It'll make the rest of the evening quite intense."

Austin was familiar with the process. He spread, chopped, cut, divided then sniffed. "Christ, this stuff is strong."

"I told you. Don't be in a hurry; take your time and enjoy." She went to the small kitchen and put the purple flowers in a cheap plastic vase from the cupboard. She turned to Austin and said, "Dip into it a bit more just for the kick. I want to see how well it works."

He leaned his head back on the white wicker chair, spread his tanned arms over the sides and let out a deep sigh. She watched him with piercing hawk eyes. "Just relax and breathe deep and slow. Oh yes," she spoke softly not moving. "I can see you are beginning to relax already. Good, good, I hope you are enjoying it."

He tried to turn his head to look at her. His speech was beginning

to slur. "Christalmighty. Wwwhaaaat d'Ya sssay's the name....
uuhh...plant?"

"I didn't say," she said as she took a few steps close to him. "But
it has many names, Virgin's Glove..."

"Oh yeah, sss'nice...that name." His head flopped to one side.

"...Fairy Thimbles, Witches' Gloves, Lady's Glove, Lady's
Finger..." She spoke more boldly, stood up straight and defiant.

Austin's head rolled over to the other shoulder. "Man...zis stuffs
making me... feel strange.. headsss.. expandin...I'm floating. Jusss
like you said.. Iguess."

She walked over and bent down to his ear. She spoke clearly
and enunciated each syllable with exploding clarity. "Dead Men's
Fingers, Bloody Fingers, Purple Foxglove, and Digitalis." She spit
out the last name.

"Digggi..taliisss?" Austin's speech was becoming more and more
slurred as he tried to open his eyes. "...the heaaart meddds?"

She stood straight, lowered her voice several octaves, and spoke
as if giving a lecture, "Yes, the same. It contains digoxin and other
cardiac glycosides that affect the heart. Digitalis is poisonous in
very small doses. The entire plant is so poisonous that ingesting a
minute portion of .5 grams dried or 2 grams of fresh leaf is enough
to kill a person."

"..pppoison?"

"Yeah, you bettcha," she snapped back.

"....how many grams?" he slurred. "How mmmuch was..."

"Oh, I would assume that you inhaled as much as 10 full grams
just a minute ago. It was probably enough to kill an elephant."

"You sonofabitch.. I'mm goonnnnaaa...killl....." Austin slumped
onto the floor.

The magnificent and powerful Austin Kaufman lay in contortion
and choking with pain. "Imagine, Austin, what you have done to
other people, especially doctors who were actually trying their best

to help their patients. Can you now feel some of the pain they had or do you still feel only your own pain? You look uncomfortable there on the floor, Austin, maybe I'd better go and leave you alone."

Austin wheezed and coughed up a choking gasp.

"Let's leave some clues for the police to study when they get here, shall we? Here on the table I put some real cocaine and scattered it around the floor, and in the ashtray are a few cigarette butts, one with lipstick and others from outside the local stop-and-shop down the road. When I picked them up, the people watching thought I was some kind of citified green-nut who just wanted to beautify their city. What a laugh."

She nudged him with her foot and waited for a response. All was quiet.

She placed the flowers on the coffee table. "Well, I have to go now, so I'll just let myself out. Goodbye Austin. Sleep well here in sunny Florida. I have a date in Boston. See you in hell."

Chapter 15

Peggy smiled and almost skipped down Tulane Ave to the lab. She was delighted that nobody called her Peggy the Lab Rat anymore. It took her awhile before she could get Gerhardt's grandmother's plant to affect erectile dysfunction, but she smiled, delighted that the old grandma was right because it worked and worked extremely well. She explained to the maintenance men what she was working on and they volunteered to be the test animals for the little green pill, and they were stimulated and enlivened by the results. Every man who tried it wanted more, and when they wanted more, they paid. She now had more money than ever and there was no stopping the need or want for their Granny's Lily product. Peggy now received respect and admiration that she'd long craved. She bounced up the outside steps to the building's front door as the security guard beamed at her and opened the door wide.

"Good morning,' Miss Peggy. How you doin' this fine mornin'?"

"I'm just fine Leroy, and how are you and your wife doing?" Peggy grinned.

"Oh, ho ho, we just fine, oh man, yes, we just fine, thanks to you. You have a good day now, ya' hear."

Full of energy, she ran up the stairs instead of taking the elevator. The empty staircase early in the morning echoed her tippy-tap steps throughout the marble walls and she tickled with excitement for so many reasons. She had money to get blue contact lenses and a stylish hair cut, and Gerhardt had turned out to be quite a pleasant addition to her life. She had new research projects to test her mental skills and finally, financial stability for the first time. Constantly thinking about her research and how to expand the possibilities, she imagined that since the beautiful white lily had a slight fragrance she might try to make a perfume and combined with the pills it could be quite a lucrative venture. She'd found out that its proper name was "Eucharist Lily' but they just called it "Granny's Lily" and the name stuck. The lily's bulbs took to the climate and soil in New Orleans, and if the heat didn't kill them and the bugs didn't eat them up, the moisture would add to their growth. It was quick and easy to get them to multiply and now they had spread all around her back yard and intermingled thoroughly with the other menagerie of plants so that the garden looked like a jungle. They were lovely and so inconspicuous that no one would suspect their potential power.

She unlocked and pulled open the lab door and flipped on the lights, and glanced at the sign on the wall: "Knowledge is power." She knew that knowledge plus her lab techniques were power and that she was in control and finally making money. It was easy, now that Mark and Adelaide were involved in producing Granny's Lily. They could continue to work with it and use other plants as a cover. How life had changed in such a short time! With the extra money, she'd bought a little shotgun house in the Garden District with enough space for the garden and a greenhouse in the winter, where they could grow and cultivate all the plants Mark sent. Peggy smiled and blushed, she never thought she'd be using pronouns like, we and us, before Gerhardt. She stood tall as she looked over her reflection, grinned, and snapped her fingers at her reflection for now she believed in herself.

Surprising enough, but with training, Gerhardt had turned into a good farmer and he followed orders very well. She picked up a new, big brown paper wrapped box from Mark that had been delivered that morning to the lab. Even with the success of Granny's Lily, they decided to continue working on the other plants as well. Peggy pulled on her white lab coat and started separating the plants into height and size.

"G'mornin,' Peggy, have you seen the new shipment of plants Dad sent?" Adelaide asked as she came through the lab door and pushed into her office. The small office was overflowing with boxes, papers, manuals, wrappers, equipment spread over the floor, on the desk, on the windowsill, and behind the door.

"Good grief, Adelaide, look at the office, it's in total chaos. God forbid if anything important should get lost in there." She turned back to the counter. "Yeah, there is a new shipment here. I try to head off and examine any package that comes in before it has a chance to disappear in your office."

"I know the office is a mess, but so many orders have been coming so quickly that it's hard to stay on top of it all."

"I haven't had time to categorize these new samples yet. Do you want to do it?"

"No, go ahead and do it when you have time. Father just called and said this new shipment was to be treated with extra special care, so be well protected. Most of these came from Australia but I can't imagine how he gets them through customs. Both my Mum and Father were interested in the way the Aboriginal people used plants, but my mum was mostly interested in the stories. There is a lot of native wisdom and knowledge that's been lost through our modern yet destructive civilization."

Adelaide shuffled the papers as she headed back to the office. "They're shipping these to us from all over the planet but many are coming from the Santa Barbara area. Well you know the Californians, they have interest in all sorts of new age doo-dads and new philosophies and new weird stuff, so I guess exotic plants would be quite normal for them."

"Oooookkkkkkaay," Peggy agreed as she snapped on the transparent latex gloves. "Now let's see what interesting specimens Mark has conjured up for us to examine. The names are on the labels, of course, but I'll have to do some digging on the internet. The website, Australia's 'Most Poisonous Plants' has been a god-send. Here's the first strange looking specimen, *Eremophila maculata* known as the Spotted Emu Bush." She read aloud, "This plant occurs extensively in semi arid areas of Australia; it liberates cyanide when the plant tissue is damaged and therefore kills insects, snails or slugs, and may kill domestic animals as well." She grimaced. "How charming."

Curiosity brought Adelaide back into the lab and she stood next to Peggy inspecting the box. "You know I studied a bit about plants when I was in school there. But Cyanide? Here, let's put on goggles. I'm concerned about getting it on us."

"Glad to know that now it is both of us opening and examining the samples," Peggy said. "Man, Mark finds the most poisonous plants on the planet. I've wondered why he wants us to research just poisonous plants. Why not other kinds of plants that aren't so deadly? What's the next one?"

Adelaide picked up the next plant between two gloved fingers and held it high, away from her. "This label reads, *Pimelea ferruginea.* Is it in the web-site?"

"Hummm… wait a minute, yep. 'The Pimelea species occurs naturally in south Western Australia and is widely cultivated in flower gardens. It has been recognized for some time as the cause of a serious disease of cattle because it produces anemia, diarrhea, and heart failure with spectacular fluid accumulations under the skin," Peggy read. "Good grief. They plant this stuff in their gardens? You Aussies are a strange bunch of people."

"But we're never boring, that's for sure." Adelaide potted the new plants with care and then continued examining the box. "Oh, my god. Look at this one. I've only seen drawings of this in books. Where in the hell did he find it? He's sent us a rainforest tree. Look up Rain Forest Tree Rhodomyrtus macrocarpa," she said as she planted it in a bigger pot.

"A what? How can you even say that word, much less remember it? Let's see… Rhodo, rhodo…here it is. 'The Rhod-whatever or the Finger Cherry Fruit trees, have been associated with cases of permanent blindness in northern Queensland. Two rainforest trees whose fruits have poisoned children are white cedar and finger cherry. Prudence suggests that they should not be eaten at all, but the local aboriginal people have used them as a food source."

"Prudence? Holy mackerel. Prudence and not total abstinence? Australians must think risk taking is for fun."

"What's life without a bit of risk, eh?"

Peggy used the tongs to pick up a small package. "Adelaide, here is a bag of seeds labeled *Abrus precatorius*. The internet says, 'The seeds of this tree are highly toxic. One seed contains enough toxin to kill an adult human.' Did you study all these in school when you lived there? Doesn't any of this make you feel a little creepy? I mean, why are we examining and experimenting to find medicines and other uses from just poisonous plants and seeds? Aren't there other kinds of plants we could be investigating or do you think he wants us to find antidotes for the poisons?"

"Hey, we're here as the worker bees, and if this is what he is paying us for, I'm ok with it. Let's put just a few of these seeds in soil and then you can take the rest home for the green house. How is it going with your little German?"

"Oh, he is turning out to be a good gardener." Peggy ignored the hidden meaning of the question and refused to talk about her private life. "What's the last plant there?"

"It says, *Idiospermum australiense,* sounds like 'idiot sperms of Australia' to me." Adelaide laughed a genuine giggle. "How typical. What does the net say?"

Peggy read aloud: "It is found in Northern Queensland. Its seeds were found in the stomach contents of cattle, which had died rapidly after feeding beneath the trees in 1971. It may be related to strychnine."

Peggy said, "Oh, jeeze, strychnine and cyanide, what next? Well, I'm glad that is the last of this lot. There is enough here to keep us busy for a long time. Have you found a use for the Ubas you were working on?"

Adelaide peered at the computer. "It says that 'the liquid from the Upas plant has been used for hunting by the natives in Java for centuries. They put the poison on the tips of their spears and just one shot will paralyze an animal in less than a minute. Even a simple skin abrasion caused by a broken branch can kill a person." She sat up and turned to Peggy. "I guess it causes a heart attack. You know, if we could find an anti-dote, it might have the opposite effect on a heart attack patient and could stop a heart attack. Let's work on this one and try to find something useful about it, but I bet we'll just manage to kill a lot of lab rats." Adelaide giggled but Peggy bristled at the reference to her previous nickname.

"Well, Adelaide, you keep working on the Ubas because there

doesn't seem to be any lack of money to buy new rats, so I'm sure you'll find something."

Peggy busied herself cleaning up the packaging and wiping the counters with strong disinfectant. "Now, I'm playing with poison, again."

Chapter 16

Robert barreled into the lab, slamming the door against the metal counters and advanced on Adelaide. She yelped and turned but she wasn't afraid of him. "Don't you ever knock?"

"Nope. Gives 'em too much warning." He threw a newspaper on the lab counter. "Stop whatever you're doing and look at this."

"And good morning to you too." She turned, showing him the latest sample of Granny's Lily, the natural male enhancement pill she'd just made. "What makes you think whatever you have is more important than creating the one thing that's making money for us?"

"Poison face creams for you silly women."

She picked up the newspaper with gloved hands. "Where in the world did you pick up the Jakarta Post? No, don't tell me. I don't want to know."

"Shit! All the crap you can find in newspapers if you just look."

Robert chuckled as he talked. "I've always said my mind is full of useless information and papers are my treasure trove where I can fill up my brain with still more worthless shit. You never know at what point some morsel of a fact will be valuable in the future."

Her eyes widened as she found and read,

"Poisonous cosmetics taken off shelves" written by Ingrid Soerdergren from The Jakarta Post, Jakarta, on Thursday, 10/27/2007 7:12 AM.

> *"TOXIC COSMETICS: The police inspect cosmetic products banned by the Food and Drugs Monitoring Agency in Jakarta on Wednesday. The agency ordered the recall of 27 cosmetic products found to contain hazardous chemicals. (USA Today)"*

She looked over the newspaper at Robert chewing on his moustache. She was a bit alarmed that he looked nervous.

> *"It seems women could indeed be suffering for beauty's sake, with some skin whiteners and passion creams found to contain the same toxic chemicals used to make paper and fabrics. Several deaths have been noted with suspicious connections to perfume and oils made from the Rosary Pea, more commonly called "Crab's Eyes." This plant is a vine with alternate compound leaves, light purple flowers, and beautiful seeds that are red and black. This is a common weed in parts of Africa, southern Florida, Hawaii, Guam, the Caribbean, and Central and South America."*

Robert leaned back on the lab stool and smoothed down his bushy beard. He was well aware that this plant grew wild around his house and locals called it Crab's Eye, and he knew that in South Florida the Seminoles threaded these peas into necklaces and decorations for their costumes. The Indians must have known the peas were poisonous and most likely they had an antidote because one seed could contain enough poison to kill an adult.

She continued reading.

> "The Food and Drugs Monitoring Agency (BPOM) said Wednesday it had banned 130 types of cosmetic products made by several different companies with different brand names. The products—mostly skin whiteners and passion creams—were banned because they were found to contain harmful chemicals, including mercury, retinoic acid, and red color dyes K10 and K3.

"Robert, everybody who's responsible knows not to use this stuff in face cream." She flicked the newspaper at him and eyed him slurping his coffee."

"Don't stop reading." He burped.

> The ban is the result of a police investigation and clinical testing that began in 2007. Use of the products can lead to burns, black spots, skin cancer, permanent nerve damage, liver failure, miscarriages, and death, the chief of police said.

Robert combed his hand through his greasy salt and pepper hair and considered the validity of the article even though it sounded too absurd to be false. He was sure the cosmetic companies were never going to let this information reach the international press because it would sure stir up shit if the public got hold of it. He flip-flopped into the office for more coffee and looked out the window staring into nothing. He wondered if the article would cause problems because women were so nuts about keeping young that they wouldn't care if there was poison as long as the crap worked to keep them young looking. Hell, they'd buy the shit anyway. He waddled back to the lab with a glint in his eye.

"Addie, I was wondering if it might be worth approaching a cosmetic company to see if they might be interested in keeping this information quiet- for a bit of money it could be deleted off the files, if you knew the right people."

"Shut up, Robert. I'm still reading."

"We have been conducting raids on traditional markets and malls since January 2007. We have confiscated 3,555 items. Some of the products were quite famous and could cost millions of dollars just for one item."

Robert pulled on his beard and said out loud, "If the Japanese and Chinese police already know, then I'd bet the USDA already knows."

"One such product was being produced in a small beauty shop inside a chicken market. An employee of the company said all its products had been withdrawn a few months ago, including from counters at its mall outlets. A neighborhood clinic has changed its name and stopped producing all such products."

"Oh god Robert. A chicken factory? How gross."

"The Vice President Director and member of the Association of Cosmetic Companies said many

dangerous products were still in circulation in markets."

<u>*Banned products:*</u>

- *Luxor Beauty night cream- Luxor Beauty day cream*
- *Poison Passion cream - Poison Passion Crystal cream*

That name looked familiar. Poison Passion Cream. Her eyes popped wide open. "I know this one, almost too well."

Chapter 17

She glanced around and said, "Rainbows everywhere. Delightful."

"And what name shall I put on the register/"

A smile coyly tickled the corners of her lips."Well, you can just put Merri Sunshine. Merri spelled with an 'I"

The manager carried her suitcase, extolling the special features of the B&B. "Just a block from the Charles River, this old Boston hideaway is discreet and acceptable to others of like mind. Inside the narrow entrance, you will see the high ceilings and long walls that are tastefully cream colored and have heavy dark red drapes that help keep out the cold and seclude the clients." He sounded like a British butler. "Please notice the multicolored stained glass windows along the long staircase and into the narrow hallway. They do give an invigorating and tickling sensation."

He sniffed with indignation when she tried to give him a tip, turned with his nose in the air and closed the door. No questions were asked when she arrived and she'd checked to make sure they had a strict 'leave you alone' policy. She threw her bag on the canopy-covered bed. The room was old fashioned with a big flower print bed cover and matching curtains that were gross. She shrugged. She really didn't mind the décor for she knew they wouldn't be watching the curtains but enjoying their escape from the outside world and all the political maneuvering, circling sharks, liars and devious self-agenda individuals.

She parted the heavy curtains and looked down at the misty wet street in front of the brownstone bed and breakfast that looked like all the other up and coming buildings on the wide, tree-lined street. She admired her reflection in the window and breathed soft and light, enjoying Boston with its quaint charm, knowing that there wasn't anything like it in Utah or Chicago. Here they could hide and feel free.

To the left she could just see one of the connecting bridges to the mainland. She felt gorgeous, giddy, feminine, and liberated in this secret place. She was free to walk the bridges and sidewalks paralleling the river, and to get pleasure from who she really was. She exhilarated in the cool weather and flirted with the men who noticed her. She laughed, "If they only knew."

She turned and sniffed the violet flowers that had a faint fragrance, then she saw the card, 'Exotic Rosary Pea.' He was ever so thoughtful. She wished they didn't have to meet in secret, but their relationship would ruin both their careers and upset spouses. They were supposed to get together in Chicago but he was murderously upset after the meeting and disappeared.

She jerked around at the sound of the phone. "Damn. Where's that phone? Sure as hell broke a romantic mood."

"Yeah? What do you want?" She snapped into the phone. "I told you not to call me on this phone unless it was urgent. What's up?"

"No! I don't give a damn how he is going to vote. He is not going to get on the National Security Committee. He's a turncoat who can't be trusted; he flip-flops like a fish in the bottom of a boat. See if he'll take a role in the Economic Recovery Committee. Don't call again until tomorrow." She slammed the phone against the wall.

She looked down at the split phone. She wondered why she ever went into politics. It was fortunate she was born good looking and tall and being filthy wealthy didn't hurt either. She turned and watched in the long mirror as she undressed. Her type of politics had been good to her and now it was time to expand her horizons, even though it might be difficult to overcome the appearance of the rich and famous in order to blend in with the ordinary crowd. Not to worry, money could buy anything and money could even buy silence. All politics has secrets.

She noticed three expensive looking bottles on the dresser. She opened, smelled, and tested each one with her fingers. He'd left her sweet smelling body oil and perfume from Paris called Poison Passion and Poison Passion Body Oil. She read the note. "The Rosary Pea passion pill is made from a plant grown in the Caribbean and South America and has light purple flowers with small red and black seeds. It is to be taken an hour or so before lovemaking." She smiled and took the pill.

She hugged a pink silk nighty, breathed deep into its fragrance then said, "No one's safe from mistakes or deadly secrets. No one." She felt the soft slinky material then slipped it on. She felt sensual, tickled and excited. She wished he'd hurry up.

Her father had been one of the richest men in Utah with more than enough political clout. But for women, it was hard to gain support for their own political desires; they had to dig the dirt like the rest of the girls and fight for every inch of gained ground. It was tough, and when a woman succeeded, many surprised men only then gave their support. Oh yes, law school, especially for women, was very useful for they learned that Flip-flopping and Kowtowing were well-used positions in all of politics.

She lay on the silk covers and hugged a pillow. Champagne with the passion pill, some slow soft music, began to stir a sensual tickle feeling over her body. She began to purr. She picked up the bottle of Poison Passion perfume and the sweet smelling body oil. The instructions on the Body Oil stated:

> *'Sensually rub this cream over every inch of you and your partner's bodies. You will begin to feel a light tingling sensation on your skin similar to numbness or tickling. The floral fragrance will soon put you in a dream state where your every movement gives heights of passion.'*

She began by rubbing the oil on her feet, and slowly moved up her legs and over her flat stomach, arms, neck, and breasts. The oil was sensuous and divine and she began to feel a slight warmth and tingling. Up and up over her body, arms, neck, and face she felt a stinging like a prickling. She enjoyed the scent and felt as if she were floating. She lay back on the bed; the tingling turned to a strange dizziness. Her arms moved in slow motion to feel her face. Her fingers tickled over her hot swollen face and she glanced down at her feet and legs. She thought they must belong to someone else because they were so big and red. She lifted her red swollen arms and tried to turn over. Her lungs were beginning to hurt when she tried to take a deep breath.

She called out. "I can't swallow, can't swallow. Nooo. can't breathe." She gulped for air. "Oh my god. Help, help, heart.. pounding. Oh god. I can't breathe. My lungs, no air, Air…. Air…."

"I called as soon as the cleaning staff stopped screaming and calmed down enough for me to understand her Spanish," said the usually calm and somewhat detached concierge.

"And this is how you found the body?" questioned the policeman.

"Yes sir. Nothing has been touched except the cleaning lady knocked over the cart on her way out of the room and the mess is still there in the hall. I locked the door and stood guard until you two officers arrived."

"Thank you. Please wait outside with the cleaning crew until we need you." The police sergeant moved to show the man out of the room.

The concierge pulled away from the policeman and turned to look at him. "We need to be very discreet about this. No press, please," he stated. "We would not want our establishment to have a bad reputation. We have a very select clientele here in Boston and we want to protect them... and us too. You understand, of course."

"Yeah, sure. You don't want a bad reputation. Now please leave the room."

"Hey, Sarge come look at the body. Look close." He lifted up the pink nightgown.

"What've you got? Oh Christ."

"It's one of them perverts, right?"

"Kevin, it is a man dressed in women's clothing, alright, but we won't know if he is a cross-dresser or a transvestite. We'll only know by investigating."

"What's the difference? They're all queer, right?"

"Shut up, Kev, you can't use words and names like that. How long you been on the force?"

"About six months, Sarge. I'm sure lucky to be working with you, too."

Sergeant shook his head. "Kev, be sure you sign up for the 'Sensitivity Training Course' next month."

"Awww man, all the guys make fun of those meetings, I mean, what're they going to tell me that you can't tell me? I ain't no social-worker type."

"You have to go or they'll dock your pay."

"Jeeze, Sarge, look at this here body.. err her. Do you recognize him? He ..er she …eer it looks kinda' familiar."

"Humm, not sure. Got to get a closer look; she's got so much makeup on. Hold on. Wait a minute. Hey, Kev, shine that lamp over here and let's have a closer look at the face."

"I don't know if we're supposed to be moving stuff around, Sarge, but if you say so…"

"ChristAlmighty! Yeah, I recognize him and boy is this gonna scream on the news tomorrow. I wonder how long we can keep this under wraps. If the tabloids knew, they would be already running up the stairs and cramming into the hotel elevators. I don't want to be around when this shit hits the news. I can hear it now, 'Senator Stephen Merriweather, Cross-Dresser, Murdered in quaint Boston B&B.'"

"You shittin' me? Senator Merriweather? From Utah? Oh man, wait until the late night shows get a hold of this one. He ain't such a bad looking woman, uh female-looking…okay whatever. Well, this dude looked good as a man, too, if you ask me but he don't look so hot any more. That make-up takes out some of them pock marks but he's got grease all over him. Man what is that stuff."

"It's smeared all over his body. Don't touch it and keep your gloves on."

"It don't smell too bad, Sarge. But just look at him, er.. her er..it. Hell I don't know what to call it."

"Just say, 'the body,' that'll do."

"Sarge, he was mighty rich wasn't he? Now look at him. Dressed as a woman, dead, all swole up in the face and dressed in a nighty-thing. Just a damn shame. How'd he get to be so rich?"

"Born into it, I guess." Sarge stood up, began looking under the pillows and bedcovers, "Check the suitcase."

"Man. There's expensive stuff in here. Well, it's for sure this Dude won't be needing 'em any time too soon."

"Don't touch any part of him. From the look and color on his face and tongue, it looks like he had an allergic reaction to something. It's going to be a while before they can figure out what got him."

"Coroner's gonna have a fun time with this one. He doesn't get too many interesting cases, mostly the usual stuff, knifing, shootin' and car accidents."

"Careful, Kev, don't disturb evidence. Everything in the room, where there is an unexplained death, absolutely everything is evidence. Make sure you keep your gloves on and be very careful what you smell or breathe."

The police questioned the hotel staff congregated in the drawing room. The staff was, as usual, discreet. No secrets were divulged. Under a dark overcoat, a red headed woman in a green silk dress tiptoed through the kitchen and slipped out the back door.

Chapter 18

Elliott was waiting for Robert in his Jacksonville office. It was Friday and Robert said he'd show up that week but you never knew just when he'd turn up and usually it was unwelcome and it was damned inconvenient for everyone. But Robert enjoyed keeping people on their toes waiting. Elliott stood at the office window and shook his head slowly disbelieving. He shrank with shame hoping their long dead grandfather couldn't see what Robert had done to the old car. The Blue Babe quietly floated down the street farting blue black smoke signals and purred to a stop in front of a fire hydrant. When Robert got out, the doors shut and locked with a whirr and click, and the whole car sank six inches like a turtle protecting itself in a shell.

Robert padded across the street in ragged cut-offs and a tent-sized Hawaiian shirt. In Elliott's office, he wiggled deep into the leather chair, propped his right flip-flop foot on his left bare knee, took out a gnawed cigar from his shirt pocket and continued chewing on the stub. "Whatcha need now, Little Brother? You got more problems your big brother can fix for you?" He sneered.

"Don't get nasty, you always get paid well because you find the dirt I need. You've perfected a talent that somebody honed well in you, but anyway, it's like a second nature to you."

"What's your problem?" Robert growled.

"Maybe I'm paranoid, but…"

"HA. You admit it. I've known it for years. But don't let me stop you, Lil' Bro. Tell me what's scaring your pants off."

Elliott glared at Robert but continued in a calm voice, "Just be quiet and listen for a short time, will you?" Elliott spoke in a low voice in order to not over excite Robert. He spoke in a quiet manner and continued, "You did well in digging up the information about the people around the table and you know that out of seven, five have been found dead. To sum up, O'Hara died at the meeting in Chicago, Johnny Collier died in San Francisco of a presumed heart attack, Oliver Michaels died in New Orleans, Austin Kaufman died of apparent drug over-dose in Florida and now the strange death and scandal of Senator Merriweather dressed as a woman. All of these men were healthy a short time ago. That leaves just two alive, Mildred Pelto, and me. You might have caught some of the news on TV. It's scary as hell that so many have died within a relatively short time."

Robert shrugged his shoulders. "So?"

"I can't believe that they were all natural deaths and I want to know if they were murdered."

"So what makes you think, my young brother, that your greedy-assed lawyers are being hacked off? Who d'you think would give a goddamn if they were? The world should be glad to be rid of cock-sucking moneygrubbers like them. You and your type are leeches that suck the blood and life out of people."

Elliott swallowed hard, sat stone-faced and doubted his own plan that he hoped his borderline insane former FBI agent brother might carry out, but it was too late to rethink it.

Robert shrugged. "Who the fuck cares? Nobody likes the voracious bastards anyway. Hell, I'd like to kill some myself, or hummm…. maybe I have already. Why the hell do you care?"

"I want to know if there's someone out there who is trying to kill me. I don't want to pay for more bodyguards; it doesn't look good to the public besides it wouldn't hurt your sorry reputation to find evidence and perhaps catch the perpetrator. You might even get your old FBI job back."

The stab sliced open Robert's ego, for in his arrogance, he refused to consider any contradiction or questioning of his abilities or to be thought inferior in any way. He started gritting his teeth and thumping his fists on the chair and you knew he was getting ready for a tyrannical rampage. He sneered through his teeth and the long grey cat-tail moustache, and snarled, "Who told you about that?"

"I have connections." Elliott looked at his hands when he spoke.

"Get them to do your dirty work." Robert belched.

"Can't trust them. Robert, here's a challenge. Think about the deaths. Who would want to eliminate high-powered lawyers-turned-politicians but another lawyer wanting to take their place? Or it could be someone with intent on revenge, which could be any number of colleagues or clients with a cause for hating malpractice lawyers."

Daggers shot out of Robert's eyes while he chewed on his yellow-stained whiskers. "Humm… I just might like to catch some of the bastards and torture the shit out of them in place of getting any of my money back. Some son-of-bitch stole hundreds of thousands from me. Shit, I'd love to put one of those motherfuckers in prison with a lot of butt-fuckers."

Elliott's jaws hurt from clenching them so tight. His fingernails dug deep into his hands and his stomach burned with acid. He knew he'd always hated his brother, for it was Robert who'd taught him that people who were near and dear could purposefully harm with intent to injure, cause pain or wound with hope of maiming and do it with gleeful evil. He took pleasure in hurting people and he was Elliott's brother.

"The pay is the usual rate, you understand," Elliott said.

"Yeah, I understand. I'll get you as much information as you want, you lily-livered cheapskate," Robert shot back.

Elliott hated him more for knowing and for keeping his secret and for using it to hold him hostage. "What do you need to know to get started?"

Robert pressed his lips together, stroked his grey beard, and looked at the ceiling. "Let's just speculate for a minute. What is the profile of the victims? They are all rich lawyers, right?"

"Yes, they were all successful politicians-lawyers and were well known throughout the legal community and to their own constituents."

"What else do they have in common? There are many lawyer-cum-politicians, that's nothing unusual. What else did they have in common: men, women, large, small, Eastern, mid-west, smoked, teetotaler, goats…what? What else did they have in common? Or who else did they have in common?" Robert was getting wound up.

"I've looked at the ones who've died, where they died and meetings they've attended. I found that O'Hara was at the Chicago meeting and died there. Kaufman attended a meeting in Tampa. Michaels was supposed to attend the Chicago meeting and had just completed a case defending in a wrongful death. It was a Warren-something case and he worked with Collier who appropriated most of the winnings. O'Hara was really livid when he found out, then Collier died a month after the meeting.

Robert perked up. "Warren? Was that the Melissa Warren case?"

"Yeah, I think so. Why?

"I know her and her family. Shit. She works for me."

"How? Never mind. Don't tell me. I looked at the list of attendees at the Chicago meeting and none other of the older crowd have died within these short months. I'll check and see what meetings Pelto is scheduled to attend. And you," Elliott said as he looked him directly in the eye. "You find a commonality and find out if there's been murder. That's what you get paid for. You get nothing until you have something factual and bring it to me. Nothing."

Robert stopped chewing his moustache. The spacious office felt like an airless vacuum with neither brother breathing or moving, and then he grunted. "When did you get balls in your shorts?" Robert heaved himself up out of the deep brown leather chair, leaving it covered in black wet stink. "Aw shit, what the hell have I got to lose?"

Elliott handed him a file. "All the information I could gather is in this file. I have a copy, in case you lose this one. There is no incriminating evidence toward anyone. Don't come back until you have something solid."

Robert thumbed through the sheets of paper and threw it back on Elliott's desk. "That file's full of piddle-shit." Robert farted and slammed the door behind him as he shuffled out.

Elliott sank his head into his hands then pushed himself up, feeling centuries of weight on his body, walked to the window, and opened the curtains to the fullest. Robert was his brother, obnoxious, filthy and a festering pain in his life but he had an unspeakable talent for digging up dirt.

He watched Robert light his cigar and wondered if being brothers was as difficult for Robert. He was a thug long before being a criminal became a popular theme in the movies and he was always in trouble. It was hard for Elliott to understand how his brother could behave in such a vindictive way toward their parents because he was their real flesh and blood son and for twelve years had received all the attention and special treatment before Elliott was adopted. Robert waddled across the street to their grandfather's old blue 1943 Studebaker in which they had both learned to drive. Robert had repaired it over and over again and had added surprises that Elliott didn't want to think about. He just knew never to take a ride in it.

Elliott remembered clearly and painfully the day Robert showed him Elliott's birth certificate. Robert had grinned as he explained that his baby brother was taken from a druggie prostitute and given to their mom and dad as their own child. The formal adoption was never talked about and their parents died in the car accident before he could ask them. The baby blue Studebaker blew out black smoke as it screeched around the corner.

Elliott turned away from the window and looked around his office. He straightened the old black and white picture of his parents, Dad was in his WW II uniform and mom was holding him and both were smiling and looking happy. Robert was there too and he looked happy, back then. Elliott shook his head and wondered what had happened and why or when did the mean streak start appearing. Robert would hit and pinch until you bruised but he was careful to hit so the bruises didn't show. But something was not right. Something felt very wrong and out of place. What was the niggling itching in his brain? What was missing? He picked up his briefcase and turned out the light. Elliott closed his office, gave the last requests to his secretary, and moved toward the elevator to the garage where his second-hand Cadillac waited. A used car was more impressive to clients than a new expensive model.

Always, after one of Robert's visits, it was hard to shake off the bad memories and emotions that came flooding in. Driving should have taken these thoughts from his mind, but it didn't help this time. He loosened his tie and threw his coat on the back seat and eased his smooth sailing car down the street. He liked the feel of the leather steering wheel with the motor purring and throbbing through it. He knew his mom would have enjoyed a ride in this car. He headed down the street toward the little brown and white house on the corner where he'd lived since law school and turned into the driveway. He sat in the car under the shade of the big old oak tree, smelled the Jasmine growing on the side fence and wondered how different two brothers could be while creeping thoughts of how similar they were began to fester. Were they more alike than he imagined? Elliott hung his head. Robert was outwardly despicable. But nagging thoughts bit into his conscious mind that perhaps he, himself, was mean on the inside and only appeared to be the goody-two shoes because he made allies of powerful unethical persons. It was the Janus syndrome of having both good and evil features. Two faced. What difference was there between the brothers?

He closed the car door carefully and paused, trying to think what his mother would advise. She knew where the most fun was, and perhaps where it was the safest. He then had a vivid memory of swimming in the ocean and he heard his mother's voice. He hung his head and listened. He could hear her say,

"Ride the waves, Elliott. Ride the top of the waves."

Chapter 19

Elliott was waiting again, this time at home and in the dark. Robert had promised to meet him late at night so it would be easier to get in and out without anyone taking much notice. The light from the street and the passing cars made the shadows move then freeze. Elliott listened and heard nothing but the leaves of the oak tree brushing across the roof.

Robert barreled across the room pushing Elliott aside and pulled the box of McCallen 25 from the shelf, threw the precious red box on the floor, kicked it under the table and drank straight from the bottle. He didn't savor the Scotch but took huge gulps and belched a liquidy burp that sounded like heaving. He wiped his mouth with his hairy arm. "Aww, you're trembling. Getting mad? Want to hit me? Go ahead and you'll never find out about your blood-sucking lawyer friends, or should I say poison-sucking friends?"

Elliott took the bottle from Robert and downed the Scotch in an effort to calm himself, while glowering and seething, he stopped in mid-air. "Poison sucking?" Elliott glared at Robert, afraid to move, afraid to think that Robert had found a murder, and afraid for his own life too. He hoped Robert meant alcohol poison, but he knew with the sly condescending look on Robert's face, that there had been a murder, or at least Robert was making Elliott think there had been.

"Well, listen up my dear baby brother." With sadistic glee, Robert began in tormenting slowness to tell his findings. "First, that meager pile of shit you gave me to begin digging the dirt on your fellow-snake-biter lawyers was piss-poor. That information was so pedantic I wanted to laugh it was so pathetic."

What have you found out?" Elliott asked. He knew Robert had some dreadful news that he would tell with agonizing detail. One thing with Robert, you had to sit and hear out his full detailed description to get to the main meat of the story. Now it looked like Elliott was in for a long, drawn-out session. "I hope the McCallen 25 will last." Elliott looked doubtful and passed the bottle to Robert.

"Don't be so god-damned impatient. I need to tell things like I remember them and in full, so you can understand the strength and significance," Robert said. "At first we didn't know if there had been any crime committed, right?" Robert smoothed out his moustache and whiskers.

"Right…"

"Well, listen up little brother, I don't know if they teach you anything useful at law school but in order to profile serial murderers, it is first necessary to link crimes to a type of common offender. To accomplish this, the offender is determined on classes of action committed at the crime scene. A sharp investigator needs to dig up the scuttle-butt."

"Right, that is why I am paying you way too much money to find out," Elliott said. "What did you find out?"

"Patience my baby brother, patience. In all cases of serial killings, there is a fantasy, whether sexual, acquisitive, or demonic. This is an important part of the killing process. In other words, there must be some idea, thought pattern, or even a sexual fantasy that propels the killer into the murderous process. This fantasy is in some cases very simple and in others quite complex, but there is always a fantasy."

"Serial killing?" Elliott questioned stunned.

"Of course serial killings. Isn't that what you hired me to find out? Serial killings."

Elliott was near to yelling but knew Robert liked to make him lose his cool to show power over him. He shuddered and took a swig of the Mc Callan 25.

"There were samples taken from each of the death scenes and they will be soon given to a specialty lab for analysis. But what we need to analyze, and that is where you and your beady little brain comes in, baby brother, we need to know the killer profile."

Elliott hated being called baby-brother but he answered, "Profiling isn't new; all police agencies have been using it for a long time."

"So, what is the difference in organized and unorganized killers?" Robert asked as he took the bottle from Elliott and gulped down the scotch.

"Smart ass. Because the FBI didn't want to use the psychological jargon of 'psychopathic or psychotic' they began using the terms 'organized and unorganized'. Ressler and Douglas described these terms in a 1988 journal article in Sexual homicide: Patterns and motives. They describe the organized offender as an individual who plans the offense to control the victim and situation, while the disorganized offender does not pre-plan but attacks suddenly to overpower the victim." Quoting texts was easy for Elliott.

"Well done. Bravo, little brother. I guess the scholarship fund flunkies did well when they chose to give you money for law school."

The priceless whiskey drizzled out of Robert's mouth which he wiped with his arm. "Now if these are murders, what we have is a person or persons who are methodically ticking off a list of people, all lawyers, and specifically medical malpractice lawyers with lots of money, lots of big-time press profile, and who are in political power or are seeking political office. And so far they were all sitting at the same table at that Chicago conference." Robert added with a flourish.

Elliott stopped dead still and stared at Robert.

"Yes, little brother, if there is such a list that means <u>you</u> are on the list."

Elliott breathed in sharply and blew out slowly. "Just as I suspected. What's the next step?"

"Well," Robert said and cleared his throat, raised his eyebrows. "I've uh…procured samples from the murder sites."

"Procu..oh shit. Don't tell me. When will the samples be ready? Where is the lab? Are the lab technicians trustworthy and competent?"

"Fuck you. I'll tell you when I find out." He yelled over his shoulder as he stomped out of the room. "Let's go eat."

Elliott waited impatiently for Robert at one of his favorite restaurants that stayed open late for night owls such as he was. There were several high-class Italian restaurants around but an authentic Sicilian restaurant in Jacksonville was a rarity. The community tried to keep this one open for business so they brought in all their clients and friends. He impatiently tapped his water glass and wondered why there was almost no information about Robert through the internet or from private sources. There was nothing official or unofficial that his snoops could find; he had learned a few things but not much.

He unwrapped and rewrapped his napkin, glanced at his watch, and looked toward the entrance. It was time to find out a bit more about his big brother. He knew Robert would show up sooner or later since Elliott had agreed to pay and the chefs had the order so when Robert came, the food would be hot and ready.

The chair scraped the floor with a jarring screech. Elliott jumped and knocked over his glass of water. "Jeeze, Robert! You scared the shit out of me; I didn't see you come in."

"Happens all the time," Robert muttered as he looked around the restaurant.

"You'd think that someone your size and décor would be easy to notice! But sit down, please." He sarcastically gestured to the seat Robert was already sitting in.

Robert growled through clenched teeth that held a chewed toothpick. "You made sure we'd be seen by choosing the table in the slap-dab middle of the restaurant." He flicked the toothpick onto the floor.

"I ordered for the both of us to save you time. Hope you like Chicken Marsala."

"It'll do." The chair groaned a little under Robert's weight. He turned red with a coughing fit, grabbed the white linen napkin, spilling the silverware on the table and on the floor, and spit phlegm into the napkin.

Elliott didn't flinch, didn't blink. He was going to find out about Robert. "Want some water?"

"Scotch. It soothes the throat."

Elliott ordered the scotch. The food, already waiting, came hot to the table. "Eat something with the Scotch. It'll help." He picked at his food as Robert shoveled the mild Italian dish into his mouth. It was hard to sit and watch him eat and not get sick. "How long have you been with the FDA?"

Robert froze in mid-chew and swallowed with a slow gulp. "So you know about that."

"Knowledge is protection," Elliott stated as a warning.

Robert watched, deciding how much Elliott already knew and how much more he would have to tell him to keep his curiosity under control. "What do you know?"

"Well, in general the FDA want people who can handle stress because they have to deal up close and personal with international terrorists, weapons proliferation, international crime, narcotics trafficking, and guerilla capabilities of rogue nations. They also want persons who are physically fit, which you are not, energetic, and able to cope with extreme situations, which I am sure you can handle in one way or another."

"You've done your research," he growled. "You're one dangerous bastard."

"They also like people who have a sense of humor, and at least there you have a knack of pulling off practical jokes, even if they do go awry, like putting cherry bombs in the university mail box, which I supposed you might find humorous." Elliott held Robert's gaze. He was not afraid of him right now; he was in control.

In a stiff, threatening, low voice, Robert asked again, "What more do you want? I'm doing your dirty work so you don't get you little white fingers dirty. I'm tired of this fucking off," He stood up and was out of the restaurant before Elliott could take another breath. Elliott breathed slowly, reached over and picked up the napkin Robert had used and put it into a plastic bag and zipped it tight. The information on Robert was spotty but with a little luck, Elliott hoped to find new information, and he needed to keep the hound dogs looking.

The waiter rushed over. "Mr. Elliott, is everything all right? Was the food not good? Your friend left in a hurry."

"Oh, yes, Andretti, it was very good. He just had an emergency. Can you send the bill to my office, please?"

"Oh, no, Mr. Elliott. The boss said it's our pleasure because you've helped us and we're very grateful."

"Thank you so much, Andretti, and thank Giuseppe for the delicious meal. Here's something just for you. I've got to run. Thanks again."

His car was already waiting and the air conditioner was turned on full blast. He flipped it off, opened all the windows and let the top down; he needed the dark sultry air to warm him. He got what he'd come for. Actually, he got more than he'd hoped. "Oh, yes. Now Robert, we shall see. We shall see."

Chapter 20

Elliott tapped the envelope on his desk, afraid to read and afraid not to read. Whatever was written would determine one of the many options in his life. He placed the envelope on the desk and paced around the room straightening the paintings and testing the weights and pendulum on the German cuckoo clock Robert had given him, then flipped the blinds to throw light on the ceiling. He'd had time to think and remember his life at home with his parents and Robert. He'd forced himself to look at unpleasant memories, but what he couldn't be sure of was if he had seen his birth certificate. Did Robert show him or did he just tell about it? Why was it that this part of his life was kept away from him? He wondered if he wanted to know or not. He sat at his desk, shaking, and opened the envelope.

It began:

Dear Mr. Edgars,

The DNA data and information you have requested is detailed in the following with full disclosure. You will find every possible test and treatment of the materials that you provided was carried out to the fullest extent.

The specimens you sent to us were as follows: Specimen A was phlegm or sputum taken from Robert Edgars. Specimen B was taken from hair from Julia H. Edgars. Specimen C was taken from hair from Elliott Edgars.

In brief, we have ascertained that from the specimens you provided, we have been able to determine that the owner of the specimen A, Robert Edgars, is of unknown birth and is not related to specimens B or C. Specimens B and C are related.

Please read the full details included in this letter and see the attached document.

Thank you for your patronage, and if we can be of help to you in any further way, please let us know.

Sincerely,
DNA Testing Center of Washington D.C.

Elliott reread the short letter several times and tried to take in the full meaning. His heart was beating like the roll of a tin drum and sweat was pouring down his cheeks soaking his shirt. He pulled out the accompanying form from behind the letter. It was an official birth certificate which stated:

Official Birth Certificate from the State of Florida

Born: Elliott James Edgars   time: 12:45 AM   sex: male

Date: December 27, 1950

To

Mother's maiden name: <u>Julia Hodnett Edgars</u>   *race: Caucasian*

Father's name<u>: Matthew Seaborn Edgars</u>   *race: Caucasian*

"My birth certificate."

His sweating hands stained the paper with his finger prints. He stared at the papers, looking from one to the other. He had never doubted Robert's account of his birth. He had swallowed it hook, line, and sinker. If it were possible for time and the world to stop, it did at that moment for Elliott. All his life he had lived under the fear that the drug addiction of his mother would attach to him. He had been frightened that one small slip and he would be like her. He had fought every inclination to drink too much and he'd grasped onto the hope that strength of willpower would help him persevere against the inherited "bad" genes. He'd feared he would one day descend into some unknown abyss of alcohol and drugs and he wouldn't have the will power to fight the negative genetic disposition when it caught up with him.

Even in his stupor, tears began to form in his eyes and he picked up the picture of his parents. "Is it true?" He stared at his parents. "Robert was adopted, not me? I am the real birth son of our parents. My mother was not a drug addict but the dear mother who raised me. Robert lied to me; he knew. He was twelve years older and was most likely jealous for a baby coming into the family when he had been the sole child for so long."

Elliott and Robert had none of the same DNA. "Julia and Matthew were my real parents."

"Ohmygodalmighty. Hallelujah," he yelled and raised his arms to the ceiling and shouted, WWWOOOHHOOO. YEEHAAA." He danced, jumped around the room' "Ohmygodalmighty. I'm Free. I'm Free." And he laughed loud and long.

The phone rang and his secretary asked, "Mr. Edgars, is everything alright? There's a lot of shouting coming from your office."

"Oh yes," Elliott shouted, "Oh yes. Everything's fine. Thank you, oh yes. Take the day off…no take the week off."

He slammed down the phone. Robert wasn't his blood brother after all but he was still his legal brother; but now Elliott no longer had to fear he would be like Robert or the drug addicted mother. He was free. Slowly, the joy turned to a burning anger for the years of abuse from Robert and all the taunting and bullying about his supposed prostitute mother. Again the uncontrollable urge to kill Robert chewed up his sense of decency.

He paced the room. Multiple murderous thoughts and plans swelled in his head giving him a headache the size of his car and then he eased into the leather chair as his heart slowed. No. He wouldn't let Robert know what he'd found out. Instead, the truth would stay with him until he'd used all Robert could find, but now he no longer felt controlled or obligated to Robert. He smiled as he leaned back into the cozy chair. He'd play along and use Robert's arrogance. He knew just how to hurt Robert in the most effective way but not kill him.

Elliott fingered his chin and slowly grinned. Yes, he knew just how to do it.

Chapter 21

Mildred Pelto talked to her reflection in the immense gold frame mirror. "You're a good looking broad, no doubt about it." She turned sideways, smoothed down her flat stomach and tight butt. She touched her temples and around her hairline where the face-lift scars barely showed. "Honey, you've got to look good tonight and get real close to some of these Jacksonville power and money people." Elliott had agreed to host a campaign meeting for her and he'd seen that no expense was spared.

The knock at the door brought her out of her self-grooming. She opened the door and turned to the porter, "Be careful. Stop slamming my bags around as if they were sacks of flour. No, no, don't leave them there. Put them on the trolley so I can reach them better." He scowled when she tipped in coins, then he left to warn the others.

She smiled to herself, satisfied that someone had remembered she enjoyed unusual and exotic plants. The light fragrance from the fresh flowers filled the room as she walked around admiring herself in the mirrors and touching the flowers. She planned to spread wildflower seeds throughout her state as Lady Bird Johnson did for Texas, and the wild flower display in the hotel room pleased her immensely, especially the huge bouquet of Queen Ann's Lace placed in the center of her room.

She turned on the light around the magnifying mirror in the bathroom, examined the wrinkles around her eyes and made a note to see her dermatologist. Opportunities had opened up for her since a few of those who stood in her way were now gone to their rewards in their afterlife. She shrugged her shoulders and told the mirror, "We all have to die sometime." She had heard rumors about Merriweather and found it hard to believe an up-standing church member would have a sexual double life; but then she knew a lot of that went on and the more she could find out, the safer it would be to climb up the political ladder. She hoped the investigation would soon determine Merriweather's cause of death, but in her experience, she knew these things would take time.

She stretched out on the king-sized bed, fully dressed in her pink suit, heels and pantyhose. She looked stiff and ready for a casket. She fingered her diamond tennis bracelet as she looked around at the gaudy gold curtains and white Victorian furniture. This was one of those times when she decided the committee would pay for the room. She enjoyed the fascinating and yet frustrating political games, for there was always the next battle, the next win, the next loss and the next recovery. She sighed, wishing that she were the king of the world or president, because she would certainly make changes.

She got up and began to examine the bottles of creams and perfumes on her dressing table. Her fingertips caressed the silky creams then she sniffed the perfumes and applied the delicate fragrance to her wrists. She spread out her medicine carrier, patted the boxes of her indispensable and essential pills that kept her alive. She had accomplished a lot in her life in spite of epilepsy since grade school and probably could've been president if she hadn't been afflicted. She began taking a mountain of pills.

She added on another layer of makeup and patted her stiff, perfectly fashioned hair and blew a kiss to the mirror, "I'm brilliant and not bad looking- well not as bad looking as others my age." Money had bought her a good-looking body and smooth face and neck. "Oh well, off to the meeting to schmooze and mix."

Mildred grabbed a golden goblet from the waiter's tray, smiled and looked for people she wanted to speak to or to be seen speaking to, when she noticed Dr. Mark talking to a fat weird man. Everyone was dressed in tux and tails but the stranger was in a cream colored cowboy suit, cowboy boots and a big white Stetson hat. She wondered how he got in, or who he was related to, or if he were an eccentric billionaire.

She small-step girdle-walked over to Mark. "Well, Dr. Mark Warren, I'm surprised to see you here. I haven't seen you since Chicago. How are you?" She gave him a wet noodle handshake

"Hello there, Congresswoman Pelto. Quite an occasion, right?"

"Yes very impressive. I have to run see some other people but before we get separated, I've heard rumors about a Grandmother's Lily pill. Would it be possible to give some a try? For my husband of course." Mildred winked and tried to flirt like a young woman.

"Granny's Lily. Of course. As a matter of fact, I have some in my car. I'd be glad to bring some to you later, if you would like," Mark offered.

"Yes, please do. I am in the presidential suite at the Westin. You could leave it at the desk and I'll pick it up later if you want. You are a dear. Who's your friend?" She asked turning to Robert.

"This is Robert Edgars, Elliott's brother."

"Oh my, you are very different looking from your brother. Do you have an interest in politics?"

Robert's voice growled from the center of his chest and a threatening scowl screwed up his face. "All politicians are snakes I wouldn't throw a rat to. They're all bloodsuckers who're out for themselves. They should all be taken out and shot, starting with the women."

Pelto didn't blink. "Well, at least you don't hide your opinions. Good that Elliott is not like you in that respect. I've got to go work the room you know. Please don't let me know when you are anywhere near me. Goodbye." She then patted Mark on his chest and moved on with her wide radiant smile but not before glaring at Robert.

Robert spat, "God, I hate women like that. She's another one who's made millions off of suing doctors. She swings her million-dollar-paid-for body at the men and she's cold as a vampire's kiss. I wonder who birthed and had those four kids of hers. She sure didn't open her legs for anybody." He grabbed a drink off the tray from a startled waiter. "How the hell did you get invited to this shin-dig, Mark?"

"I met some of these people in Chicago at that meeting where you and I bumped into each other. I brought some Granny's Lily for some of these…men and women." He watched Mildred fawn over some rich contributor. "And you? How'd you get rooked into being here?"

"Investigating." They both turned to see Peggy and Adelaide walk into the room. "Nice, Elliott took my suggestion and invited the lab rats to this shindig. It's good for them to get out of the lab and see the snotty-nosed upper crust."

Mark nodded. "Yea, the girls look right spiffy." He took another glass of champagne from the waiter's tray. "Robert, you shouldn't be too hard on Ms. Pelto. She's a plant lover, like you, and she's particularly fond of exotic plants and flowers---and how she loves exotic flowers."

"Yeah?" Robert's bushy eyebrows lifted up into his shaggy hair.

"Yes, I saw someone take a bunch of Queen Anne's Lace to her room."

"Queen Anne's Lace?"

"Well, that's what it looked like. Funny how close it resembles the Water Hemlock. It's hard to tell them apart."

"Yeah, I know."

"The Water Hemlock's the most violently toxic and fatal plant in North America. It contains the convulsing cicutoxin which causes Grand Mal seizures and it always is followed by a quick death."

"You don't say," Robert mumbled and looked over the crowd to find Mildred Pelto.

"Socrates drank hemlock when he was convicted of corrupting the youth of his day by making them think for themselves and to think through their problems. He encouraged them not to accept the ways and lives of their parents. He shook up the boat of the established way of life. So they killed him."

"Well, there you go. That's what happens when you rile the political snakes."

"You're such a bloody bastard."

"Yeah, Mark, you're right. In a way we are just alike."

"Yeah. That's two of us, Mate. Two of us, like two rosary peas in the same pod."

Near midnight the porter opened the hotel entrance door for Mildred Pelto. "Good evening Congresswoman, hope you had a pleasant evening."

"Boring and my feet hurt."

"Sorry to hear that. There's a redheaded woman waiting to see you. She's in the lounge. She has a basket of fruit and a package. Shall I bring her up?"

Chapter 22

The Chief Coroner of Duval County, headquartered in Jacksonville, grumbled as he pulled into the dimly lit parking space in front of the Coroner's Office. For many years he'd asked himself why he'd ever run for this office and couldn't figure out why people voted for him, except he was the only candidate. He rested his head on the steering wheel and wondered if he'd been out of his mind or drunk when they talked him into becoming Coroner. The pay was lousy and he was at the beck and call of every politician in the area who needed a favor for some constituent even at two god damned o'clock in the morning. At least all the patients were dead and he didn't have to worry about getting sued for killing any of them.

The door handle tore the pant leg of the dirty green scrubs he'd worn all day or maybe all week. At any rate they looked like he'd worn them for a long time and he didn't seem to notice or care.

He was warm and cozy at home and had fallen asleep dreaming of retirement on a foreign island with palm trees and all the free booze you could drink. The call came for him to perform an autopsy on one old bird who was past due her trip to never-never land and was probably so tightened with surgeries that he'd have to be careful the scalpel didn't bounce off her. Politicians thought they deserved special treatment.

He trudged through the heavy door and nodded to the night watchman. "Evening, Pete."

"Evening, Doc," said the night guard without looking up. "Thought you'd be comin' in soon."

"Christ, Pete. You've been working here longer than I've been alive and that's a hellofa long time."

"Prolly be here after you long dead and gone too, Doc."

"I got a call that Mildred Pelto's body was found in a hotel. They want to make sure of the cause of death because the press is going to be all over this in the morning. Where's the body?"

"Room three on the right."

"Grrrr... don't like that room; there is something suspicious about it. An autopsy takes longer and turns out to somehow be more complicated. Certain rooms just have bad outcomes and that is one of them."

"Yep. That's what they all say."

"Hey, let's change it over to room two, there's more light in there." He yelled down to the guard, his voice echoing down the empty hall.

"Nope, no can do, it's already got two bodies, Chief, one gunshot, the other a knifing," he said without lifting his head from the desk.

"What do we have in room one?" the exasperated Coroner asked.

"Two more from City Hospital, not sure yet what they are. They don't tell me unless I ask."

"I hate room three. It's against me. Oh well, can't be too superstitious. Just got to get this over with."

He pulled on his plastic gloves and pushed through the double doors and bowed. "Madam Pelto, please forgive an old man for digging into you. I hope you didn't suffer. They say you had epilepsy. Shouldn't be too hard to figure this out."

He called out to the night watchman, "Who's here to help out? Do we have any medical students?"

The guard turned his head slightly and called back, "Yup. I called them soon as I knew you were coming in. They're newbie's. First timers. You gonna' have fun with these two." He laughed into his arm that was cradling his head.

The Coroner chuckled when he remembered one of the few pleasures in this work was seeing the uninitiated faint or throw up at their first autopsy. After his first autopsy many ages before, he'd thrown up for a week but at least he hadn't fainted like some of his classmates.

The two young medical students hesitated in front of the cold morgue room. The Coroner held open the door, gave them gloves and white lab coats. "Oh ho, freshmen medical students. Welcome. Well, have either of you seen a dead body before? Let me lift the sheet for you so you can get your first look at what mortality looks like." The coroner lifted the sheet. "You and everyone else, at the end of our lives, will be in this same state of repose. And this is what you will be avoiding for the rest of your lives."

The two medical students tiptoed up to the body and turned pale.

The old Medical Examiner showed just a touch of sympathy. "Let's take the instruments and begin, shall we, hummm.....? If you need at any time, the bathroom is the second door on the right. Hurry back as soon as you can. I'll be needing your assistance."

Paint had long since peeled off the old wooden desk. Sitting in the front office behind the desk, the coroner scratched his graying stubble which was appearing faster than he expected. The two medical students sat across from him stinking from various surgical solutions and nervous sweat. "Well, this is one of the rare times when this old man is stumped. It doesn't add up." He enjoyed teaching but he didn't lecture, instead, he liked to ask questions and probe the minds of the students urging them to think for themselves. He guided their thoughts so that they would discover the answers. "Pelto had epilepsy. Have either of you guys studied epilepsy yet?"

One tired student shook his head, no. He was too tired to remember even if he had studied it. He'd spent a good amount of time retching in the bathroom and just wanted to lie down. The other student, a bit more awake and appearing somewhat interested, answered, "Well not really, sir. My cousin had seizures when she was a kid. They said she would outgrow them, and I guess she did. It has something to do with the neurons in the brain, I think."

He looked at their glazed-over eyes; they were tired and this lecture was a bit beyond their comprehension this late at night and after their first autopsy. "In simple terms, seizures are transient signs and/or symptoms of abnormal, excessive, or synchronous neuronal activity in the brain. Epilepsy is more likely to occur in young children or in people over the age of 65, which Madame Pelto was even though she would have denied it, and epilepsy most of the time can be controlled, but it cannot be cured with medication. The mainstay of treatment of epilepsy is anticonvulsant medications. Often, anticonvulsant medication treatment will be life-long and can have major effects on the patient's quality of life."

One student sat glassy-eyed while the other scratched a few notes. "What is the prognosis?" the half-awake student was able to ask.

"Most people with epilepsy lead outwardly normal lives, like congresswoman Pelto for example. But while epilepsy cannot at this time be cured, for some people it does eventually go away, like your cousin. Most seizures do not cause brain damage. It is not uncommon for people with epilepsy, especially children, to develop behavioral and emotional problems, sometimes the consequence of embarrassment and frustration or bullying, teasing, or avoidance in school and other social settings. For many people with epilepsy, the risk of seizures restricts their independence and recreational activities. Some states refuse drivers licenses to people with epilepsy. You will note that Congresswoman Pelto did not drive, she always had her driver, but she claimed it was a work-related issue because she worked in the car. People with epilepsy are at special risk for two life-threatening conditions: status epilepticus and sudden unexplained death."

"Perhaps Congresswoman Pelto just had a big seizure and died," suggested the student. "What medicines did she take?"

The Coroner shifted scattered papers around his desk. "I think the report said she took Lyrica. At present there are 20 medications approved by the Food and Drug Administration for the use of treatment of epileptic seizures in the US. One of the first medications was Phenobarbital which was first used in 1912 for both its sedative and antiepileptic properties."

He loved to explain whenever a student was alert enough to ask. It made him feel that his medical studies were still tucked away in his brain somewhere and he could recall some of the lectures some of the time. "Oh my" he said stretching and yawning, "it is getting late."

The now wide-awake student read the report and began to ask questions. "Mrs. Pelto was found on the floor dead of an apparent seizure. Her pillbox where she kept all her meds, in particular the barbiturates, were clearly marked and all the pills were missing. Did she overdose?"

"I can't be sure but there was not enough of the barbiturate residue in her GI tract to suggest an overdose," the surprised coroner answered.

"I just don't have the answers young man. But it is perplexing. What we do know now is that Congresswoman Mildred Pelto had a severe seizure but didn't call for help. Her pills are gone and there is an unusual mixture of martini-like liquid in her stomach but it will take further tests to find out what flavor of martini it was. There were also bites on the abdomen as possibly a result of the smashed brown spider found in her room. I'll have to send that to the Insectarium in New Orleans where my son works to verify it. He's always liked those crawly things. It's a puzzlement. I wonder if that new lab in New Orleans will take a look at the samples."

Jacksonville Daily News announcement:

Congresswoman Pelto found dead in hotel room after an apparent Grand Mal seizure. She has had a long fight with Epilepsy. A memorial service will be held in her home state in a private ceremony. Full results of an autopsy will be released within the week.

Chapter 23

Mark's phone rang.

"Hello, this is Mark at 323-643-8991. Please leave a message at the beep...beeeep."

"Well, hello there Mark, this is Robert. Sorry we keep missing each other, I was kinda' tied up- literally- but the other guys are dead now so no worry. I need you and maybe your Dad's expertise with some rare plant poisons. Can we talk? I'll be in California in about two weeks. See you both at Dad's farm."

Robert's phone rang.

"Hello your own God-damn self. This is Robert. Leave a message. I might call you back or not, depends on how I feel or if I like you or not. Beeep......"

"Hello, Robert, This is Mark. I'd be glad to help if I can. We'll be waiting at Dad's Farm."

Dad's phone rang.

"Hi there, this is Dad of Dad's Farm where all things are grown natural and friendly. I'm probably just out in the back field and can't hear the phone. Please leave a message and I'll get back to you as soon as I wash my hands. Thanks."

"Hi Dad, Mark here. Got to talk to you. Robert Edgars is coming out to see you and wants me there too. Around the 14th, something about plants, do you know why?"

Mark's phone rang.

"Hello, this is Mark at 323-643-8991. Please leave a message at the beep...beeeep."

"Hi, Mark, this is Dad. Nope, don't know what Robert wants. Come up anytime. Your room's always ready. Bye."

It never rains in Southern California, except when it floods, then houses mud-slide into the ravines, the canyons and the Pacific. Now was one of those times. The rain pounded for three days and three nights without letting up for a breathing second. La Niña had stirred up some tropical storm that bashed, bruised, and slickened the whole countryside. Several of the richest home owners in defiance of common sense, had their homes built on the precipices of the high cliffs to show off their wealth and contempt for mud slide danger. These few affluents refused to evacuate.

To Mother Nature, her La Niña was just having some young childish fun with the small tropical storm she had kicked up. What trouble could one small La Niña cause anyway? Mother Nature looked down at the homes on the cliff that seemed like weak match-box toys and let little La Niña knock them about like a child playing with sand castles on the beach. She watched La Niña cry for three days causing hills to slide into the lowlands and she patiently allowed her child's temper tantrums to set off earthquake tremors. When she was suitably calmed and pacified, Mother Nature led her away to water the dry Western Plains filled with waiting wildflower seeds, eager to sprout and bloom.

Rescuing the crops around the Santa Barbara area was paramount- not only for Dad but for the entire region. Neighbor helped neighbor. Robert, Mark, and Dad worked for four days trying to save all they could from the farms. When the worst was over and on the last night, the three men sat in the kitchen around the solid maple table just big enough for four people, or three men, a very large pizza and three cartons of beer. The aroma of the Italian five meat and cheese pizza curled around the table, counter top, curtains and crept up to the ceiling while the beer-burping men added to the smell.

Dad took a heated pillow from the microwave and put it across the sore muscles on his shoulders. "God, I've never been so tired in all my sixty-seven years."

Mark moaned, "I don't think sixty-seven years has anything to do with it, Dad." He rolled his shoulders loosening the tension, "My forty-three year old bones are aching. But Robert doesn't look too bad."

"Shit, I've taken so much Ibuprofen my stomach is used to it by now and it's beginning to think pills are all it'll ever get." Robert grabbed a big piece of pizza. "God damn this is good! Dig in chumps."

Dad groaned as he massaged his shoulders. "I've worked hard all my life."

"And what did it get you but a fucking law suit that took away your license, your practice, sent Mark to Australia, and broke your wife's heart." Robert spat out, "Fucking bastards."

For a moment all sound was sucked out of the room. In the intense silence they could hear the run-off rain bubbling down the furrows in between the rows of plants in the garden and in the quiet, the soft ticking of the kitchen clock sounded as if it were a grandfather clock.

"What did you want to see us about, Robert?" Mark grabbed a piece of pizza and took off the meat.

Dad stopped eating but played with the pizza crust, never looking up from the plate. "What's so important that you had to see us both?"

"There might be a serial killer out there poisoning people….. Might be, not sure. There're some strange findings in the victim's blood and liquid samples you two might be interested in."

"Serial killer? Who's getting killed?" Dad asked.

"A few high profile and highly paid medical mal-practice lawyers have died in the past year."

"Great going. The best news we heard in years." Dad tilted back his hat. "I'd be glad to donate to their expense account."

Robert pushed back from the table. "There's a secret investigation going on." He waited. "I'm leading it."

The tiny kitchen seemed smaller and smaller and the air was heavy to breathe. Mark, in a low monotone voice asked, "Why should this concern either of us?"

"Bottom line, there could be a lot of money in it and certainly recognition." Robert smacked his lips anticipating either money or more pizza. Who knew, who could tell. "Also, I thought you two might be curious because there are elements in the samples which so far have been undetectable. Mark's lab in New Orleans has been working with exotic plants and I wondered if these undetectables could be from plants."

Dad slowly sat straight up and his ice-calm demeanor slightly cracked. "Samples? You have samples?"

Robert stared at Dad for a brief millisecond and registered the emotion, the dilated eyes, the momentary flush and trembling hands and Mark's sharp breath intake. *Hummm...interesting... will have to keep this in mind.*

Mark recovered first. "It might be exciting to test some examples and I'm sure the lab would be the perfect place. When do you want us to start? Peggy and Adelaide are well trained and could run the tests. Where are the samples? Why do you want Dad?"

"I thought Dad would know about less familiar poisonous plants and their components or at least be able to suggest what to look for." Robert added a mysterious touch. "All the victims died of seemingly natural causes."

"So, Robert," Dad said as he pointed with his piece of pizza, "let me get this straight, an old man has to have things laid out plain. You want my help because I'm familiar with exotic plants, right?"

"Yep."

"And the connection is that the deaths seem natural, or the victims seem to have died from natural causes?"

"Yep."

"Who were the victims?

"Senator Steven Merriweather, Tom O'Hara, Austin Kaufman, Michael Oliver, Johnny Collier and now Mildred Pelto."

"Ass-holes all of them. Why should we give a flipping fart about how any of them died?" Mark barked.

"Money. Like I said, I am getting paid really well, by my brother by the way, to find out any connection in the deaths, and there will be people who will want to know our findings. Some may pay to know and some may pay to keep it quiet." Robert stroked his beard and raised his bushy eyebrows and waited for the information to become clear. "Either way it's a win-win situation."

"Bribery. You sonofabitch. Paid to find out and to keep it quiet," Dad whispered.

"No, not bribery, no, no, no. Intellectual property information." Robert pounded on the table. "Intellectual property information," he said and roared with laughter. "We can't lose." His laughter transitioned into a hacking pleurisy cough, rolling, gurgling and spewing. Mark and his Dad watched without moving, without offering to help. "We get paid no matter what we find out. What a sweet deal. Besides, if you want to help find out if these ass-holes were really murdered or not, you'll be heroes. Or if they died of natural causes we can at least put the conspiracy rumors to rest. Your Dad will gain some his medical reputation back and we could make money. He could become famous as an expert and wealthy in the process."

"So you have the samples frozen somewhere?" Dad asked.

"Yep, different locations, and they're divided up so no one can destroy them before they are all tested." Robert scraped his chair across the linoleum floor and stood up.

"We'll think about it and let you know," Mark whispered as he folded the limp pizza slice into small pieces.

Robert left in the slackening rain as Mark and Dad sat, neither wanted to speak. The forgotten pizza was cold, greasy and sticking to the cardboard box.

"Dad, why should we care? Why should we help Robert?"

"He's asked us to help. He knows we're experienced." They looked at each other, both with questioning care for the other. "I wouldn't mind working in a lab again for a while. It might be a welcoming change from farming and put me back in the medical world, at least for a little while. I'd like to know if I could still be useful in a lab."

"Sure you'd be useful in the lab but I'm suspicious. You know Robert hates malpractice lawyers as much or more than we do. Those lawyers who died are sorry examples of human beings. Why should we do anything to help?"

Dad gathered the sticky pizza leftovers and empty bottles, put it all in a big black trash bag and tied the top. "Who is it that wants to know? Robert's brother? Why would he be interested?"

"Elliott Edgars is also a lawyer who's sued medical pharmacies very successfully and he's got a successful practice in Florida." Mark stared down at his fingers as they drew circles in the grease and moisture left from their meal.

"So, Elliott is the one with the money. It figures. He must be another get-rich-on-the-backs of the medical establishment lawyer."

"Remember, he's Robert's brother."

Dad watched as small drops of sweat popped out on Mark's forehead. "What would we gain by finding out if these slime-balls were murdered or not? And who would care?"

"There's the conflict Dad. These evil people have been possibly murdered and now have been taken out of the path of harming more innocent people."

"You think they were murdered?" His shaking hand reached for another piece of pizza.

"I don't know. I was just assuming someone hated them so much they wanted them put out of commission."

"So again, Son, why would we want to help Robert find out the truth?"

"Do you want to know the truth about the deaths?"

"No. I don't care how they died."

"You could use the money for the farm. Why shouldn't you get some money for all the wrong done to you? How much money have you lost because of a deceitful lawyer? How much of your life was ruined? What about Mom? The pain broke her heart; you said so yourself. Where's the price in that?" Mark was uncharacteristically yelling at his father. "And the lawyer who cheated Melissa. She's footing most of the bill to care for Melody."

Mark turned away. "Sorry. Sorry I yelled. There is no right and no wrong, only hurt and more hurt."

After a quiet moment Dad said, "Let's sleep on it, but for right now, pass the Jack Daniels"

Chapter 24

Robert pulled the Blue Babe up to the curbside of the New Orleans airport in front of Mark and his Dad. Just looking at the car made Mark grimace and Dad chuckle. Robert yelled over the noise of the airplanes, "Hello there you two jet-setting bastards. Good to see you Dad; you been baby-sitting Mark? How was your flight?"

Robert pulled on thick rubber gloves and wrenched open the trunk with a crowbar he had in the back seat of the car. In the trunk were various sizes of cans rusted and leaking, dilapidated toolboxes, wires, rope of different sizes and lengths, odd-looking pieces of equipment, batteries of all sizes, headlamps and everything smelling of age and rust. "Let me put your suitcases in here but don't touch anything. Get in and hang on," Robert ordered. "I picked up Adelaide this morning. She was at a conference in Tampa and she cursed the whole way into town. Don't think she trusted the Blue Babe or me."

"Hi, Robert," Dad said with a hiccup. "Boy does the Babe bring back memories."

"Shit yeah. We've been together a long time and boy does she purr. Wait until I get her out on the I-10; the cops can't catch me." Robert spun off, scattering passengers pulling their suitcases across the road toward the parking garage. "Get out of the way you mangy bastards," Robert growled at the tired straggling tourists.

"Hey, Robert. Be nice. We need all the tourists we can get," Mark said as he turned to his Dad in the back seat. "Dad, don't touch anything metal; you could get a bad shock."

Dad's eyebrows shot up. "Oh yeah, I remember. This thing can electrocute."

"Only when I feel like it," Robert said. "It's turned off now. Relax."

The Blue Babe hummed into the airport exit lane with wires and cables dragging in the road. The other cars gave it wide berth because it looked like it would fall apart with the slightest nudge. The Blue Babe didn't have air conditioning but the night was moderate and dry so the windows let in streams of docile warm air similar to a gentle massage. It was quite pleasant after the long stuffy airplane flight.

"This sultry air makes me feel mellow," Dad said, his voice slurring.

"It's not the air Dad," Mark said, "It's the two high balls you had on the plane on the short flight from Houston. You sure put those down in a hurry. You also had a few on the flight from Santa Barbara."

"Well, I ordered one and when I realized we had more time, I ordered another one. I wanted to drink them before we landed. Waste not, want not, I always say." Dad giggled.

"Good to see you both in good spirits. You will be staying at Peggy and Gerhardt's home in the Garden District. Her mail order husband is Gerhardt from Germany," Robert said over his shoulder to Dad.

"Hey, mail-order husband sounds like a great idea. Is there an age limit? Mark's told me a bit about them." Dad was happy and feeling the effects of the alcohol on an empty stomach. It had been a long time since he had been away from the farm for any length of time and he was truly enjoying his vacation. Even the aspect of working in a lab again was exciting. He knew he just needed to get out more often.

"Dad, are you talking to yourself again or mumbling to me?" Mark asked.

"What? No, I don't know, just thinking out loud I guess." He was used to talking to himself, which he did even when there were workers on his farm because the workers usually spoke some form of Spanish. He continued having a wonderful conversation with himself as they sped along toward the Crescent City.

"I want you two to get a good night's sleep because we've got a lot of work to do in the morning," Robert ordered as he swung into the pothole-filled small street. Mark groaned as they hit hole after bump after hole and Dad giggled in the back seat.

"Why didn't you tell me New Orleans would be so much fun, Mark?" Dad asked. "I think my stomach just bounced into my throat, at least my bladder did."

"Here, Dad, here's their house. Go water the plants. You know which ones thrive with bladder-water." Mark jerked open the back door after wrapping and protecting his hand with a sweater he'd worn on the plane.

Robert laughed at Mark. "Sure scared you with that shock-story didn't I?"

"Well, is it true or not?" Mark asked.

"Sure it's true. I just don't always remember to turn it off and sometimes I shock the shit out of myself. Don't worry. This time I tested it before I came to get you two. It's off."

"Just out of curiosity, how do you test it?" Mark asked with his hands on his hips.

"Simple. I just take a cat and throw it on the hood of the car. That'll tell me real fast." Robert laughed. "Shit. It's so funny to hear them yowling and to see all the cat hair standing up all over. It makes them look like big fuzzy hedgehogs. Sometimes it's hard to find a cat; they pretty much try and stay away from me these days."

"Yeah, I don't doubt it," said Mark.

"Hey, you got some pretty interesting plants around here. I can't wait to see them in the daylight." Dad was a bit perkier now. "Let's go meet the young couple."

Mark struggled with the two suitcases up the short steps to the porch when the door opened to a heavily pregnant Peggy, a shy, curious Gerhardt and Adelaide.

"Grand-Dad! It's so good to see you." Addie gave him a big hug.

"Dad, this is Peggy and Gerhardt," Mark began.

"Welcome, Dr. Warren," said Peggy. "Robert's told us so much about you. Hello, Mark. Come in. come in." Gerhardt gave a firm handshake, a nod of his head and took the suitcases.

"Ooo, now I see you two are going to have a baby soon. That's great, that's just great. Congratulations to you both. Is it a boy or girl? How exciting." Dad almost drooled on the couple. "Call me Dad or Grand-Dad. No formalities, please."

"Dad, you are never having high balls on a plane again. You feel ok?"

"Never felt better. I just feel great." He was rocking back and forth with his hands in his pockets, beaming as if Peggy were having his grandchild.

Peggy flitted around the guests. "Are you hungry, thirsty? Would you like a beer, anything?"

"Ya, I get beer." Gerhardt said.

"You must be tired. Please sit down. Adelaide was just beginning to tell us about her grandparents in Australia," Peggy said.

Grand-Dad hugged Adelaide. "Now that's something I would like to hear. Mark doesn't tell me anything. He says there's nothing to tell. Damn kids." He squeezed Adelaide. "Please tell us Honey, I'd just love to know."

They all settled in close and comfortably except Mark who picked up the suitcases and left the room. "I don't need to hear this."

Adelaide had the story-telling gift from her mother and the Kaurna Aborigines who were her friends from birth. She began by imitating soft, sleepy sounds of the birds from the nightlife of the outback. "In the outback at night, you can see more stars in one quadrant of the cosmos than ever possible in the townships. The incredible breath-taking view of the night heavens is enough for any doubter to believe that there was a Godly plan for our universe. In the scrublands, with the Indigenous Australians, you learn how to live with the plants and animals without encroaching on the other's space and lives. Poisonous plants, spiders, animals, snakes are all a part of living in the wilderness and surviving. There is a reverence and respect for all living and dead, for both people and animals. Death is just a passing phase and those who have gone on to the next stage of existence can be brought back to comfort and guide those who are left behind."

"So, where were your grandparents from?" Peggy asked.

"My grandparents originated from Ireland and were either moved by force to Australia by the authorities, or came on their own free will. No one's really sure and they wouldn't talk about it. At any rate, they came to the Adelaide plains to begin a new life, or in actuality, to dig and hoe out a new life. They hoped for a better and freer existence than the one they had in The United Kingdom. What was important to them was how each person lived their life in the present for no one wanted to know what was in the past. Everyone came for a fresh start. They settled on the rich plains next to the Kaurna Aborigines and because they treated the natives with respect, there wasn't much violence and crime like in some of the other provinces. They learned their language, customs, stories, and how to use medicinal herbs, all in an effort to survive in that hostile but beautiful land."

Even Robert was quiet as he listened. He grunted and said, "You're a goddamn poet. You should write these stories down."

Mark had stayed in the shadows and listened to Adelaide; she sounded just like Yhi when she told the Kaurna stories. He leaned against the wall, listened and allowed his thoughts to remember. Yhi and Mark had met in college during their undergraduate studies and had found kindred spirits in each other. From the beginning they had been inseparable, and shared in the delights and problems of the other's career interests. They blended medicine, literature, and nature into one life, and enjoyed the variety of ideas and experiences of each other. They found each other exotic; Mark, the American Yankee who came to live with his Aunt Bertie, and Yhi, the Aussie who loved the wildness of the outback and the native people. Mark called Yhi a hippie and she laughingly called Mark a Yankee invader. Their life seemed completed with the birth of Adelaide and they wished for no better or happier life.

Mark had given their baby girl the name Adelaide, because this was the town and the people who had welcomed him into their lives and had rescued him from the horrors of his small American home town. This new place and its people had changed his life. The Australian way of looking at life and giving everyone a new chance and a new start was refreshing and salvaging for him. Even though he was close to his father, mother, and twin sisters, he never planned to return to the States.

He walked into the living room and faked a big yawn. "Addie, these folks are tired, and Grand-Dad needs to get some sleep. You can tell stories some other time. Robert can you take Addie home?"

"I guess you're pushing us out. What choice do we have? Come on Addie, time for beddy-by. Let's leave these old and pregnant folks. I'll get you home safe."

"Cripes. I'll be lucky to get back to my apartment in one piece if I have to ride in the Blue Babe. But what's life without some risks? Good night all." She kissed her dad and granddad and left.

"Dad, don't you think it's time for you to go to bed?" Mark almost pushed his father into the spare bedroom where Gerhardt had slept for a long time before he and Peggy got to know one another better.

"G'nite all. Thanks for your hospitality. See you in the morning." Dad smiled and waved to everyone in the room.

"Gerhardt, show Mark where the towels are. Ask if they need anything. Thanks." Peggy waddled over to the small sofa and clumsily let herself down into the soft, comforting pillows.

"Ya, ya sure." Gerhardt had stopped to smell the cigarette smoke that had wafted into the house on the airline passengers. "Ya, I'll be right back."

The last thing in the world Peggy wanted was to go to the lab tomorrow. Her small framed body with a slight sway back did not carry the pregnancy well but she was intellectually very alert and active. "Well this is going to be the only child in this family. That's for sure," she said.

When Gerhardt had made sure Mark and his Dad were comfortable, he asked, "Peg, is someting I can get for you?" Gerhardt had become very timid around Peggy as she was touchy and snappy in her last months.

"Yes, my dear, yes, you can help me get up off the sofa and get into bed, please."

"Yes, my flower blossom. You are getting bigger as I watch you. But getting you into the bed is how you got a big stomach, ya?" Gerhardt grinned as Peggy swatted him with a sofa pillow. They were indeed getting along very well now.

"Ya mein herr, I remember very vell," she teased. "But I have to sleep before going to a long day at the lab tomorrow. I think there are going to be a lot of surprises before this is all over."

Both of them groaned as they levered Peggy off the sofa. Peggy muttered to herself, "Oh yes, I think there certainly will be lots of surprises, and not all of them will be pleasant ones I'm afraid."

Chapter 25

"Robert, where did these specimens come from? What is the name of the lab? Who was the person in control of keeping the samples clean and pure? Did you get these legally? What are they for? We can't work with them unless we know they are safe."

Adelaide was giving Robert the third degree about the samples. She needed to know for safety's sake, but Robert wouldn't divulge any information and the women refused to work with the samples until they knew. She wasn't yet aware that they'd be testing samples from crime scenes.

Peggy crossed her arms over her now abundant pregnant chest and said, "I will not work with these anymore until I know something definite."

"Alright, alright." Robert threw up his hands and pretended to surrender. "These are samples taken from a place where someone died. They're from some bodily liquids or from liquids or creams or lotions that were in the rooms."

"We are testing plants and their uses, we are not Police Forensics, for God's sake!" Adelaide yelled. "We're not the police here."

"Ok, wait. Let me explain. Just calm down and I'll tell you what you need to know." Robert squirmed on the stool and chewed the ends of his mustache. He took a deep breath as the girls watched and waited.

"These samples were procured from several cases where...."

"SEVERAL cases? What the hell are you getting us into Robert?" Adelaide hadn't calmed down.

"OK, wait. These samples are suspected to be from exotic plants that would not be easily recognized anywhere in the states. This lab and your expertise is the preeminent place in the states to do this work and it needs to be done in secret."

"Exotic plants, Robert?" Peggy asked "Is that why Mark's Dad was brought here? To help us test for plants we might not know?"

"Yes."

"But why not just tell the FBI and use Grand-Dad in another lab? Why this lab?"

"I guess you girlie-girls don't realize how unusual your work is and how far advanced you have become in the herbal world. This lab is well known and unique," Robert said.

"Well then, you will pay us triple what we would normally charge to run the tests. We're not doing this for free," Adelaide said.

"I have a client who is very wealthy and he will pay but I am not sure how much."

"Well, we'll tell you our price and you tell your money-bags to fork it up or there won't be any testing."

"Goddamnfuckingbroads!" Robert yelled. "Ok, you'll get every penny you ask for, but I want the work done accurately. And I want it now."

Mark and his Dad came sauntering into the lab. "The ladies giving you a hard time, Robert?" Mark asked.

Robert swore and slammed out of the lab.

"Hi, Dad. Hi, Grand-Dad." Adelaide beamed as she hugged them both, "I love having the three of us here together."

"Ok ladies, let's see what we have here. Robert will be back, don't worry," Mark said.

Peggy turned to Mark and said, "Robert told us that these samples came from a crime case, or maybe several crime cases and might be from exotic plants. He explained that's why Grand-Dad is here with us, to help us recognize some of the plants, if that's what they are. This is all very strange." Peggy blushed. "Your father told us to call him Grand-Dad and I think it's wonderful."

"Well yes, let's look at it this way. This is an opportunity on several levels. If we can show that we can identify what these samples are it'll give our lab more publicity and positive recognition, and by doing so we can charge for other companies or the police force to use our lab for testing. If we are successful, we could set up our own lab with more technicians working as your subordinates. You two, Adelaide and Peggy, would be the bosses of the lab." Mark was very convincing.

The women blinked, stared at Mark and each other taking in the situation. Adelaide let out a long breath. "Well, I guess we'd better get to work."

They showed Dad where to put his things, where to get a white lab coat then they took out the samples and set up.

The cases that held the samples were labeled, O'H, J.C., M.P., A. K., S.M., and O.M. They decided to all work with the same case at the same time and compare the results as they proceeded.

The morning moved along peacefully and in a continuous stream with the three working compatibly together. Mark was absent most of the time and stayed in the closet office making phone calls. "He isn't that necessary to lab work anymore as we pretty much know the routine," Adelaide explained to Grand-Dad.

"Peggy, have you found anything yet from O'H's samples?" Adelaide asked when she saw Peggy sitting and playing with the sample and not testing it.

"No. There is a substance that is not at all familiar to me and I tested it for all sorts of things. Maybe Grand-Dad can check over my notes and think what I might have left out." Peggy massaged her round belly and winced.

Grand-Dad asked tenderly, "Peggy, are you having contractions?"

"Contractions? Oh, I don't know. Or I don't think so. OH, I don't know. Am I?"

"Honey, I think you'd better go lie down. We'll handle this for a while. I'll check over your notes. You have an excellent penmanship. You could never be a doctor, they can't write worth a darn." Dad shooed Mark out of the little office and helped Peggy lie down on the worn out sofa.

"Peggy, you might be having Braxton-Hicks contractions," Grand-Dad said trying to comfort her.

"Oh, ok…uh what's that? Is it serious? Do I have to go to the hospital now?" Peggy was getting anxious.

"No, no, not to worry." Grand-Dad spread a blanket over her. "Braxton-Hicks contractions can start early on in pregnancy but most of the time there're late in pregnancy. In the days or weeks before labor, Braxton Hicks contractions may intermittently become rhythmic, relatively close together, and even painful, possibly fooling you into thinking you're in labor. But unlike true labor, during this so-called false labor the contractions don't grow longer, stronger, and closer together."

"You sound like a doctor. Ohhh, that feels better. Thanks. Just give me a few minutes and I'll be back out to help," Peggy said as she was falling asleep.

He walked back into the lab where Adelaide had her testing section set up. "There is something I don't recognize." She held up the small vial. "It's yellowish green liquid. Wanna help?"

"Sure do," Grand-Dad said and he rolled up his sleeves.

"Test for sleeping potions and I'll put my thinking cap on and try and remember plants that have sleeping properties."

"Right. I'm on it. I think I'm going to like having you around here."

Grand-Dad looked up at Adelaide. "Do you know that Hippocrates described a yellow-greenish liquid that came from the Valerian plant and it was used as a remedy for insomnia?"

Adelaide reached for another sample and got to work. The typical, cheap, easy and quick method of testing for certain chemicals, is the "Color Test" which is a chemical solution added to blood, tissue or urine. The test will show whether a specific chemical or class of chemicals is present in the material being tested.

"Grand-Dad?" Adelaide called out softly, "I'm getting a positive reaction to the color test. What do you think?"

"Hummm… let's add a little bit of this." He shook the tube and held it up to the light. "Ok, now we have a positive proof. My guess would be a natural herb such as Valerian root. The concentration was enough to put a horse to sleep."

"Valerian Root, like what we can buy in the natural drug store?"

"Valerian Root is used for sleeping disorders, restlessness, anxiety, and as a muscle relaxant. When the concentration is as much as was in O'H's body, it was fatal. It's a shame the plant is so lethal because it has sweetly scented pink or white flowers and they are perennials. I have a few in my garden."

"Grand-Dad, why or how would O'H have taken such a large quantity? If Valerian has a bitter almost metallic taste, it would have had to be mixed with something to hide the bitterness, like a cocktail or red wine." Adelaide shuddered and carefully placed the vial on the counter."Then O'H either took an overdose or was given the valerian in a drink by someone else. What did the medical examiner's report state?"

Dad read: "The medical examiner states in Part 2 that O'H had Diabetes Mellitus and Hypertension and it lists the immediate cause of death as Pulmonary Embolism, and sequentially lists congestive heart failure, and acute myocardial infarction with chronic ischemic heart disease having been evident for a period of eight years."

"Wow, not very healthy I'd say. He was a prime target for heart attack death by overdose."

Adelaide held up the test tube. "There was something else that I didn't recognize. Maybe if we can find out what else is in these, we might be able to tell if he was poisoned or OD'd. It's gonna take a while to run a whole bunch of tests."

A groggy Peggy came out of the office where she had been sleeping. I'm sorry I left you folks to do all the work. I must have been very tired."

Dad just laughed and put his arm around Peggy. "Well, you just get all the sleep you can now because after the Little One shows up, you won't sleep for years."

"Oh no," she said and tears rolled down her face.

"I was just joking Peggy. Don't cry. Don't get upset now. Some babies learn to sleep very early, in a few months. Don't worry. Gerhardt will help you take care of it... is it a boy or girl?"

"Oh, we don't know. We want to be surprised." Peggy yawned and asked sleepily, "Any results yet?"

"O'Hara was a big glob of mucus, hairy as a Grizzly and as mean as a Kodiak," Robert spit out. They were so intent on their findings that no one had noticed him coming back into the lab. They all turned and looked at him, waiting for an explanation.

"I was in Chicago when I met Mark and heard O'Hara's key-note address to the audience which turned out to be an invective diatribe against the medical profession. I felt like killing him myself- on the spot. But there were too many lawyers in the room. I met Mark after the meeting."

"So, O'H stands for O'Hara and you and Mark knew him?" Adelaide asked what everyone else in the room was thinking.

"You know what, we've had enough surprises for one day. Let's get out of here and go have a drink. Well, Peggy can have a cup of tea, but I need something stiff. We've done enough for one day. Lock up everything and let's go." Grand-Dad was giving the orders. "Where's Mark?"

No one noticed Mark had left. He had been on the phone all day talking to his lab back in Los Angeles. "He's around somewhere, call him and leave a message Grand-Dad, and tell him to meet us at O'Henry's in the Quarter." Now it was Adelaide giving orders. "Bring the report and let's see what else is there we might have missed. I'll call Gerhardt to meet us."

Dad took Peggy's arm and led the way out of the door. "Everything locked up? Let's get the hell out of Dodge."

Chapter 26

Everyone at the lab the next morning walked on tiptoes and talked in whispers with Peggy grouchy with pregnancy and the others heavy with hangovers.

Adelaide raised her head from the lab table with as little movement as possible. "Does anyone remember what we talked about last night? Peg, you and Gerhardt left early, right?"

"Yeah, there was too much smoke for me and the baby. Gerhardt was enjoying the secondhand smoke but we did leave around 9:30. I remember all that was said while I was there but since we left early, I don't know what you talked about."

"I never would have believed that Grand-Dad could put down so much whiskey and still leave walking straight up," Adelaide whimpered into the table.

"You young whipper-snappers don't know how to hold your booze," Dad teased. "You should have been around when I was young."

"Uuugh.. I never would have survived." Adelaide moaned and lowered her head back to the table.

"Well would somebody tell me if ANYBODY remembers …oh forget it," Peggy snapped. "Can we start all over? I want to know what the police report said. Who has it?"

"Well, I rescued this from all the spilled drinks last night." Dad smiled and pulled the rolled, stained, and wrinkled report from his coat pocket. "But it doesn't look too good. But it's got interesting patterns with various colors and splotches."

Peggy snatched the report from Dad. "There isn't a responsible person in this whole group," she spit out. "How are we supposed to get any decent work done around here?"

"Oooo Little Mama is a bit touchy this morning," Robert whined through his nose.

"Shut up, Robert. I'm here to do a job, and as I remember we have a potential murder on our hands."

"Ok, ok, everybody, let's all take some aspirin and start over. Here, I've made some strong coffee in Adelaide's tea pot," Dad offered. "And there's plenty of water and orange juice to dilute the alcohol."

"My tea pot? You used my tea pot? You put coffee in my tea pot?" Adelaide would have been more distressed if she had felt any better but as it was, she could barely lift her head. "You've ruined my tea pot," she said as she slowly lowered her head back down on her arms. "But I sure could use some coffee- black and strong."

"I did read over the reports this morning before we came here and we can discuss them from top to bottom after the aspirin and the coffee takes effect. Here, have some donuts from the cafeteria down stairs," Dad said.

Robert poured a quart sized cup of coffee and threw ice cubes in it. "OK Pops, give it to us in brief."

"O'Hara was at a conference in Chicago. He left the meeting after dinner and went to his room. At some point in time he took sleeping pills or sleeping medicine of some sort. He was known to have insomnia. He died in his sleep."

"Yes, well, we have a problem, don't we? Any ideas from this brainy group?" Robert looked around and saw all his potential collaborators, all the people he would trust with the information he was about to share with them. "Mark, you got any ideas?"

Mark looked into his coffee cup, "Suicide or murder. The only reason we care is because of your br..."

Adelaide moved in slow motion trying to massage the stupor from her head.

"Was anything taken from the room? Was the room in good order or did it appear as if someone was looking for something like money or a computer or a watch or... anything?" Peggy poured another round of coffee and watched each face intently. She wondered if anything could ever be accomplished from this group. She knew at the moment that she was the only one with a clear head. She crossed her arms over her chest and pouted.

Robert puffed up his big round chest and spread his arms out wide, as if to encompass them all. "You are all very bright and dependable. Like I mentioned before, there is a lot of money and prestige in finding out the answers from the samples that I brought in." Robert was skillful in buttering-up people when he wanted something from them.

"You do know how to be opaque when you don't want to tell us anything, don't you." Peggy was miffed at the condescending and pedantic way Robert was talking to them, but she realized she was probably the one sober person who could understand what he was saying. "We know you were in some covert organization so why isn't the FBI interested, why can't they do their own work? What are you going to get out of this? Are we protected in any way because this might be a murder, and….."

"Goddammnit woman," Robert shouted. "Stop with all the damn questions and let me finish."

Everyone groaned and Peggy broke into tears. "I don't trust you, Robert. And you don't have to yell and be so mean."

Dad and Mark reached over to control Robert as Adelaide put her arm around Peggy and comforted her. "OK, guys, just settle down," she said tenderly. "We're all a bit tense today and this questionable murder has us all edgy." She turned to Robert and said, "You know we do excellent work here, that's why you came to us. But you have to be up-front as to what you are doing and why we should be involved." She was surprised that she could have such a hangover and still be coherent.

"Robert," Dad also spoke softly, as he knew this was the best way to deal with a person with anger management problems. "Tell them why this is so important to you."

Robert chewed the ends of his bushy gray moustache then wrapped his arms under his big belly. He still had on the same Hawaiian shirt from last night's French Quarter trip, or he could have had it on for several days. "Hummm…. I don't know if I can trust you." He glared at them all through his squinted eyes.

"TRUST? What are WE supposed to do? Trust you with blindfolds on and earplugs in our ears? This has to be a two-way street you know." Peggy still had a lot of fight through her tears.

Robert glared at her and then looked at all the faces around him, watching him. "OK. Here it is. I think there is a serial killer out there with a list and one person on the list is my brother, Elliott Edgars."

The lab was so still you could almost hear the wheels churning in their hangover stupor brains.

"Wheeeuuu, boy, Robert you sure are full of surprises." Adelaide whistled. "Elliott Edgars, the big shot lawyer from Florida is your brother? How did you two ever come from the same family?"

Peggy looked at Mark and Dad and said, "You two knew this already, didn't you."

"Yes we knew it Peggy," Mark answered in a matter of fact manner. "He thought that it would keep you safe if you didn't know what you were getting into."

"No *he* didn't think about our security, *you* did. All he wants is for the samples tested by the best team possible and you know we're the best. We have been specializing with plants for a long time since both you and Robert have been bringing in all these specimens, and we've been rather successful." Adelaide was back in her business executive mode with none of the tenderness that she had just shown to Peggy. "What are we going to bc paid?"

Robert growled, "It's harder working with you women, than putting a condom on a cockroach."

"I'll bet you've tried it, haven't you," Adelaide countered.

Dad and Mark burst out laughing. The tension in the air was broken and congeniality slowly settled around them like an old friend. Hangovers lifting, donuts eaten, coffee gone, and aspirin working, the lab rat pack was back together slowly getting ready to work. The business details Adelaide would work out on paper with Robert and Mark to give to Elliott Edgars. They would agree to absolute secrecy and Elliott would agree to the cost of the lab tests plus additional money for each of them.

"Well there are more samples to test." Dad was excited and eager to get to work. "Let's see what else we can find out, shall we?"

"I, I...I have to tell you something." Peggy folded her hands in her lap and stared at them. Without raising her head she said, "I haven't been honest."

Robert growled through clenched teeth, "Don't, Peggy. Don't."

"I have to Robert." All eyes flipped between the two. "Robert swore me to secrecy last week. He wanted me to test these O'H samples in secret."

"Stop!" Robert yelled.

"No Robert. They have to know." She turned to Adelaide and said, "I'm sorry. I should have told you sooner, but he told me not to. Now that it seems we are involved in quite a few cases, it'll just save time to tell you. I tested OH's samples last week"

"You were doing some of this last week, Peg? And you didn't tell me?"

"Yes, I am sorry, but Robert made me swear not to tell you." Peggy twisted her fingers around and around. "It seems a moot point now. But I do feel better now that you know."

Adelaide turned to Robert. "You bloody bastard. You knew she was pregnant and vulnerable but you made her swear to secrecy. I could cut your balls off. Don't you ever use her again like that." She turned to Peggy. "Well? Tell us. What did you find?"

"Coral snake venom."

"WHAAT? Coral snake venom?" Grand-Dad and Adelaide said at the same time. "Coral snake?"

"It looks like there was enough concentrated venom to flatten an elephant. I couldn't believe it. I still can't figure out how in the world that much coral snake venom could get into the body. The person would have run or screamed before the snakes could have bitten multiple times and Robert said that coral snakes are very shy creatures that would rather run than attack."

"Unless he was asleep," Grand-dad whispered. "We found Valerian Root in his sample yesterday." He squinted and glared at Robert. "What made you think of coral snake?"

"Surprisingly, the hotel restaurant staff found one curled up in a corner of the kitchen and the whole place had to be shut down. Sure caused a shit load of panic." He bit the end of his moustache. "It was just a hunch."

"But why coral snake venom?" Adelaide asked.

"Somehow, having snakes around a medical malpractice lawyer just seems suitable," Robert said.

"Were there any reports of snake bites?" Peggy asked.

"No." Grand-Dad flipped through the report. "There is no report of fang bites or any bites on the body but because coral snakes have very small fangs, they make small punctures that are hard to see. You have to know what you are looking for to find the puncture bites. And if the person was a very hairy person, you might never notice the bites."

The report stated that a pygmy rattlesnake was found in his room and it was killed. There was no evidence of any rattlesnake venom in the body. There were no skin punctures noticed, and no edema. Could it have been a false positive?" Peggy questioned as she looked at Robert. "What do you know about coral snakes?"

"Shit, I know a lot about corals. I grew up in Florida where there are lots of them and we learned as young kids how to handle them safely or stay out of their way." Robert was beginning his lecture. "Coral snakes are found in scattered localities in the southern coastal Plains from North Carolina to Louisiana, including all of Florida. They can be found in pine and scrub oak sand-hill habitats and in pine flat woods, far from the damn Yankees who pollute the rest of Florida."

"I guess that leaves all the Northern states free of them, right?" Grand-Dad asked.

"Right. They don't strike like a rattler." Robert demonstrated by using two fingers to strike against his arm like a rattler. "Corals have a pair of small fangs fixed in the front of their top jaw to deliver venom and they hold onto a victim when biting." He pinched the skin on his arm to show how a coral snake would hang on. "There is little or no pain or swelling at the site of the bite, but later the person will develop breathing difficulties and ptosis, or lazy eye, which can occur within hours."

"What about antivenin?" Adelaide asked.

Robert's upper lip curled into a snarl. "Don't interrupt. I'm just coming to that."

"However, if untreated by antivenin, the victim will have slurred speech, double vision, and muscular paralysis, ending in respiratory or cardiac failure. You might think a person is having a stroke or is just butt drunk. Any coral bite is a medical emergency that requires immediate attention. There is a high percentage of fatalities from the coral snake bite every year."

"The hospitals must have some antivenin available," Adelaide said.

"Don't rush me," he spat. "That's a very interesting point and a bit contentious. Antivenin is found in the Deep South, not in Chicago. And the anti-venom serum which hospitals had stored, expired, so they were forced to throw away their out-dated supplies. The Wyse Pharmaceuticals, the sole company to make the antivenin, announced it was going to stop making the antidote in part because demand was so small."

"So the murderer must have guessed that there would be no antivenin in Chicago," Grand-Dad chimed in.

"Yep, most likely. There are some sleazy exotic animal shops that might have had some, illegally of course, but for some reason, the victim didn't alert anyone or didn't know he was being bitten. It would have been essential to receive the antivenin during the first hours after a coral bite; it would have been too late to administer the antivenin when someone found him the next morning."

The lab was quiet. Dad turned to Peggy. "You are not to test any more samples and it would be best for both you and the baby to stay away completely. We have a murder."

Chapter 27

"Goddamnit, Dad, we have to find out faster what killed the others. I have to know and I have to know now!" Robert slammed his hat on the lab counter. "Yesterday's hangover day was a waste of time."

"Robert, you know good and well that Adelaide has been very busy with writing contract specs, working with lawyers, trying to protect our work here. It takes a lot of time. And, also, we have banned Peggy from the lab and Gerhardt too because of the risk of poisons. Since the coral snake find, we have added more protective gear and precautions. It is absolutely necessary. Right now I am the one person who can work the experiments since Mark is back in LA. You have to get off my back and let me work in peace." Dad was not afraid of Robert. He took the rolling straw hat off the counter, pushed it into Robert's stomach and headed him toward the office. "Now, why don't you go see if you can help Adelaide and give her some ideas on how to protect the farm and the new lab. Your expertise should be invaluable there."

"Humm…" Robert mused as he chewed on the ends of his moustache… "Guess I'm in the way here. I'll go see what Gerhardt's up to. It'll be good to get out of this stinking lab anyway." He flip-flopped out of the lab, leaving Dad to work in peace.

Dad shook his head and prayed that Robert wouldn't get involved in the business end of the new lab. He remembered all too well how Robert tried to get him to invest in growing mushrooms under his house or the time when he had a plan to have a butterfly farm and charge people to come look at them. Robert had a love of plants and screwy schemes, but no real sense of business.

"Hi, Grand-Dad" Adelaide strode into the lab, confident and glowing. "You talking to someone?"

"No, no … just me." He laughed.

"Well, the deal's all sewed up and we'll be getting a new lab…but it'll take time of course. Dealing with the lawyers is both a pain and a pleasure. I thought I was a stickler for data, facts and paperwork but I'm not as bad as any of those guys. But it's all for our protection." She threw the papers in the office and came back to see what he was working on.

"What cha' got? Found out anything new?" She peered over his shoulder. "You know, if we can find out anything substantial that caused the deaths, there is a clause in the contract that allows us to expand the lab into this forensic-testing area if we want to."

Dad turned and looked at Adelaide in admiration. "You are absolutely amazing. You are way ahead of any of us in all this business. You have blossomed in this adventure, haven't you?"

"I guess I never gave myself credit for my own abilities. I never trusted myself to do anything out of the ordinary or anything spectacular. I was always afraid that someone would find out that

I was a fake and not smart." She pushed her red curls off her face. "Yeah, it's exciting to see myself successful. God, it feels wonderful. Woooh." She danced around a bit and then said, "Ok. Let's get to work. At least now we know the names on the samples. OH for O'Hara, JC for Johnny Collier, MP, for Mildred Pelto, AK for Austin Kaufman, SM for Steven Merriweather, and OM for Oliver Michaels. Somehow that makes the testing personal. What are you working on?"

"Johnny Collier died in San Francisco right after the meeting in Chicago. I've gone over the police report and the death certificate. This is what I've come up with: He had a long history of heart disease, and the immediate cause of death was a pulmonary embolism with congestive heart failure, acute myocardial infarction and chronic ischemic heart disease. Typical definition for a heart attack."

"Well, there's nothing unusual about any of that," she said. "He was known for his high-rolling lifestyle and unhealthy habits."

"Listen to this. The police report had a few more curious things to say. That evening, he had a female visitor just before he died. Before the cameras in the lobby were shut off they picked up a red headed woman in a green dress; his office staff knew he was going to have a visitor and had the cameras turned off soon after she arrived. Long red hair- natural and not dyed, was found on the sofa, in the bathroom and around the bar. There were high heeled shoe prints in the plush carpet, red lip stick on one of the glasses, small finger prints- which were not matched, and the toilet was stopped up with a bloody sanitary pad."

"A bloody sanitary pad? Women getting all dressed up to meet a man don't use those things at that time. That's weird. And besides, all women know not to put those things in the toilet; they put them in the trash can. There had to be a trash can in the bathroom, right?"

"The report doesn't say. What's strange is that the woman was not small due to the large shoe size but the fingerprints on the glass were small and at last check, the lipstick print on the glass hadn't shown up in any files."

"Well, those are things that might not ever find their match. What else do we have? Give me something solid I can work on. Are there any fluids or blood samples to test?"

"Yes, I'm just getting to that. Because Collier was such a high-profile trial lawyer the forensic police went over his office with every imaginable kind of new-fangled gizmo and tested everything. For example: They took a sample of the water where there were some flowers, water from the toilet, and from the glasses they drank out of. The whole place was microscoped for anything unusual. That's when they found the red hair, and they said the shoe size was large for a woman but..."

"Hey, don't knock it, Grand-Dad; some women do have big feet. Take mine for example." She held up one of her sandaled feet and wiggled it around. "I call this size infinity and beyond. I could easier wear the shoe boxes instead of the shoes."

"Bet you're a good swimmer as well as a long distance runner, like Mark. The police used inference holography to find and examine the foot prints."

"Holography?"

"Yeah, it's a technique which uses a split light beam to create a holographic image of the print, and that image can be transferred to photographic film."

"They'd need a huge piece of paper to take my shoe print size."

"Well, all it does is to show the size and structure of the shoe. She was wearing high heels and the heel had a tiny point."

"Like stilettos?"

"I guess. Those are fancy, right?"

"Oh, yeah. A girl knows what she's going for or she's on the prowl when she puts those things on. What about the fluid samples?"

"Here you go, liquid from the vase with the flowers, the water glasses, and the toilet. Which ones do you want to start with? There are also some samples of blood and fluid from the stomach. No other blood was found in the room."

"Ok, give me the stomach and blood, those are things that I can get my hands on…oh sorry, didn't mean that to sound bad. You take the flower water since you're the plant man. Let's see what we can find out."

After hours of searching, Adelaide stopped. "I don't get it, Dad. I keep coming up with some trace element in the blood and stomach but I don't recognize it. I've tried everything I can think of and now I'm beginning to think he did have a heart attack, or he is going to give me a heart attack trying to find out. Have you found out anything?"

"Nope. Same here Addie, but if there was a plant poison present, it was quickly metabolized by the body and is very hard to trace now. There is one more thing I would like to try; it's a long shot but since we are dealing with plants and their components, why not go out on a limb and try anything."

"Ok. What do we try?"

"There is a poisonous plant in the Gelseium species that can be lethal. But whoever in the world would know about this had to be a serious herbalist indeed. I don't know. It's worth a try, I guess. Here, you test your samples, too, for this Gelsemin and let's see what we come up with."

The lab was quiet. The clock ticking on the wall sounded like gunshots and the dripping faucet was like a drum beating a slow funeral march. Every now and then either one of them would lift and stretch their shoulders and back and bend down again to their work. It seemed that hours passed in a flash. Or did time stand still for the two lab workers?

"Addie, I'm getting a positive from the Gelsemin. Are you getting anything?"

"Grand-Dad... I think I have a positive too. What plant does the Gelsemin come from?"

"Yellow Carolina Jasmine."

Adelaide pushed back the thick protective glasses and stood looking incredulously at him with her rubber-gloved hands on her hips. "You've got to be kidding. Those beautiful yellow flowering vines that come out every spring? They're sold in every nursery in the South and in some greenhouses in the North. It's poisonous?"

"'Fraid so. The root of Carolina Jasmine can be made into a drug that is a powerful spinal depressant; it's most marked action being on the anterior cornus of grey matter in the spinal cord. The drug kills by its action on the respiratory center of the medulla oblongata. Shortly after the administration of even a moderate dose, the respiration is slowed and is ultimately arrested, this being the cause of death. It looks like a person has had a heart attack."

He looked out of the small window, seeing his house on the farm. "Your grandmother loved those vines. Had them growing all over the house up to the roof. I told her to be careful around them."

"Where was your sample taken from?"

"The flower vase. And yours?"

"From the glass."

"Oh my god. The second murder."

Chapter 28

"Can this get weirder?" Adelaide stood with her hands on her hips and stared at Grand-Dad. "Sorry to say, but I'm anxious to start on the other samples.

"Hang in there, kiddo. Let's see what else we have to work with."

She handed Grand-Dad a few rumpled pieces of paper from Robert. "Here, see what you can find from these, and I'll finish up a report on the Carolina Jasmine."

Grand-Dad smoothed out the sheets and looked over Robert's notes. "Let's see what we can find out about the Lady Pelto. She had a severe seizure but didn't call for help and all her pills were gone. The Medical Examiner wrote that there were spider bites on her abdomen, so let's check to see if there was any venom in her blood samples. Then let's see if we can isolate the unknown liquid from her stomach. We can set these tests in motion and then while we wait a few days for the results, we can be working on the men. Let's test for venom."

"Let me see, Grand-Dad." She gently took the rumpled notes from the counter and read. "Oh boy, do we have a lot of things to sort through with Ms. Pelto; this lady is going to give us trouble. What's really bizarre is that the world's deadliest spider, the Brazilian Wandering Spider, was found in her room which evidently caused the spider bites. The housekeeper was from South America and recognized the spider and killed it. The smashed bits were kept by the police and sent to the Medical Examiner who then sent it to the Insectarium here in New Orleans. Poor woman who found that spider, I bet she is still screaming." Adelaide shuddered. "Have you heard about the Wandering Spider? Is it really the deadliest spider in the world?"

Looking over her shoulder, Grand-Dad said, "Oh, yeah. This spider has a neurotoxin known as PhTx3 of which 0.0006 mg of venom is enough to kill a mouse. A person bitten by the spider will have breathing problems, loss of muscle control, paralysis and certain death. But I guess you know your spiders since you're from "Down Under." Did you know that another interesting thing about this spider's bite is priapism?"

"Priapism? An uncontrollable painful erection?"

"Yup. Real nasty. Ready to begin?"

"Aye, aye mon Capitaine." Adelaide saluted with a glass vial and a snap of her heels.

"When you get a chance, look in the police reports. There's got to be photos from each of the murder scenes. Oh, boy. I'm afraid I just lumped all the cases into murder. What a bad omen."

He looked over to Addie. "I just remembered that a plant that causes Grand Mal seizures is the Water Hemlock which looks like Queen Anne's Lace."

"Queen Anne's Lace? It's a wild flower that's white and looks like lace, right?"

"Right, but the Water Hemlock looks just like the Queen Anne's Lace."

"So? Ooh….is it related to THE hemlock?"

"Yep. You must have studied history somewhere along the way. The famous poison hemlock drunk by Socrates was fatal, and the Water Hemlock is just as fatal. According to the USDA, the roots of the Water Hemlock contain chambers that are full of a toxic sap containing the convulsant cicutoxin. Grand mal seizures are followed by a quick death if even a tiny amount is consumed."

"Grand Mal Seizures? And Pelto had Epilepsy and recurring seizures."

"Yep. See if there're pictures of flowers from the scene of the crime. Let's test the liquid again, both from the vase and from her stomach, and see if it matches with hemlock. That test shouldn't take too long to give up its answer. And as long as we're at it, let's test for other poisons as well. If there is proof, we might just have a serial killer on our hands."

Hours later Dad spoke. "Adelaide, look. It matches. The liquid from the vase and from Pelto's stomach are a match and the liquid is water hemlock."

"Are you saying she drank water hemlock? It must have been mixed with something like a cocktail."

"There is still something about the liquid from her stomach that doesn't match up with the results from the hemlock. We have to keep testing."

"Well, would you mind if I started on the last samples, the ones from Oliver Michaels and Kaufman?"

"No, sure, go ahead. I'll just take some samples here and run them through a few more solutions to see what results we might get. The results are coming up faster now that we know the path we need to follow and all these samples so far are related to plants of some sort, plus some spiders and snakes."

He sat back on the stool, pushed his glasses to the top of his head and asked, "Adelaide, did your mother ever make you take castor oil as a child?"

"Oh, my goodness, yes." She shuddered. "Every summer we were forcibly spoon-fed a whole regimen of it to get rid of all the worms in our system, even if there were no signs of worms. She just knew that we had them since we ran barefoot in the Outback all summer. I think we had ringworm and hook-worm and I don't remember what all. But, oh yeah, we tried to hide when it came time for the cleansing. It was disgusting."

"Me too. I had an old aunt who believed that anytime we teenagers got out-of-hand she would say that it was the meanness coming out of us and she'd come with the castor oil."

Adelaide laughed so hard that she spilled some of the liquid she was working with. "You ought to write a book. You lived in a time and culture that doesn't exist anywhere, anymore. Have you ever thought about writing any of the stories?"

"Well, I don't know that many folks would be interested. Everything is so technical, futuristic, and outer space now."

"Why did you ask me about castor oil? What were you thinking?"

He stopped working and stared into space, shaking his head. "I just found the unknown substance mixed with the water hemlock. It's from the castor bean, the same bean plant from which castor oil is taken. The ingredient in the castor bean is likened to ricin and one bean is enough to kill a person within a few minutes."

Adelaide stopped working on her samples and stared at Grand-Dad, all the laughter gone now, replaced by chills. "Oh, my god, another murder."

He turned to Adelaide. "That's what it looks like. The castor bean plant is one of the most deadly plants on earth, and amazingly enough it's grown for decorative purposes all over the States, especially in California. Ms. Pelto's death was no accident."

Adelaide shuddered, "Another one. A serial killer. Oh my god."

"Hello?" Elliott's sleepy voice grumbled into the phone.

"Hello, your own Goddamn self," Robert answered.

"Robert. It's 2:00 AM." Elliott was groggy. "What the hell do you want?"

"Thought you'd want to know that O'Hara, Pelto, and Collier were murdered. Poisoned. Don't eat anything that you don't cook yourself until this thing is solved. Don't mention this to anyone yet as we are still investigating. Now go back to sleep." The phone went dead.

Elliott sat with the phone in his hand. When Robert called it was never good news. Elliott sat on the edge of the bed wide awake now and felt like a Mack truck had just hit him. Three murders all from the same table. He knew it would not stay quiet for long. It would soon get to the press. Someone would find out. He walked into the kitchen to make coffee but spilled the grounds and gave up. He knew that the police handled all unusual deaths, but their deaths looked natural and these people died in separate states and each state had different sets of rules for the police and for the coroners. Robert and his team were the only ones who were putting it all together. He took out the McCallen 25 and drank from the bottle. There were three more deaths they needed to investigate. He felt helpless but determined that his life would not stop, and he refused to be controlled by some mad-man or mad-woman.

Chapter 29

"Good morning, Sunshine," said Grand-Dad when he picked up Adelaide. "How's Peggy? I'm anxious to get to the lab. Six dead and we know Pelto, O'Hara and Collier were poisoned. Three to go; let's get to it." Grand-Dad questioned as he dodged the potholes in the narrow streets. "Who would gain from their deaths?"

Adelaide held tight onto her seat belt. "Wait, Grand-Dad, my phone's ringing. Hang on; it's Dad. He gave me this dang thing, now I can't hide from him anymore. Here, you talk to him."

"Hey Son, what are you doing up so early there in LA? Isn't it 5:00 AM there?.... Fine. Fine. Just fine. We found the third person, a John Collier, was killed by Carolina Jasmine. Yeah. Oh yeah, they're taking real good care of me. I feel right at home. Are you going to come back to New Orleans for a visit sometime soon? Oh, ok. Don't get too stressed out. Go for a drive or a run. Take care. We'll talk later. Bye."

"Dad's a workaholic, isn't he?"

"Yeah. I think he is still mourning your mom. He also blamed himself when he wasn't here when his mother died. Sometimes I wonder if he will ever get the grief out of his system. I just don't know what will help him."

"I'm so sorry, Grand-Dad. All of this must have been hard on you too."

"Life never turns out the way you expect it to. There're just too many things that happen beyond your control. My life isn't too bad; I've adjusted. Now that you're here, things will get even better, I hope."

"How did you ever get so knowledgeable about all these exotic plants?"

"Oh, it's in the blood, I guess. My dad was a farmer during the depression and lost everything. He moved out to California and started as a fruit picker, then after a long time, got his own small farm. I always liked biology and botany in school and just kept reading up on these things. I don't know." He shrugged as he kept one eye on the road. "It just interests me. They say my grandmother was American Indian and she was a healer who knew the healing natures of plants. I don't know. No one could ever prove she was Indian after she died. I never knew her."

"We studied a bit about plants but I didn't get too involved with them in college. Grand-Dad, you need to make a U-ie at the next turn."

"It's important to know the poisons and their components," he continued talking and didn't slow down for the U-turn. The car screeched and kept on going. "The pharmaceutical companies are developing new drugs so fast that thorough testing doesn't always occur, and even if it did, there are so many things the new meds could affect, that the companies just can't know all the results. The FDA has strict controls on new medicines, but the natural medicines or natural plants are not under their control yet."

He hit a pothole and sailed over the next speed bump. "Driving in New Orleans has definitely broadened my education."

"Well, I for one will be very glad when we have finished with Robert's project and can continue on our own. Wait. Stop here at the parking gate. Here's my ticket to open it. Push it into that little slot there. Wait, you'll get it back. It's one way the office can control if anyone leaves during the day instead of working."

"Whoa. Big Brother watching a bit too close for me," he said while giving back her parking permit. But to change the subject, I was wondering, is there any certain place you need to set up the new lab? Well, I mean, could it be set up in California also? Like, near Cuyama where I live? The weather there is quite dry, compared to New Orleans, but it might be a good place to establish a new business. Have you thought about moving somewhere else?"

Now it was Adelaide's turn to be surprised. "Well.... No, I never thought about any place but New Orleans. Let's think about it. Maybe we could work something out. We could branch out, maybe have two smaller labs instead of one large one. I'll spend some time looking at the finances."

"Let's get to work. Where's my tea, uh, coffee pot?"

Grand-Dad stood with the remaining samples on the counter top. "What we're doing here with testing these samples is in the arena of biological forensics; I never thought I would be testing to find poisons for murders. Robert must have procured these samples from the FBI's National Crime Lab which does offer these services to law enforcement throughout the country."

"Do you think they lent these samples to Robert?" Adelaide

started pulling on the haz-mat suit and gloves. "Maybe because these deaths looked so natural, they were not interested in furthering their investigation. Do you think anyone else is looking into why six of the most prominent lawyers in the country have died all in a relatively short time?"

Grand Dad shrugged his shoulders, "Do you think anyone else cares? It seems to me they had reputations of being very unpleasant people. And now that they are gone, the sharks have already circled and have taken our dead persons' places."

"Well, for me, I just want to get this over with and get on with building a new lab, or maybe two labs, one here in NOLA and one in CA? With the money pouring in from sales of Granny's Lily, we could manage two labs."

"Sounds great to me Addie. Just great," he said with a big grin on his face. This whole project had rejuvenated him and had given him an eagerness that he hadn't felt in many years.

"Let's get to work." Adelaide was getting frustrated. "We have samples from the last three lawyers who were sitting at the table: Senator Merriweather, Kaufman, and Michaels. It looks like they had heart attacks. Let's find out if that's all they had. Here, you take Kaufman and I'll take Michaels. Maybe we'll find something faster if we skip the regular tests, go straight for the exotic plant poisons. We might save time.

"Ok, give me Michaels. I knew him. He's the bastard lawyer who was supposed to help Melissa get a good settlement for Melody, but the pig took most of the money and left her with almost nothing. I could've killed him myself."

"Grand-Dad, I've never heard you talk like that before."

"Melissa is working with Robert in his green house trying to help pay for Melody's care in the nursing home. It's not much but it helps some, and she's learning a lot about plants and gardening."

"Do you think Aunt Melody will ever come out of the coma?"

"No. No chance, and Melissa has power of attorney and won't let Mark or me withdraw the life support."

"I'm sorry. I lost mom and that was hard but to lose a son-in-law, a grandchild and a daughter all at once must be unbearable." She put the tray holding the samples on the counter top.

"I'll take Michaels. It might be easier for me." He stared into the past with tears clouding his vision. She nudged him. "Come on, Grand-Dad. Work will be good for us."

❀ ❀ ❀

Adelaide took off the plastic gloves, coat, and goggles, stretched long and tall and yawned big and loud. "Come on, it's almost midnight. We can wrap up now. We've got everything under control. Let's get out of here. I'm dead tired."

"Ok. We've got the tests going and by this time tomorrow we should have some results, not everything, but at least something." He hung up his lab coat and shifted papers on the desk. "Where are those police reports? We can look over them in the meantime."

"NO! No more work. We're done for now. You can't come to New Orleans just to work. This is a fun city, didn't you know that? I have to show you some hot places in town."

"You're right. We've done all the damage we can do right now. Let's go get something to eat. Hey, is there anything open this late?"

"Good grief, Grand-Dad, this is New Orleans. We can always find food to eat, and it'll be delicious. Come on, some of the best food is found in the Quarter right across from the cathedral."

"I'm not dressed up and I don't have a coat. We can't get in a real fancy place, can we?"

"Stick with me, pardner,' I'll fend for ya." She nudged him with her elbow.

It was past midnight and Muriel's was still packed with diners both upstairs and down. This red-orange restaurant sat on the corner looking out onto Jackson Square in defiance of the pure white St. Louis Cathedral across the street. Muriel's décor was bordello red with long heavy drapes, giving an old-world comfortable feeling.

There were two available seats at the Courtyard bar where Grand-Dad and Adelaide chose to have a hurricane drink while they waited for a table. When their drinks were brought to them, the young waitress said, "If y'all are interested, there's a fortune-teller up stairs telling fortunes. It don't cost nothing." With all the problems they were dealing with the new labs, new business ventures, six possible murders, Adelaide and Dad both said, "Yes." They wanted their fortunes told.

The rooms upstairs were also decorated in dark red with long, elegant, heavy velvet red drapes giving the character of a house of ill repute, which it actually had been in the past. The small plush rooms with deep cushioned red sofas harkened back to the time of pre and post-civil war where rich men spent lavishly on beautiful young courtesans. One room was called the Séance Room. This was where the resident ghost Pierre Antoine Lepardi Jourdan preferred to spend most of his time and where they found several people waiting for their fortunes to be told.

They were surprised to find the fortuneteller well dressed in a slim-fitting long black sequined evening dress, her hair well groomed and her makeup impeccable. She looked as if she were ready to go to the opera. They had expected her to be dressed in fancy gypsy high head-gear, shawl, long bangle earrings and snakes draped around her neck. Adelaide and Dad were both flabbergasted and a bit giggly after the hurricanes.

"You can tell fortunes?" Adelaide asked.

"Oh, yes, and there is no charge, just so you know that I am genuine and sincere. Give me your palm, you first my dear. Don't tell me your name. I don't need to know."

The fortune teller grasped Adelaide's hand and turned it over.

"Oh, what a colorful life you have had, and there are so many more adventures to come. Your first husband was not a successful match but your second one will live with you a very long time. You have a long lifeline with a lot of travel involved. It is a good life for you. Make the most of it." She closed Adelaide's hand and patted it fondly.

Grand-Dad looked at Adelaide in surprise, but Adelaide was very quiet.

"And now you sir; give me your hand." She took his hand and gently ran her hand over Dad's callused farm-worked palm. Tears welled up in her eyes. "You have many deep wounds and I am sorry to tell you but there are more to come. But there is a sunshine, also, a bright sparkling that will last you a very long time, one that will bring you more joy than you have ever had. For you, my friend, the worst and the best is yet to come. Keep your friends close to you. You will need them." She closed his palm, hugged it tightly then turned to read to another person's palm.

Dad and Adelaide sat still and didn't move or speak, both absorbing the messages. Then Adelaide began to laugh. "Grand-Dad, I've never been married before. So the first husband isn't supposed to be so good? Man. I can hardly wait for the second one to come along. Maybe I'll just skip the first one and go straight to the second one."

"Her reading scared me."

"Don't worry, everyone has had troubles, and for sure we'll all have more. She didn't mean anything special by it. Stop thinking so much. You'll spoil the fun. In a couple of days we'll find out what killed the three last at the table and then begin a new life."

"Here's to life. Cheers." They clinked their hurricane glasses together and headed for the dining room to their table.

Chapter 30

Adelaide read the police report and reported to Grand-Dad. "Kaufman ingested cocaine. And an awful lot of it from the police report. Did he think he was invincible? The higher you go, the harder you fall, I guess. Witnesses said that a red headed woman with a green dress went into his apartment and later drove off. Grand-Dad are you listening?"

He stood staring at the display of samples with one twirling in his hand. He didn't respond.

"Grand-Dad, wait a minute. Red hair was found in Collier's office, the woman had on a green dress…and, and here it is again. That can't be a coincidence." She flipped through the police reports. "Goddamn that Robert, this is such a mess. He's such a fucking slob. Pelto, Pelto, yes. The doorman said a redheaded woman in a green dress was Pelto's last visitor. GRAND- DAD are you listening? I think here is another red thread."

"Humm… yes Addie, a red thread. Nice."

"You're not listening. What are you working on?"

"Addie, we have three deaths we still haven't investigated, Merriweather, Kaufman and Michaels. Those are the three last from around the table. The only one alive is Elliott Edgars." He stared at the samples as if daring them to move and wanting the solutions to foam up out of the vials. "I wish this was simpler and quicker."

"I'm surprised at you. You've always said how slow the lab investigations should be to make sure the results are accurate. We started these samples last night. They'll soon be ready to examine. What's the rush now?"

He rubbed his hands over his face and head to relax the tension and stress. "Addie, I just have such a bad feeling about this. I wish it were all behind us and we could get back to our normal lives."

"Well, then, let's light a fire under our asses and get to work. Three completed and three to go. Let's move."

"Remind me not to work for you in the new lab. I'd have a stroke or heart attack."

She jokingly put on an Outback accent, "Yeah, mate, but you'd bloody well get the work done." She snapped a towel at Grand-Dad. "On with it, you lazy bush-whacker."

Grand-Dad grinned, pulled the samples toward him. "How am I so fortunate to have a spunky granddaughter like you?"

"I dunna know. Lucky I guess."

"Slave-driver, hand me one of the victim's leftovers, how about Senator Merriweather, the cross dresser." He pushed his glasses on top of his head. "Now there's results I'd like to get a hold of."

"What? You want to get a hold of a cross dresser? Grand-Dad!"

"Oh sorry, that came out wrong. I just thought his data seemed interesting and a bit unusual."

"Ok. Here you go. You take him and I'll take Michaels from New Orleans and I bet I'll get something first, Grand-Pops!"

"You're beginning to sound like Robert."

"Grand-Dad? You ok?"

Arms stretched out and bracing himself against the counter, he hung his head down. "I'm ok Addie. I just never thought that lab work could take the positive stuffing out of me. To think that we're working on murder cases instead of finding cures, or inventing drugs or, or anything constructive." He stood up and stretched his back. The mixed smells of cleaning solutions and fumigation liquids permeated the small lab like grease on a hole-in-the-wall fried-chicken shop.

"From the police report, it was more or less obvious that Merriweather had an allergy to what now appears to be shellfish, which was ground up in the body cream and smeared over his body. That could have been enough to set off an anaphylactic reaction from the body lotion, but liquid from his stomach shows a form of another poisonous plant, the rosary pea." He turned and looked at Adelaide.

"So Merriweather had rosary pea poison. Another murder. I can't do this much longer. I thought I was stronger. " Adelaide ran to the sink, retching. "I'm going to be sick."

"Addie. Eat some chipped ice. It'll help. Sit down. Wipe your face. You didn't throw up much since we haven't eaten since breakfast. We have to stop this pace even though we're close to the end. What about Michaels?"

"Thanks. I'm sorry. I'll be ok." She wiped her face with some cold water and antibacterial lotion. "I feel better, and, yeah, we can't keep going like this, but Grand-Dad, Michaels was easy. He ate oleander and some kind of mushroom. He was poisoned, too."

"We only have Kaufman to go. We should be finished by tomorrow. Do you know what happened to the photos from the death scenes?

"Robert has them," she whispered. "So two more murders." She wiped her hands, stored the leftover vials in a locked cabinet and sprayed room freshener in the air.

"Addie, let's keep quiet for just a little while. I just can't talk about this right now." He took off his white lab coat and put it carefully in the laundry. "Let's go to the baby shower at Gerhardt and Peggy's. It's got to be more cheerful than this place right now."

They gathered in the Garden District in Peggy's little dream home, the shot-gun house which now smelled of fresh crab gumbo, Wiener schnitzel, garlic bread, and Robert's now cold- coffee and dry beignets from Café du Monde.

Robert was in control and the mood was gloomy. "Dad, never play poker." He talked with one side of his mouth while with the other he chewed on a cigar. "Your face looks like gloom and doom. What did you find out today? Give it to me brief."

Dad sank into the old sofa and clasped his hands together. "We started the tests a few days ago and today got most of the results. We lined them all up according to the victim then added the testing solutions little by little. Addie and I made..."

"Goddammit Dad, get to the fucking point."

"Don't be so damned impatient." He sat back even deeper in the sofa. "We have a lawyer murdered in Chicago by overdosing on Valerian root and coral snake venom, one lawyer dead in San Francisco from Yellow Jasmine. Pelto drank Hemlock and had poison spider bites. Now, we have a cross-dressing senator murdered by allergy to sea food and rosary pea."

The pendulum on the cuckoo clock sounded like a death toll.

Robert squinted and from underneath his eyelids looked at Dad. "Have you noticed each was murdered by a flower?"

They all looked at Dad. "Yes," he whispered. "Someone has to know a hell of a lot about plants."

Adelaide jumped up and clapped her hands to get everyone's attention. "Stop it. Right now. This is a party for celebration. Now it's baby gift time. From me, I give you two new parents one year's supply of diapers in graduated sizes." Dad bounded for the front door. With great difficulty he hauled in a package from the front porch so big it just fit through the door, and put it in front of Peggy and Gerhardt. "If you need more, I'll supply it."

Peggy started whimpering and Gerhardt stared, "Oh mein Gott.. tat is lot of baby shit." And everyone laughed. "Oh, so sorry…tank you, tank you very much it will save much money. Ya, Peggy?"

Peggy whimpered softly into Gerhardt's shoulder and squeaked out a small, "Thank you" as Adelaide and Dad gave her a hug.

Dad stuck out his chest in pride and said, "I will offer to baby-sit for 50 hours anytime you need. I am the best grandpa babysitter in town. And you can come and stay with me on my farm for as long as you want."

Applause went around the room with Gerhardt and Peggy looking at each other thinking of the possibility of moving to California. What a wonderful gift. The ideas just started spinning around in their heads and they were excited with the prospects.

Robert threw a check at Gerhardt and said, "Here, here's a check. Go out and buy yourself something you need. I don't buy gifts."

Adelaide stood again. "I asked my Aboriginal friends to make something for the baby. They have magical talents in their fingers. Wait one minute." With that she rushed to the car and nervously carried back a flat package wrapped in thin tissue paper and placed it on the low coffee table. Peggy was too big to bend over to open it so Gerhardt, not knowing exactly what to do, pulled at the thin paper string holding the package. The wrapping fell open to a mess of string and colored paper. All the guests just stared, wondering what to do.

Dad stood, took the top piece of paper and with great care slowly stretched and pulled the string up toward the ceiling. Gentle as a breeze, the mix-mash of colored pieces drifted up to the ceiling with hundreds of colorful origami swans floating, swaying, and spreading out in all directions. It was enchanting and hypnotizing. Everyone sat in awe. This was the most beautiful mobile they had ever seen. Some of the swans were made of sparkling paper that reflected the light and sent rainbows flitting around the room while red, orange violet fragile and delicate birds dipped and swayed around the ceiling.

Peggy started to cry again. "Oh, it's so beautiful. It's just beautiful. Thank you. Thank you so much."

Gerhardt jumped up. "I go get hammer and nail to put it up now. Ok, Peggy?" He ran out the back door to the shed where the tools were and came huffing and puffing back into the house. "Peggy, this is for you and our baby." Now it was Gerhardt's turn to be proud. He put in front of Peggy a handmade cradle of rose wood, polished to a mirror sheen, and carved with intricate Germanic designs. "It's big enough for one or two years and took almost as long to make."

"You made this? Yourself?" Peggy asked.

"Ya. Is custom in my family to make sure baby has his own bed. And after the baby comes, I put his name here on the top."

Now, Peggy caterwauled as Gerhardt held her and patted her fondly.

"Good God, woman, will you stop howling! You're making everyone miserable. You're ruining a perfectly good party. I need a drink. Anyone for something strong, like whisky?" Robert headed for the back porch. "You think this fun is going to last? Plenty of shit's gonna hit the fan."

Chapter 31

"No, no, Gerhardt, it doesn't look good over there either. Move it back next to the changing table. There, the cradle looks good there but it is too far from the bed and I want it next to me so I don't have to get out of bed all night. Can you move it back next to the bed, please?" Making decisions wasn't easy for Peggy right now. She was uncomfortable, swollen, bloated and hungry.

"Ach, mein dear, I vish I make it out of feathers now. It's damn heavy. Can you decide for the last time, please?"

"It really is beautiful, Gerhardt and I do love it. Yes, right there next to our bed. Thank you."

"Ve have now tree veeks to vait and vunder?"

"We…Weeks…Wait… Wonder…. Gerhardt, to say the 'W' you have to round your lips like you are going to kiss and then blow… like this Woo, Woo… try it." Peggy pursed her lips and blew.

Ever ready to please, he puckered up his lips, blew, but nothing came out but bubbles. He looked so ridiculous that they both laughed. "Ach, English. You look like fish to speak. I teach our son to speak good German, you work on English."

"What do you mean son? This baby is a girl. And you will spoil her rotten, I'm sure. You are such a softy."

"Ya, well, we'll see, we'll see. Don't be too sure."

"Life for us is going to be so different. We are going to need a lot of patience. I've always worked and never thought about being at home with a baby. Now that I've been home this week, I miss working in the lab but I am excited about the baby, too."

"Ya, well, two years ago I never tought to be here with you and now have a child come. Never before tonight I could ever know this kind happiness. Tank you Peggy. Danke."

"Gerhardt, I am happy too. We'll be good together. I am glad that Grand-Dad is staying with us. He is pleasant to have around, but I bet when the baby comes he will want a quieter place to live. It worries me that he hasn't told me much about what they are doing in the lab. I think he doesn't want to worry me. I'd like to talk to him."

"Yah, he sometimes comes in late from Quarter like young man. He sleeps late, he used to wake early- remember, and then he works all day. He is strong. Would you like to go to California and see his farm sometime?"

"Oh, yes. I've never been in that part of the country and they say it's beautiful out there. When the baby is old enough, it would be lovely to take a trip out there."

"Goot. We will go. I want also to go there." He sat thinking. "So you think baby is a girl? Maybe? Ah, Little Bleumchen, hah?"

"Bleumchen… what does that mean?"

"Little Flower. She is like little flower in our garden. Yes?"

"It sounds beautiful in German but in English it sounds like someone from the 1960s flower children." She giggled. "Try the 'W' sound again. Pucker up your lips and try to kiss; you have to practice to get it right. Woo…woooo."

"Woople…whoop.. stupid language. Wooop…"

"No, like this, pucker your lips and blow.…OWWW… AAAIIII…"

"That's not pucker."

"No, aiieee…Gerhardt, the baby! Oaawwaieiii The baby. Contractions. Pains! Ohmygod my water broke."

Panicked, Gerhardt spewed out,

"ThebabycomesnowvhatdoIdovhereisthecabdoIcalldoctorvhereisbagvhatishospitalnumbervaitvegonow…"

"GERHARDT, SHUT UP. Give me the phone. This is too early. I have to call the doctor. GIVE ME THE PHONE."

"Ya, Ya surewhereisdamnthing? Here, Mein Liebchen, here phone."

"Liebchen… Beloved? You've never called me that before. AAAIIIEEEEE. Oh Gerhardt. AAIIIEE."

Grand-Dad phoned. "Adelaide, Peggy's water broke. Gerhardt kept yelling in a terrible German and English mix and they had to go to the hospital. They took a taxi. I'll pick you up. We need to get over to Touro Hospital. The baby is three weeks too soon, but babies have their own timetable. Let's go. I think we'll need to take care of Gerhardt."

"I'll throw some clothes back on. I've never been an Auntie before. I'm excited. "Bring the police reports and all the photos you have from the murder scenes. I'm curious about them. We can look them over while we wait. Hurry up. I'll be outside waiting."

"What took you so long? Get a move on, Grand-Dad. Let's go."

"Boy, Addie. You're nervous."

"I'm glad you're driving. I'm too nervous."

"You, nervous? After all you have been through and a birthing baby can make you nervous? You are supposed to be a tough lady."

"Well, I've never been this close to a real birthing before. Even in the Outback they always shooed us younger ones away. And it's Peggy, who I know and have worked with for so long, and I'm going to be Godmother. Hurry up. This is my godchild being born!"

"Well, hang on. They might give her some IV Magnesium to stop the contractions, if it isn't too late. It's better to have the baby cook a bit longer in the womb. We'll have to see when we get there. I brought some Scotch for Gerhardt, but you might be needing some before the night is out."

"Just hurry up, will you?"

Chapter 32

"They're going to keep Peggy overnight to see if the contractions stop." Grand-Dad patted Adelaide's shaking hands. "Peggy's lost a little amniotic fluid so perhaps the baby will wait a bit longer before making its appearance. Gerhardt will stay overnight with her and will call if anything happens…if he's not too nervous to remember how to use the phone. Poor guy."

"Come on, Grand-Dad. The Blue Bird Café is just down the street and they always have the best breakfasts in town, all day long. Let's go over there. I'm starving. I always get hungry when I'm nervous."

"Yeah, I could stand a good cup of coffee, too."

The Blue Bird Café was not noted for its décor. It was a true hole in the wall diner with aluminum tables and folding chairs. But on any given morning the line was out the door and down the street with people waiting for up to two hours to get in to eat a most wonderful breakfast. The long-time owners were getting ready to retire and when the news got out about their upcoming retirement, the lines got longer. Folks knew there would never be another couple who could cook such great breakfasts, and customers came from all over the city to eat here one last time. At this time of night there wasn't much of a line, so Dad and Adelaide got a rickety table with no waiting.

"I don't know how Robert comes up with these things, but he got pictures from each of the murder scenes. I shudder to think how he procures them." Grand-Dad said as he pulled the manila envelope out of his folder.

Addie made a face, "We can look over the crime-scene pictures and eat. Ugh, what an un-jolly thought. I could never imagine that I would ever be doing those two things at the same time." She sipped on her black coffee. "What is so interesting about the photos?"

"Well, you know I'm a plant man and I was just curious about some of the flowers in the rooms."

"Flowers? You know what they look like already. Why relook at them?"

"I'm an old man and I can take time to look at flowers and smell the roses...or this wonderful coffee, and sit, and just enjoy. Here are the police reports and pictures of the rooms where the bodies were found. Enjoy." He handed the files over.

"Man, I bet you have low blood pressure too," she said as she poured cream in her coffee. Gotta' have café o'lait tonight; it'll be easy on my already upset nervous stomach. I hope Peg holds that baby in a few more weeks."

She flipped through the photos and tossed them back on the table. "Oh no. I can't right now. You look at them."

Grand-Dad slowly examined the photos. "Let's see what we have here. You can tell if the dead person is important or not by counting how many pictures were taken, or saved, from the death scene. It seems these people were pretty important 'cause there're lots of pictures."

"I've never noticed, not having ever been this involved with any crimes before. And, I hope never again." Adelaide ordered the full Southern breakfast: ham, grits with butter and cheese, pancakes, homemade syrup or honey, sausage, two eggs, and biscuits with gravy. Dad had a bran muffin.

"Here, take half of the stack of pictures. See if you can find pictures of any other flowers in the room, in vases, or on, or near the body." Grand-Dad encouraged. "We still have one murder to examine. I just wonder if we could cut to the chase and pick out the flowers before we test the solutions. I bet it would lead us straight to the poison."

"You know what, I think you are looking for some more plants to put in your nursery," Adelaide teased. "Do you think these flowers are a symbol? No… they are the poison. Do you think there might be pictures of other flowers in the rooms with the other deaths?"

"Yes, possibly. Do you think the killer left the flowers as a sign?" Addie stopped eating.

"Perhaps. It's known that for various reasons, a serial killer might leave a sign behind."

With gusto and renewed interest, Adelaide began poring over the pictures. "It doesn't seem the photographers were interested in flowers. Oh, wait, it's not very clear, but here are some frames from the woman in the Collier's murder and she's wearing a green dress and holding a bouquet of yellow flowers. Are these Carolina Jasmine?"

"Humm.. it's kinda' hard to tell, but we can have these blown up and focused on the flowers to make sure. Good eyesight, Adelaide. Look again and see if there are any more pictures of the yellow flower. Where do they wind up?"

Where do they wind up?"

"Yeah, are they in water, on the chair, on the desk... where do they wind up? Residue from the poison could be left behind."

"This picture's real fuzzy, but it looks like they're in a vase on the desk. That must be why we got a positive from the vase water, right?"

"Could be. Let's see what else we can find. Well, there might not be flowers at the O'Hara murder, but look anyway."

"Good that Senator Pelto was such a high profile person. There are so many pictures that it'll take days to go through all of them. But as luck would have it, there are several very good shots of a vase with flowers that look like Queen Anne's Lace. See here, Addie?"

"Queen Ann's Lace is poisonous?"

"That could be Water Hemlock. Water Hemlock is a bit more yellowish than Queen Ann's Lace. There's also something reddish mixed in with the white flowers. Can you see these closer? What do they look like to you?"

"They look like fuzzy red triangle flowers, I don't know. It's not all that clear and I'm not familiar with flowers, except Australian flowers. I don't know. You're the plant man, not me. I don't know flowers too well, as you can tell."

"Well, maybe with a magnifying glass or under the microscope we can see clearer."

"What do you think they are?"

"I'm not sure, but the Castor Bean has a small reddish group of flowers that might shape up into a triangle. I'd have to see them up close to make sure. Castor Bean was what we just found in the Pelto fluids."

"Grand-Dad, I don't think I can take any more surprises; I've had enough in this one day to last a lifetime. Can we stop for a while.... please? And while you're at it, pass the syrup."

"Okay, okay let's just eat in peace and think of pleasant things...

like setting up a lab in Cuyama, California. Close to your old Grand-Dad. What about that?"

"You know we would need to look into the real estate prices to see if there are small empty houses or small warehouse-type buildings where we could set up a lab." She started twirling her fork in the air. "We won't need much space, but it would be great if we had the possibility to expand once we got going. What are the state taxes and how difficult is it to bring new factories or businesses into California? There are so many questions that need to be followed up and explored." She dug into her pancakes. "Are there cost effective housing and shopping places for the employees? We could begin with maybe ten workers, counting the farm help. Then there are the costs of setting up a larger farm, with plants and fertilizers or pesticides and all the equipment that you might need."

"Whoa. Slow down. You're going too fast for an old man. I guess you've been thinking about this. And I thought you were just over in your side of the lab being quiet doing the experiments with no other thoughts in your mind. Boy was I wrong."

"These tests are so routine now, that I can do them and make other plans at the same time. No big deal."

"Well, I had to concentrate. Once today I looked all over for my glasses and then realized they were on my nose under the protective glasses. I had to laugh at myself for that one."

"Absent-minded professor. Let's eat. Oh, yummm…ham, eggs and grits, two pancakes, fresh homemade biscuits, butter and jam and red sauce on the side for a bit of spice. More coffee please."

Grand-Dad watched her eat with gusto and smiled, remembering that Mark used to eat the same way.

"Oh, man, this is delicious; fat does make everything taste good. I might die tonight but I am going to enjoy every mouth-full of this. Amazing how these people can really cook down here."

Several minutes went by with just the sounds of munching, and smacking of lips. "Let's go back to Peggy and Gerhardt's place and look at these pictures. I'm just dying of curiosity to see if there are other flowers or plants."

"Sure, but let's make one last check on Peggy."

"…and Gerhardt."

"Yeah, poor guy. I hope he doesn't stroke out before the baby comes. Bet he wishes he hadn't given up smoking."

The little shotgun was dark and the street light had been out for months. No telling when the city would come by and put in a new light bulb.

Adelaide asked, "Hey, how many New Orleans City workers does it take to screw in a light bulb?"

"Oh, uh, I don't know. How many?"

"Well, first someone has to remember to report it, then it goes to the answering service, then it goes on a list which is put on someone's desk, then the city commission has to look at the list and decide which are the most important repairs and if there are any 'big-wigs' who live in the area, then it gets put on another list for the street light workers, then it goes to the supervisor of the committee and then they try and figure out if they are going to be in the area anytime in the next six months. By then everyone's forgotten that there ever was a street light that worked. So who cares anymore?"

They laughed as they walked into the house and turned on the light.

Grand-Dad yelped. "Good God, Robert. You'll give us all a heart attack. Why didn't you tell us you were coming and that you'd be here at Gerhardt's house? Why are you sitting in the dark?"

He was incensed that Robert was casually sitting in the big armchair, feet stretched out on the small coffee table, and smoking a cigar in the dark. But then, Robert didn't need a key and no one knew when he was coming and going.

"Heard the Little Sparrow is getting ready to pop. That true?" Robert didn't move or rise to Grand-Dad's anger.

"Hi, Robert. We ate without you, since we didn't know you were coming. How did you know about Peggy? Oh well, don't answer. Never mind." Adelaide had heard Robert say once that he treated everyone with the same amount of disrespect, and she was practicing that same treatment on him.

"Yeah, well, they are trying to stop the contractions and hopefully the little one will cook a bit longer." Grand-Dad seemed tired all of a sudden.

"You find anything interesting in the police records?" Robert had noticed the file under Dad's arm.

"Robert, we might be able to use some of your exotic plant expertise. Turn all the lights on and let's have a real close look at these pictures. You like flowers, don't you?"

Robert puffed a big ring of blue smoke into the air. "Depends. Whatda'ya have?"

"We have one murder to go. If we can recognize the flower, I guess we can call them murders now, we might find the poison sooner."

"Hot damn! Let's have a good look." Robert exploded out of the chair and grabbed the files. "Come in the kitchen where there is more light," he ordered.

"Robert, put out that cigar. It will make Peggy sick when she comes home; cigar smoke lasts a long time in a house," Adelaide said.

Under his bushy, unkempt eyebrows, Robert shot angry looks at Adelaide but doused the cigar in the kitchen sink. "Damn all little bastard babies."

They showed him the pictures that looked like the Water Hemlock in Pelto's room and the yellow flowers in Collier's office, that might be Carolina Jasmine. They then divided the rest of the files between them and for a quiet hour, they poured over the pictures.

"Look at some of these pictures from Senator Meyer's room; you can just make out the small vase that has some purple flowers. They could be Rosary Pea." Robert mused. "You found Rosary Pea in his stomach, right?"

"Yes, along with ground up shellfish and crustacean powder in the creams. It looks like someone wanted these people dead and didn't take a chance of just one thing killing them," Adelaide said.

"We can't be sure until we see them up close. I suppose we can choose a few good pictures and you can get them blown up and clear for us to use, can't you Robert?" Dad asked.

"No problem. Let's go through the rest and see what else we can dig up."

"I'll have them all blown up tomorrow and we'll see if there is anything useful," Robert offered.

"Here in Michael's hotel room there's a huge bunch of flowers, in all colors, but lots of white ones. Good grief, Robert, look at these and put out that stinking cigar, it's still smoking." Dad slid the photos over to Robert. "Do these look like oleander?"

The smell of a crushed cigar, wet and steaming in the sink, was worse than the original smell. "Hope that satisfies you two." Robert sank into the metal kitchen chair. "Could be oleander, could be. Shit, if you're right, it's one of the most poisonous plants on the planet and it grows like weeds everywhere." He looked over the top of the photos at Dad. "You knew Michaels, didn't you."

Dad pretended to examine the photos, sweat slid down his cheeks. "Yeah, he was the lawyer who cheated Melissa out of Melody's long-term care money."

"Look, you two. There's someone out there who knew all the people at the table and who knows plants. No, not someone who just knows plants but someone who knows how to work with them, handle them, use them and dispose of them," Adelaide said. "Could it be more than one person?"

"Guys, there aren't many flower pictures from Kaufman's file; I guess he wasn't as interesting to the police and press as Merriweather and Pelto. Kaufman was obese and was in a small, unknown, rather cheap hide-away condo near Sarasota. It says here that 'he died of an apparent heart attack and a possible overdose of cocaine.' All the pictures are grainy. There were cigarette butts and some with lipstick, and there was cocaine found in the room. Here, see if you can find any flowers in that slimy mess."

"Well, I'll be," Grand-Dad said. "Robert, have a look at these. What does that flower look like to you?"

"Shit. That's Foxglove. Digitalis ….so that was his poison. Jesus-God."

They put the pictures on the table. "That's it then," Adelaide said. "The last murder that we know of. We should be able to prove it tomorrow. Only your brother, is left from that horrible table."

"Why just these six people around this particular table? Are there others who have been killed but were not around this table?" Grand-Dad was full of questions. "The sooner we get a good look at the pictures, the more we will know, and then we have to turn this over to the police, Robert. We can't keep this to ourselves. If your brother is the one person left alive, then you have to warn him about all food, drinks …almost every goddamn thing on the planet."

"He knows to be careful. I'll contact him again. For now, let's get some sleep. Tomorrow may be longer than today."

"Jeezums," Adelaide squeaked. "With all this excitement, who can sleep now?"

In seconds Robert was snoring loud and strong in the big arm chair while Adelaide crawled into the bed next to the cradle. Grand-Dad went into his room with ear plugs.

Chapter 33

"Elliott is so shit-ass scared he is in lock-down mode. What a wimp-ass brother. Crap."

"Well, maybe it's your calling in life to be there to protect him," said Adelaide. "Would you like to taste all his food or drink his drinks before he did? You could even search his room and closet every night for strange critters crawling and slithering around." Adelaide was getting tired of Robert's complaining. "Why don't you go to Café du Monde and get us some coffee and beignets while we finish up these tests?" She was anxious to get rid of him so they could work in peace. "It's going to take a while, yet."

"Ain't you getting a bit big for your britches?" said Robert as he picked up his hat. "Good luck, Grand-Dad."

She turned to Grand-Dad as Robert slammed out of the lab. "Good. I want to discuss the results in quiet with you before he gets hold of them. I've got to be sure and give him a bill also; that'll give him something else to think about."

He brought in these enlarged pictures of the flowers we suspected." Grand-Dad spread the pictures out on the table top. "Here you can see the yellow Carolina Jasmine from the Collier murder and the light violet colored Rosary Pea from both Pelto's and the Senator's murders. The Castor Bean plant has star like leaves, which are very distinctive, but its flowers are quite small and inconspicuous; you can just see a trace of them in this photo from Pelto's room." He picked up the picture of the Carolina Jasmine and stared hard at the picture.

Adelaide leaned over to examine the other crime scene pictures. "The pictures of oleander from the Michaels death are very clear and distinct in the pictures. Those flowers I recognize easily. They're all over New Orleans."

She turned and looked at him, "Look at these from the Kaufman death. These beautiful bell shaped purple flowers are foxglove. We guessed that the flowers looked like foxglove or digitalis. We were right."

He looked at her thoughtfully. "Yeah, the sample of digoxin from Kaufman's stomach was a high concentration. Digitalis is poisonous in even small doses. The entire plant is toxic, and ingesting just .5 grams, or two dried up and crushed leaves, is enough to kill a person. When you ingest too much, you have an actual heart attack."

"So, with Kaufman being obese and having a heart problem already, the killer didn't need another poison to help his victim find the next life. He or she left a bouquet of Foxglove as a sign. This is so bizarre and creepy. What about Michaels?"

"Well, we know that he had a lot of oleandrin and nerine from the oleander in his system and both have a powerful effect on the heart. Anyone who swallows even a small amount of oleander will have drowsiness, an irregular heartbeat often followed by death."

"You said often, but not always?" Adelaide asked.

"Yes well, we don't know. Maybe he did ingest enough to kill himself. I guess we would have to imagine so."

He gathered the photos and stuffed them back in the envelope. Adelaide looked and thought that he was acting a bit strange. Why was he all of a sudden evasive and not direct? "Did you find anything of interest?"

"No, no, nothing more. I think we have pretty well wrapped this up, and now Robert can take it over."

"Would you like for me to have a look, Grand-Dad?"

"No, no, I don't think that will be necessary." He waved her away, "I'll take the photos Robert got for us and then let's give Peggy a call. You never know she might come home with bed rest for the last two weeks of her pregnancy. She may want to have us at home when she gets there. In fact, we could go and get her from the hospital, since Gerhardt doesn't drive very well, and Gerhardt might want us there to help him."

He strained a laugh, put the photos under his arm and ushered Adelaide out of the lab.

"Grand-Dad, are you nervous about something?" Adelaide was getting concerned.

"Oh, well, you know, this is as close as I have been to a birthing in a long time, too. I guess I am kinda' giddy. Let's go see the kids." He rushed to the elevator, impatiently pushing the down button repeatedly.

"Alright. Slow down. I guess Robert can find us later. You're as nervous as a pregnant nun."

"I guess I am kinda anxious to get this behind me and get back to my farm.

"Grand-Dad, let's talk about who would want to kill these people. Somebody has a vendetta or a hate campaign against them. Are there other people? Why poison? Who would want to see lawyers or politicians suffer- well, lots of people I guess. But why just those people at that specific table?"

He angrily punched the elevator down button. "There is no way we can know; everyone knows these six- seven people; they are known and recognized all over the country. That is the reason no one else has thought about these people being part of a serial killer's plan. It's for the police to take up now. Let's hope they will take up the cases, and let's also hope nothing will happen to Elliott Edgars."

"Aren't you interested anymore? You seem to be apathetic."

"Well, I just am eager to get home. My job is done here, now, and I am sure the weeds are growing so thick all around my door I'll have to use a machete to get into my house. I think I'll go home just as soon as Peggy has her baby. Or maybe I'd just better scoot home soon and come back later, when things have settled down a bit."

Adelaide looked at him long and hard as he was driving to the hospital. He grasped the steering wheel as if it were going to get away from him, his face was tense, and his jaw clenched tight. Something had changed him dramatically; he was no longer interested in the cases and was eager to head home before the mystery was finished or Peggy had birthed her baby. Maybe that was what it was like getting old. You change your direction as quick as you want; and maybe your interests have just a short span of time. Who knew? "We will all miss you very much, me in particular, but you know we have grown very fond of you and have profited by having you around."

"Thanks, Adelaide I appreciate that, but I really do need to be getting home."

She tried again, "What about finding a place for a small lab out in your town when you go back? We could talk about it later and see what you have found."

He was slow to answer, "I'm not sure it's a good idea anymore. I've been thinking about it, and California has lots of taxes and tons of red tape that might make it impossible to find good profitable growth out there. Even the computer companies are leaving."

Adelaide was stunned and sat very quiet the rest of the ride to the hospital. Something was definitely wrong.

By the time they had Peggy and Gerhardt settled at home, with a nice meal under their belts, Grand-Dad had found airline tickets to Los Angeles that very evening. He packed his bags, said he didn't want to be a bother to the young couple, promised to return after the baby was born, called a taxi and headed for the airport. It was surprising, but with so much concern on Peggy needing to rest, he felt it was best to go and return later. He said he missed his farm. Adelaide just watched.

As he was getting ready to go through the airport security, Robert showed up, put a firm grip on Grand-Dad's arm and guided him to one of the quiet chairs in the middle of the waiting area of the airport lobby. Robert leaned in close with the cigar smell blowing around them, "So, tell me what you found out that you don't want anyone else to know."

Grand-Dad sat still and looked at his hands, took a deep, long breath. "Robert, you knew all those people who died, you hate lawyers and politicians, and you know how to handle plants. You have a brother who is now primed to go to the top of his career since these others are gone. You could be the murderer." His shoulders sagged. "I don't want to stay around here anymore."

"Humm….. you're right. I could be the killer, but so could you. You have had bad luck with lawyers. You know plants. You were around at the time of the murders. You could be the killer."

The men locked glances, neither showing fear.

"What're you hiding?" Robert asked.

"Goodbye." Grand-Dad got up with the heaviness of depression and walked through the security to catch his plane.

Adelaide and Robert worked in the lab both quiet in their own thoughts. Robert was looking over the pictures; Adelaide wrapping up their testing.

"Adelaide, some of the pictures are missing. Did you take any?"

"Why would I take any pictures? Are some missing? Can you tell which ones are gone?"

"There are only two here from the Collier murder. I know damn well there were at least six." He counted the pictures as he chewed on his moustache.

She looked through the pictures. "Where are the originals?"

"I have them. Why?"

"How soon can you have them enlarged?" she asked.

"Won't take anytime at all. Why?"

"I think we'd better have another good look at them. Get the pictures and we'll see. Go, now."

Robert lowered his eyebrows so they covered the stare he gave to Adelaide. "You suspect something don't you?" He turned and flip-flopped out of the lab.

Robert's phone rang.

"Hello your own God-damn self. This is Robert. Leave a message. I might call you back or not, depends on how I feel or if I like you or not. Beeep......""

"Robert, this is Adelaide. Meet me at the hospital. Peggy is going into labor and this time it's for real. The baby will be born today. Bring the pictures."

The hospital gown was falling off Gerhardt as he paced from Peggy's birthing bed to the windows and back to the bed and over to the door and back to the bed. "Robert, Adelaide. Tank you for coming. The baby comes fast. Water, water everywhere and baby jump into my hands almost."

"So, it's a little Fraulein, huh? Congratulations, you old bastard. I didn't know you had it in you," said Robert as he gave Gerhardt a big fat cigar. "Here, at least you can chew on it. Don't even attempt to smoke it until you are in the back part of the garden. The Little Sparrow there will turn into a huge hawk and peck you to death."

"Ya. She is beautiful. Right." He looked like he'd lost fifty pounds, was red faced and drenched with sweat, just like Peggy. Gerhardt beamed while Adelaide held the baby which Peggy had nicknamed Little Flower. Peggy was exhausted and cried a bit while Robert acted as if it were his baby and knew everything about babies, which he didn't. Gerhardt with tears in his eyes, whispered, "We call her Kerstin after my mother."

"Come on, Adelaide; let's leave the little family alone. We have some things to talk about."

"In a minute, Robert, this time won't come again, so I want to enjoy it as long as possible."

"Aw, hell, Adelaide, you'll be pretty tired of it when she shits and cries all night. Put her down and let's get out of here. We can get some mud coffee from the cafeteria."

"You are such an ass-hole, but you know that don't you, Robert." Adelaide seethed, but walked out of the birthing room and down the hall trying hard to keep up with Robert. She wondered how someone so large could be so fast and forceful. He looked like he was full of muscle.

The smell of the bitter chicory coffee knotted her stomach. "Can't people in this country make a good cup of tea or coffee?"

"Sit down. Tell me what you found out in the lab today. I know you were redoing some of the tests Grand-Dad did two days ago.

What did you find?" Menacing was a mild word to describe Robert's hiss through his tight teeth.

Robert was not pleasant to deal with, but right now he was the only person she wanted to tell her results to. "Then you'll show me the pictures. I know you have them or you wouldn't be here." She pounded her little fist on the small table.

"Ok. Now tell me what you found in the last tests," he said gently but forcibly.

"Grand-Dad was acting kinda funny after we tested the last of the samples, so I went back and retested them all. There was not just one poison for the Michaels murder, there were two."

"What was the other one?" Again Robert spoke softly.

"It took a long time to figure it out. I had to do and redo so many tests."

"What did you find out? Come on, Adelaide, get it out; you'll feel better when it is out."

"First was oleander, like we thought. The second poison was from a rare exotic Australian mushroom called The Angel of Death; it's the world's most poisonous mushroom. It is quite rare and is found around the locations of Canberra and Melbourne. Only someone very familiar with this mushroom would know it or recognize it or know what to do with it."

His big stomach fell on top of the table and several of the middle buttons of his Hawaiian shirt were open or missing. He pulled the manila envelope from under his butt and Adelaide groaned.

"You've crunched and messed them up." She grabbed the file out of his hands.

"Hold it, Adelaide. Go slow. You're not going to like what you see." Unlike the usual Robert, he spoke in a soft and gentle voice.

When Robert spoke in a tender manner, it was time to be frightened. She knew from experience that when he put on his kind face, he wanted something or something really bad was about to happen. She was alert and trembled as she took the envelope.

He put his big calloused hands over hers to slow her down. "Go slow. These are the missing photos from the Johnny Collier murder. Look closely at the photo from the hotel lobby. Take a good look at the red-headed woman in the green dress."

She stared at Robert. She knew there was trouble and she was scared. With shaking hands and a queasy feeling in her stomach, she opened the large envelope and took out the crime pictures.

She spread the pictures out and bent close to examine them. She gasped, choked, "No. Oh, no...something's wrong, how, why? No it isn't." She struggled for breath then buried her head in her hands and cried uncontrollably. It wasn't unusual to see people crying in a hospital, so no one bothered them.

"I'm sorry you had to find out this way. Take a deep breath. Drink some of this." He handed her his pocket flask. "I'm going to call my brother. Then leave the rest to me. I have a plane to catch and I think you have a god-daughter to take care of."

Robert waited with uncharacteristic patience. He patted her sobbing head and her tear soaked arms. "It can't be. It can't be," She moaned. "Oh, my god, Aunt Melissa."

Chapter 34

"Curse you, you know I am right." Melissa turned and scowled at the tearing and panicking tarpaulin roof pushed by the screaming winds. The light diffused through the colorless canvases that surrounded her father's small greenhouse while the incessant wind ripped and frightened the angry sheets causing them to pop and whip, and strain to pull free from the killing toxins held in each flowerpot inside the greenhouse. Many beautiful blossoms were deadly poisonous.

Dad's greenhouse was like a second home to her and she was anxious to transfer some particular plants to Robert's garden in Florida. The fragrance of the plants, the moist soft soil, and the slight humidity gave her the confidence and strength that she sensed from no other place. She felt invincible and excited as she chose each plant carefully for she knew that her knowledge and abilities with poisons would soon eliminate the world of evil people who had been chosen to die. People would call her an angel, a quiet grey drab angel with the power of death.

She raised her voice above the wind, yelling at the havoc ripping at the tarps. "You will not stop me. You know why I have to do this." The veins in her neck swelled, causing her face to contort into a gargoyle-like grimace, as her gloved fist clenched the garden knife. "Leave me alone." she bellowed above the furious wind. "I didn't ask for this. They have to be stopped."

She lowered her head to the planting task muttering, "Calm down. Think clearly. Slow, deep breaths. Get in control. The wind is just making you jumpy. Don't let it bother you. Keep going. You know what you have to do. When they know, they will see you're right, and things will change afterwards. You just wait and see." Her inner voice had been her best companion for many years. It had never led her wrong but had given her confidence and courage. "A psychiatrist once told me that the self is one of the most intelligent persons to talk to and to share my thoughts with." She laughed. "The psychiatrist was right, if only he knew how right he really was. And those stupid pills he gave me were useless. Valerian root would have been better, but I don't need anything for what I have to do." She used the Hori Hori knife with its extra sharp curved serrated blade and sliced open the castor bean seed and mashed the oil into a small vial. "There, my lovely. Beautiful and deadly. You will be very useful one day soon."

She shuffled around the exotic plants, talking to them and defending her actions. "How can there be so many evil people in the world? Really evil. I mean, there are people who hurt others on purpose. Sometimes it's for financial gain, like my lawyer, that Michaels bastard. He took advantage of all of us and we trusted him - he lined his pockets and we got nothing. We have to care for Melody but lost everything we'd saved. Where is the justice in all that?"

She continued moving around the small greenhouse, watering, talking to the plants, and fertilizing when needed. She was comfortable in the greenhouse; plants were her friends who responded to her care with abundant growth. "You, my friends, are so thankful just to be alive and you respond to the dedicated care I bestow on you."

The wooden framed tarpaulin door swung open and with a bang, hit the side of the wall. Mrs. Amies walked in, holding her multi-flowered straw hat tight onto her head. "Hello, Melissa, my dear. My goodness, but that wind can certainly blow up a good storm when it chooses." She was one of Dad's best customers, as she preferred plants that had been raised without chemicals and sprays.

"Oh, hi. I didn't hear you drive up I was so busy talking to the plants. How are your monarch butterflies doing, Ms. Amies?" Melissa relaxed and turned to greet the old family friend as she closed the makeshift door.

"Well, the caterpillars are just gobbling up everything I put out there. There must be hundreds of the hungry little critters. What have you got for me to feed them?"

"Since the milkweed is all gone, try some parsley or dill. I really think you ought to try planting several of those big butterfly bushes. The butterflies will drink the nectar but will only lay their eggs on the milkweed, and the bushes won't be nearly as much work to keep up with."

"Alright. I am sure you know what you are talking about." Ms. Amies crossed her arms over her big stomach that reached her now drooping and very ample breasts. Menopause and old age had not been kind to her. "I'm getting too old to continue working so hard in my little garden. I am thinking of putting in concrete so I won't have to be out there all the time." She sighed as she put three large pots of butterfly plants into the trunk of the beat-up old Camry. "I'll get my son to plant them this weekend when he comes by."

Ms Amies reached into her car for a large paper bag. "I am sorry. I can't pay you right away, but I have some juicy ripe tomatoes and cucumbers if you would take those until the pumpkins are ready. Would that be alright?"

"Sure, Ms. Amies, that would be fine. Don't worry. I understand. That will be fine."

The older woman nodded her head, drove away with tears in her eyes, too humiliated to say thank you.

Melissa stood watching the car whirl up the dust in the gravel road. "Don't worry. The day will come when your grief and ache of losing everything to unscrupulous lawyers will be revenged. You will feel justified knowing of their deaths. Others will be satisfied too, many others." She walked back into the greenhouse pulling the frame door shut.

"Protests will begin soon. There may be martyrs. But others will take up the fight and demand change. Someone has to defend the innocent ones." She sighed as she put down the knife on the wooden bench. "Someone has to fight. Only the evil will die."

She turned and listened. Another car was coming up the gravel road. Creeping. "No one drives that slow." The hairs stood up on her neck and shivers ran down her legs. She couldn't see through the canvas but turned to where the sounds were coming so slowly that the dust did not kick up. She tightened her grip on the Hori Hori knife. "I won't run. Whoever it is will find me waiting. This can't end, yet."

The car came to a quiet stop. One person stepped out and the car door closed with a little snap. The heavy footsteps crunched on the gravel. The steps, deliberate and cautious, came closer and closer to the makeshift greenhouse and stopped. She waited, holding her breath. "Who is it? How could anyone know?"

The door yanked open.

"Bet you didn't expect to see me so soon, did you?" The voice slivered across the rows of plants and sent electric shocks down her spine.

Robert walked in.

The knife shook in her hand. She was afraid of what he knew, what he could find out in torturous ways.

"I'm not paying you to work in Dad's greenhouse. What're you doing here?"

Her tongue and throat felt like a swollen aloe plant. "I..I came to see Melody and to pick up some plants for your garden. There's no change in Melody, but I can't let her die. I have to keep hoping something will happen to bring her out of it."

"You can never trust the quiet mousey ones.....Dad'll be here soon; he took a side trip to Mark's apartment in L.A. to look for you. I thought you might be here. Anything you want to talk about before he gets here?"

"No. Nothing. What would I want to tell you, anyway?" She gripped the knife and swung it towards Robert. "Leave me alone." She backed away.

"Nobody hates lawyers more than me. Were you so mad at Oliver Michaels for taking the six million settlement that was supposed to help Melody, that you killed him and then started killing the others from the Chicago meeting?"

"I don't know what you're talking about. I don't trust you. Get away from me, Robert." She stepped back around a wooden plank table never taking her eyes off him.

"You were around in all the places where the murders took place, New Orleans, Florida, Jacksonville, Chicago, San Francisco, I checked." His flip-flops sank into the mud as he slowly stepped toward her while looking nonchalantly around the green house.

"I can go wherever I want. You gave me money to travel and it's nobody's business. Back off." She swung the knife at him again.

"You know enough about poisonous plants from Mark and Dad

to know exactly how to get rid of anyone." From the corner of his eye, he recognized a Hori-Hori knife and knew it was extremely sharp, but it looked puny in her hand.

"Everybody thinks I'm dumber than they are just because I'm quiet. That's what Michaels thought too."

"Put the knife down! You look stupid," Robert said.

She grinned at his confidence, "Not so stupid when it's saturated in ricin. One knick would kill you. I learned a lot from Dad."

Robert stopped. The knife was moist and it could be ricin. He couldn't be sure. He stepped again, this time his sandal sunk deep in the mud, threw him into the plank table and up ended it, throwing him with a thud into the sludge. Melissa screamed. "Noooo. You can't tell anyone." She held onto the upended table, the knife jabbing as she lunged toward Robert scrambling in the mud.

A car roared down the gravel road, the horn blaring nonstop. They both stopped to listen. "Melissa. Melissa." Dad yelled as he jumped out of the car without turning it off and ran to the greenhouse. "Melissaaa." He yanked open the tarp door and froze. Out of breath and holding his heart, "Melissa, oh god no. Melissa no. No more. It's enough."

With tears running down her face she whispered, "Dad, I love you. Take care of Melody." She turned the knife dripping with ricin and sliced her jugular.

"Noooo." Dad cried and ran to her. "No, no Melissa, no."

The blood spurted over Robert's and Dad's hands and clothes. Robert wrapped his hands in a cloth to protect from the ricin and put pressure on the sliced vein. Her head wobbled in Dad's hands. "Dad, forgive me. I made the solutions." Her throat gurgled. "I gave them to Mark." Her head flipped over, she drooled blood and stopped breathing.

Chapter 35

"Everything should be in order, said Mark in a voice that was content and satisfied. "I've wanted to take you on this ride on Route 1 from Santa Barbara to San Francisco for a long time. It's one of the most exhilarating drives I've ever taken. Here we are with the top down, the sun beaming warm and caressing."

The spirit image of Yhi sat next to him with her hair blowing in the wind and she chided him. "You know, Mark, you should be wearing a cap to keep the sun from creating skin cancers. We don't need any more cancer in the family."

"Oh, Yhi, what does it matter anymore? Look at this scenery! There is nothing quite like it in Australia. This is truly one of the most picturesque rides in all America. This ride should be taken with no hurry, with a feeling that, ok, I have arrived and I am successful.

No one can touch me; no one can bother me... I am the ultimate. And you are with me, and I am feeling oh so mellow."

"They told you I was dead," said the spirit image. "But as you know, we never leave the earth. We just take different forms. Remember that our Kaunas friends talk to their loved ones in the spirit world as if they were in the same room, same space, same car, like I am here with you today." She smiled and caressed his arm like the soft breeze.

He turned and smiled at the empty spot in the car next to him. "I see you whole and beautiful as always. Perfect as you were before the cancer ate you up. "Mark pulled the opened bottle of red wine from the basket. "Dad gave me this great bottle of red wine, and now let's drink and salute the haughty, proud and defiant rock face of Big Sur.

The cliffs rose straight up as if stretching in fear, to escape the grasping and beating ocean. The grey craggy wall stood determined never to be beaten down, never to succumb to the groveling waters below. In retaliation the waves below were furious that the land had escaped the watery floors and the rugged bluffs dared to stand rebellious against the demands of the ocean's grasping fists and fingers. "Henry Miller wrote of Big Sur, 'Here is the face of the earth as the creator intended it to look. And as the earth, we, all mankind, are made from dust and it is to dust we return.'"

"Only our bodies will be dust, my dear Mark. As you can see, I am here with you. My spirit is free and rides with you as we rode the outlands near the farm. It's only my human body that is gone."

Mark reached into the basket and pulled out a glass, put it in the cup holder, then filled it with the wine. "This is a good wine. It helps me unwind. I have such a happy feeling and am pleased that all the work I have concentrated on in the past year has been very successful. Not bad, not bad."

Yhi's spirit reached over and smoothed down Mark's flying red hair. "My Love, feel the constant back and forth, this winding small road is soothing like a cradle rocking, rocking, rocking. The tension is leaving your shoulders and you are relaxing more with each mile. Mark, that's the way to enjoy life. Pour yourself another glass."

Mark squinted at the bright sunlight and reached for his dark glasses.

"Soon our spirits and thoughts will be as intertwined as the clouds around the mountains," she caressed his cheek. "Do you remember the story of the Indian River maiden whose father wouldn't let her live with her lover? Sorry, but you know I'm always telling stories."

"Yeah, I remember that one. That's one I could never forget." He changed to a higher gear and sped around the curves. "The lovers threw themselves into the sea; he became a rock island and she became the clouds that flowed around the island, never leaving, always caressing. That is the way I have thought of you, my love. You are like the white soft and caressing clouds always around me, always near no matter what I do or where I am. Even now, I can smell your White Shoulders perfume; see your strawberry blond hair flowing in the breeze and your fingers touching my cheek. It's hypnotic."

"You are getting quite poetic in your old age, my dear. You were never this romantic when my body was with you. It must be the wine going to your brain."

"True, I am in a dream-like state. Yhi, do you remember on our honeymoon in Sidney, we were walking in the park along the bay and people were staring at us? I turned and said to you, 'I wonder what those people are thinking, because here I am an ugly, gangly, funny-looking fellow walking along, holding hands with a beautiful and elegant woman.' You turned to me and with no hesitation said, 'They must be very jealous. I believe they are wondering what he's doing right because she looks so happy.' It took my breath away. I thought I could not love you any more or any deeper than at that moment. But my love and respect for you grew with each new adventure. I would watch you with our Aboriginal friends and feel pride as you talked and laughed with them. I watched you with Adelaide, how you raised her and how lovingly you led her to grasp your death. How I have longed to join you."

"Soon, my Love. Soon," she whispered.

"The wine is beginning to have a slight bitter or metallic taste, like Valerian root. Maybe it's been in the sun too long; I'd better just polish it off before it gets any worse. I feel a bit separated from my body, like floating." Mark grabbed the bottle and drank.

The landscape was beautiful but treacherous with jagged sheer boulders that plunged directly into the crashing waves far down below. The peninsular land dotted with trees, jutted out into the Pacific beckoning, don't leave me, stay with me a little while, come surround me and let's dance and weave together. The round hills rolled into the sea, intoxicating and comforting like old lovers caressing softly.

Mark watched the white caps on the vast ocean. "Yhi, the sea is azure blue and turquoise like the opals I bought you. You wore them until I took them from your body and gave them to Adelaide. Now she never takes them off."

"My spirit never leaves my daughter's side. Soon you will see."

"I think Dad knows. He was quite teary-eyed when we said good-bye and gave me the wine and wished me a good trip. He asked me if I knew anything about the Angel of Death mushroom. Why would he ask me about that if he didn't know? He's sometimes a strange fellow."

"Mark, there are storm clouds around the hill tops and the road will be slick."

"No worries. This wonderful car rides soft and smooth and takes the curves like silky glass at whatever speed I drive. Look, everything looks straight and flat; there are no curves anymore, just straight, straight roads. Watch how fast we can go. We're flying like clouds lifting us into the sky and beyond and I am rocking, rocking, rocking like in a cradle, sleeping like a baby in my mother's arms."

It took several days to wrench the tangled debris from between the jagged cliffs and the thrashing Pacific. The violent waves, wind, and rain had beaten the car and the body debris into shards and pieces. Along with the rubble, the police found a waterlogged cardboard box, a torn silky green dress, a soaked red wig, and a pair of stiletto heels.

Chapter 36

The memorial service was held up on the hills behind Dad's farm with just a few migrant workers, Peggy, Gerhardt, the baby, Robert and Adelaide. What was left of Mark's body had been cremated as soon as the autopsy had been completed.

Robert stood next to Dad while others mingled and looked at the blue green mountains and hills around the property. "Dad, did you see the autopsy report?" Robert was unusually quiet and solemn.

"I don't want to know what's in it," Dad snapped. "Mark's dead. Melissa's dead. What does it matter now?"

"I think you know why it matters and what really killed him." Robert bent his head and pretended to wipe his eyes. He spoke through the white handkerchief he was carrying.

Dad clenched his fists together and wrapped his arms tight against his body.

"Dad, you have Addie here now. You have a new start on life. She is going to need your guidance." Losing two people close to him made Robert uncharacteristically gentle. "She's a beautiful, smart girl who is going to be lost in many ways. She is going to need you."

Tears streamed down Dad's cheeks. "I won't be here long. It doesn't matter anymore."

"Dad, you saved my life once, long time ago, now I don't owe you anymore." Robert's eyes never left the ground. Dad looked at him with suspicions. "It seems the autopsy report disappeared for a while and then was found again. Strange, don't you think?"

Dad watched Robert who still stared at the ground.

"It seems that the police findings stated that there was Valerian sleeping component in the stomach of the deceased and that it was an apparent suicide."

Dad groaned. Robert waited. "Funny how that part of the autopsy report got deleted. Also, the part about the red wig, the silky green dress and shoes being in the trunk of the car was somehow wiped from the record. Remember that one time several years ago for Mardi Gras, Mark dressed as Rita Hayworth? He sure was a fine looking woman in that red wig, green dress and high heels."

Dad began to moan so that his chest ached.

"When Adelaide and I looked at the pictures, we thought the woman in the Collier picture was Melissa. But you knew it was Mark. When did you figure out that Melissa was involved?"

Dad sank to the ground in sobs. "Mark must have snapped and Melissa...I thought she was ok since she'd been seeing the psychiatrist, but together they killed six people. They probably didn't see any other way out."

Robert sat down on the ground next to Dad and put his arm around the sobbing father. "If Mark had been caught and put through a trial, and into prison... well, you all would have gone through more misery and suffering. You all have suffered enough. You put the Valerian in Mark's red wine didn't you?"

Dad's cries were muffled into his arms. "Oh God, help me. Oh God, help me."

Robert whispered, "Dad, No one will know. There is no record. Now get hold of yourself, get up, and go comfort Adelaide."

Dad looked up from his soaked coat sleeves, turned to Robert. "You're a son of a bitch, you know that, don't you." he spat out.

Neither man moved.

"Yeah, Dad, I know. I love you, too. None of this has a pretty ending but you have to live with it."

"I wish I could die, too."

Robert caught sight of Adelaide standing apart from the group. He smacked his lips, "That Addie is the prettiest thing I've seen. She's tall and lanky like Mark, but she just glows."

"What? Glows? Have you been smoking something?" Dad was becoming more aware of what was being said and wasn't sure he liked what he heard.

Robert glanced at Dad and realized that he was breaking away from his sobbing. "Her hair is her crown; it's like honey, flowing honey, soft and sensuous caressing her shoulders in spontaneous relaxed waves laced with sunlight and sparkles with copper. It's damned hypnotizing and sensual as hell."

"Stay away from her, Robert," Dad growled. He stood up, shook himself, and controlled his sobbing. "She's all I have left." He looked at Robert with bottomless hatred. "You touch her, and I'll kill you."

"You have Melody, too. She's going to need you more now that Melissa's gone. And Dad, I won't touch Addie, I promise." He stood up and spit. "I'm not staying for the tear-jerker end. Elliott left a message that he has some papers to talk to me about and something about doctors being killed off. So I'll just..." He looked over at the mourners, spun around and walked off.

As Dad gathered the small knot of people together under the bare almond trees, Adelaide looked around, not really seeing the faces. Numbness tightened around her, making it difficult for her to breathe, much less greet anyone. She stood aloof while her thoughts swirled, dizzying her. She knew she had to do this to free her father's spirit.

Grand-Dad was barely audible. "Thank you all for coming and sharing our grief in this very difficult time." The sadness almost bent him double and he looked years older. This was hardly the vibrant man who laughed, drank, and sang with the lab rats in the French Quarter only a month ago.

"Mark and Melissa would be pleased to know you came to be with us today. As you know his body has been cremated and sent to his friends in Australia, and Melissa will be buried here next to her mom. Adelaide will say the Lord's Prayer in the language of the Darling River people where Mark and his wife and Adelaide lived."

Adelaide slowly withdrew from a stupor and looked at all the faces in the small semicircle. Slowly she lifted her snow-white arms and raised her palms to the sky and began chanting in Darla.

"Our Father who sits in the great sky,
Blessed is your name, your kingdom will arrive,
Your wish is done, on Earth as in heaven…
Give us bread every day, forgive us,
As we forgive others,
Save us from Bad,
The earth, power and praise to you. Amen."

Chapter 37

That night, Peggy, Gerhardt and baby Kerstin settled in the guest room on the second floor of Dad's house, and Adelaide had Mark's old room. Adelaide sat by the open window as Mark had done for many years as a boy and a few times as a man. She watched the night birds chase the mosquitoes and counted the stars slowly appearing, dotting the blue-black sky. She took a round black clay bowl from her suitcase and put it on the window ledge.

She stood before the open window and lifted her opened hands to the sky and prayed, "Great Spirit who rules the destinies of all his children, I beg you to restore my father's spirit and my mother Yhi's spirit together. Hide and control all the evils and pains they had during their time on this earth. May their light never stop shining."

She took the Lord's Prayer she had read and placed it in the bowl. "Great Spirit, take this offering." She lit a candle.

"Father, walk about. If you walk far enough and long enough, you will come out the other side. There the spirit of Yhi will be waiting for you. Be at peace."

She touched the candle to the paper and watched it burn to black ashes, then she took the ashes and blew them out the window into the night. She watched the ashes lift, twist and turn like black snowflakes, then mingle with the dipping, diving night birds. She prayed for the last time, "Great Spirit, make sure he will never feel evil again. Let the story end here."

Acknowledgements

First, above all, Dr. Vehaskari would like to thank her co-author, Dr. David Clark, who was inspirational, enthusiastic, encouraging and patient. It was an exciting educational journey to write this book with him. Thanks to my long-suffering sister, Mary Der, who read through every scrap of material since the book's inception and to the two editors, Glenda Goss and Constance Adler who gave enlightening suggestions and formative corrections. A fun and helpful thank you to Stephen Rea and his delightful Creative Writing courses and students.

Dr. Clark's successes are the end product of the influence of numerous members of his family, friends, colleagues, mentors and many children. Collectively they have encouraged, collaborated, admonished, constructively criticized, and cajoled him through the hard times and the good.

Of special note is this collaboration with the coauthor, who initiated the over decade long interaction which resulted in this book. The majority of the credit goes to her.

Printed in the United States
By Bookmasters